GOUDA FRIENDS

OTHER TITLES BY CATHY YARDLEY

Ponto Beach Reunion

Love, Comment, Subscribe

Smartypants Romance

Prose Before Bros, Green Valley Librarian book 3

Fandom Hearts

Level Up
Hooked
One True Pairing
Game of Hearts
What Happens at Con
Ms. Behave
Playing Doctor
Ship of Fools

Stand-Alone Novels

The Surfer Solution
Guilty Pleasures
Jack & Jilted
Baby, It's Cold Outside

GOUDA FRIENDS

CATHY YARDLEY

This is a work of fiction. Names, characters, organizations, places, events, and incidents are either products of the author's imagination or are used fictitiously.

Published by Montlake, Seattle
www.apub.com

Amazon, the Amazon logo, and Montlake are trademarks of Amazon.com, Inc., or its affiliates.

ISBN-13: 9781542030021
ISBN-10: 1542030021

Cover design and illustration by Philip Pascuzzo

Printed in the United States of America

*To Kerry Koda, Kathy Sun, and Glori-Ann Burnett—
the ones who secretly taught me to drive (sorry, Mom),
went with me to prom, and basically helped me enjoy
life when it was really, really hard. And to Brian
Chambers, Felix Lu, and Donovan Steutel, because
some friendships just last, no matter what.*

CHAPTER 1

Tam Doan probably shouldn't have detonated her life over seven ounces of cheese. But, in her defense, it was really good cheese.

It was almost three in the morning when Tam had stumbled out of the elevator and down the hallway that led to her apartment. She was used to coming home late. But tonight she wasn't even supposed to *be* home, which made the late arrival that much worse. She'd been setting up a weekend off site at a spa hotel for the ad agency account team that she assisted, with the promise of having time to enjoy herself. That is, until her boss, Lydia, told her she'd given up Tam's room to a VP who had unexpectedly decided to join their outing.

"I'm sorry, Tam. But he's a vice president. What was I supposed to say?" Lydia had then pointedly glanced at her watch. "You can take tomorrow off, all right? Now, you'd better get going. The hotel people say the last train back is at eleven, and you don't want to get stuck."

So Tam had caught an Uber and barely made the last train back to the city. She'd even taken a picture for Instagram of a deserted Grand Central Station with the clock showing 2:30 a.m.: *Just another day at the grind. #GhostTownStation #TwoA.M. #QuestioningMyLifeChoices #IfIDieDeleteMySearchHistory.*

She'd probably delete it in the morning. Not that she had a *huge* following, but she did run the social media for the agency as well as a few accounts, so she had to be circumspect. Still, for now, she was sandy eyed, frustrated, pissed.

Worst of all . . . it felt too terribly *familiar*.

Of course she'd put in an eighteen-hour day with nothing to show for it.

Of course she wasn't going to get what was promised.

Of course she was getting screwed.

She unlocked the door to the apartment she shared with her boyfriend, Brent. The lights were out. As a client finance manager for a global communications firm, Brent had to work long hours sometimes as well, but she figured he would be home by now despite recently being busy on projects at work. She'd invited him to the resort with her, but he'd said he was slammed and couldn't get the time off.

She'd thought spending a long weekend at a luxury retreat might be good for them as a couple. It turned out to be good that he hadn't come with her. If he'd had to take the train to Manhattan this late, he would have been furious. He would have caused a scene at the hotel, maybe even gotten her fired, and fumed all the way back to Manhattan. No, better that he'd stayed here at the apartment.

Since it was so late, she tried to be quiet as she cleaned up in the bathroom, washing her face of all makeup. She left her roller bag, the one she'd packed with four days' worth of clothes for her supposed "vacation," in the living room rather than the bedroom. She'd deal with it tomorrow. Or rather, later today.

Her train of thought was immediately derailed as she slowly noticed something odd. *Brent must've eaten dinner in front of the TV,* she thought. Then she registered that there were two plates on the coffee table.

And two wineglasses.

He had a friend over?

Not that he had friends over very often, especially without her there, she puzzled. Usually he—they—went out with friends, for rare celebrations.

But . . . maybe . . . ?

She turned on a light and stared as her already punch-drunk brain tried to put the clues together.

Two glasses.

One with lipstick on the rim.

Obvious evidence of take-out containers and plates.

Clothing strewn around. She recognized Brent's suit—those wrinkles were gonna need dry-cleaning to get out. She didn't recognize the black skirt and sapphire blouse, though. She looked at the high heels that were by the couch.

Smaller size than hers. Expensive brand.

She shut off the light. Then she sneaked into the bedroom.

It took a second for her eyes to adjust. Slowly, in the low blue light from the humidifier that Brent insisted on, she finally saw.

Brent. In bed.

With another woman.

Tam felt floaty, in a daze. Like she'd hit her absolute limit of tomfuckery and her higher brain functions had decided to simply nope out.

Can't do it. Can't deal with one more thing. Not right now.

She could drink, she supposed. Unfortunately, she tended to have the stereotypical Asian flush when she had alcohol, so she rarely had any. Besides, all Brent had in the apartment was some weird hefeweizen that tasted like you should eat it with a fork. She wasn't choking down that crap just to look like a strawberry *and* not feel any better.

Option two: sweets. Chocolate was always a good choice, but she hadn't had any in the house because she'd been trying to be good. Brent had been making noises about her gaining weight, and she'd largely tried to eat healthy since. But she'd allowed herself one lone, luxurious indulgence. It was her "in case of emergency, break glass" food.

This looks like a job for cheese.

She crept out, shutting the door silently behind her. Then she headed for the refrigerator and dug into the very back of the vegetable drawer, where she'd tucked away her prize: seven ounces of heaven, a.k.a. Cloud City Creamery's Signature Sensation, a semihard sheep's milk cheese, one of her favorites. It was her little guilty pleasure. She'd special ordered it from Seattle, and shipping had cost as much as the cheese itself.

Was she self-medicating with food?

Yeah, probably.

Did she care?

She thought back to the spectacularly shitty day she'd had, and the fact that approximately ten feet away, her boyfriend was currently naked and wrapped around a strange woman like kudzu.

Nope. Don't care at all.

She frowned, her motions getting a little noisier and more frantic. Finally, she pulled the drawer out, dumping the contents on the counter.

The cheese was gone.

"What the hell?" she hissed, tearing through the rest of the fridge. "Where is it? *Where is it?*"

That, unfortunately, was the moment when she snapped.

After slamming the fridge door, she stalked into the bedroom like a woman possessed, throwing the lights on with force.

"Where is my cheese?"

Brent sat bolt upright, his light-brown hair sticking out like a hedgehog's spines, his eyes wild. "Wha? Huh?"

"My *cheese*," Tam growled, aware she probably sounded like Gollum whining about his precious. "Signature Sensation. My *emergency cheese*! What did you do with it?"

He stared at her, then quickly and nervously looked at his naked companion, who was scrambling to pull the sheet up to cover herself. "I . . . I thought . . . why aren't you in Rhinebeck?"

"I was supposed to be, but as usual, it fell through," she snapped. "All I want is my cheese. So *where is it?*"

"I can explain!" he said, starting to get up. "Daphne came over, to talk about the pricing for the latest client proposal, and . . . we had some wine, and one thing kind of led to another . . ."

Tam was momentarily thrown out of her cheese-finding fugue. "Daphne. Daphne Long," she repeated, looking at the other woman, who had a tiny smug smile on her face. "Daphne, your *ex*."

He rubbed the back of his neck. "Daphne and I have a lot of history, Tam. You can't just—"

"The married one," Tam interjected.

He reddened. "It's complicated."

"And I can't express enough how much I don't care." Tam felt like her head was going to explode. "The *cheese*, Brent. You don't even like cheese, you said. So what happened to it?"

He stared at her, then glanced at Daphne, then back to her. "Are you really asking me about cheese at three in the morning?"

"YES!" she shouted.

He took a deep breath, then shot her a mulish look. "I threw it out."

Her hands balled into fists. "You *what*?"

"It was taking you forever to eat it," he said. "I figured I'd clean out the fridge."

Which was bullshit. In her mad search, she'd dug through take-out containers, half-drunk bottles of white wine, and some weird protein bars he'd bought ages ago.

"Besides," he said, "didn't you say you wanted to lose weight? Do you really think cheese is a good idea if you're dieting? I was trying to *help* you."

She blinked slowly, her mouth working silently as she tried to figure out what to say.

The audacity was *breathtaking*.

After a brief moment of fantasizing about setting him on fire, she pulled her phone out of her pocket and quickly snapped a picture of the two of them in bed. As her brother always said: *Anger is great, but have you tried evidence?*

Daphne finally squawked in protest, all trace of smugness removed. "What are you doing? You can't do that!"

"Right. I'm going to leave," Tam said, tucking her phone away. "I'm done. I've had it."

Brent did get up at that point, rushing to her side, putting a hand on her shoulder, his junk bobbling ridiculously in his nude state. "You can't just leave like this," he wheedled. "I made a mistake, yeah, but we've both made them. We need to work through this. You can't just—"

"Trust me, I really, *really* can," she snarled, shrugging his hand off. "I'll be back to get the rest of my stuff when I get a chance. We're done."

"We need to talk about this!" he yelled. "This isn't just my fault."

"Are you serious?"

She shouldn't have bothered. It opened the door for a discussion—for him to keep talking. She should have simply walked. Or perhaps hit him with something heavy.

His expression was pleading. "I only cheated on you because you haven't had time for me." He was rallying—she could see it in his eyes, hear it in the imploring note of his accusation. Like blaming her for his infidelity was somehow logical and rational. "And you know sex has been problematic with us when we have had time too. I was with Daphne for a long time, and we were both a little sad and lonely, and you were gone." He waved a hand between Daphne and himself. "You can't just blame me for falling into old patterns. It was *one* mistake."

"I don't even give a shit at this point," Tam said. "You really don't get it, do you? You don't care about what I care about. We're *done*."

"Is this still about the cheese?" He sounded dumbfounded. He stared at her. "You're not . . . seriously, Tam. You're going to throw away a six-year relationship over fucking *cheese*?"

She thought about it. The lies, the deception. Making her feel bad and then making her feel responsible for his actions. The gaslighting, if she was honest with herself, which she hadn't been. And now, the boundaries he'd gleefully leaped over, pretending to "help" her.

It had taken seven ounces of prime semihard sheep's milk cheese to finally push her over the edge.

"Yup," she said. "Cheese. Let's go with that."

She strode out, grabbing her roller bag as she walked past the dirty dishes and floor-strewn clothing in the living room, then past the chaotic food mess on the kitchen counters, hurrying away from the naked couple even as Brent made squawking noises about how she couldn't do what she was obviously doing. She slung her computer bag over her shoulder and stomped out the door.

She'd made it all the way to the street before she realized: she had no idea what she was going to do next.

CHAPTER 2

"You gettin' tired over there, boss man?" Josh O'Malley's executive chef, Amber, said with a grin as she moved in a flurry. "Been a while since you've been on the line."

He grinned back. He was the owner of Ghost Kitchens Unlimited—five different restaurant concepts in one large commercial kitchen space, delivery only. He leased the entire building, which he and the staff playfully called "the Tombs." He subleased one space out, subcontracted another for a large national chain, and hired his own chefs for the other three independent restaurants. It was true he didn't do much actual cooking anymore, focused more on the administrative and business side. But one of their chefs, Eduardo, had a sick kid, so Josh had covered for him at their Oaxacan "restaurant." He'd also jumped in when French Bistro got in the weeds and covered breaks for chefs on two of the others.

"I can handle it," Josh said breezily as he assembled street taco "packages" and tortas before boxing them and popping them in the bag, stapling it shut with the order slip, and then putting it on the conveyor belt that rolled toward the delivery area. "At least we're almost done. French Bistro has been closed since ten, and Healthy Bites has been pretty slow."

"Still think staying open later is the right choice?" Amber asked, reading his mind.

"We're getting the stoner market—all those munchies mean money," Josh said with a shrug. "But I need to double-check if the numbers back it up. I'm not loving the sales on Healthy Bites. I think we may need to pivot on that. Complete overhaul, ground up."

Amber nodded thoughtfully even as she didn't break stride, assembling food and barking a quick order at the chefs in the Monster Sandwich kitchen. "We're paying you to work, not talk! If you can lean, you can clean! Move your ass!"

"Yes, chef!"

She shot Josh a surreptitious wink. She was nearly as tall as he was, with spiky black hair and onyx gauges in her ears, along with full-sleeve tattoos. She looked like a pirate, in the best possible way, and her kitchen was the definition of a tight ship.

They finally closed out all orders and got stuff prepped for the next day. The actions were repetitive, clear, soothing. Josh was able to go through the motions as his brain churned away at possible changes for Healthy Bites. It would mean looking at the research, determining what kind of restaurant concepts would fit the Ponto Beach/North County San Diego area, but he had that at his fingertips with a custom-built search engine and data tables. Once he chose the concepts, that's when the work would really start: developing menus that would travel well and reheat easily as well as reduce spoilage and work with their overall ingredient orders; packaging that was sturdy yet sustainable and of course fit in with whatever branding they came up with; and finally, the marketing they'd need to do, especially if he was launching a new restaurant from scratch.

It was hard, consuming work, and he loved it, for a number of reasons. Not the least of which was the proof that he'd come a long damned way from his childhood—from scrounging for whatever food he could find, wearing raggedy-ass clothes, hiding whatever cash he could get his hands on before his mother took it, mopping up at a diner in exchange for tips and free meals. Now, it was midnight. He talked to the night cleaning crew, the ones who would make sure everything was sanitized before tomorrow's opening, then headed to his car, waving good night to Amber as she got into her car. He stretched a little. Amber was right—it *had* been a while since he'd worked the line. Because cooking itself wasn't actually his passion, or even his talent, if he was being honest.

But *making things work* was.

He was just pressing the button to unlock his van when his phone rang, and he frowned. Nobody he knew actually called him. Or anyone else, for that matter. They texted.

He glanced down at the display, not recognizing the number, but recognizing a New York area code.

Spam from New York? At midnight?

He probably should just ignore it, let it go to voice mail. But . . .

Damn it. He knew people in New York, and maybe it was an emergency.

You only know two people in New York, at least well enough for them to call this late, and it's been years.

He grimaced, then accepted the call. "Hello?"

There was a pause, a long one. And he was ready to hang up when he heard a short impatient huff, then a woman's low voice. "Goldfish."

Every muscle in his body tensed.

He knew that voice. And he knew what it meant when she said that word.

"Do I need to kill someone, baby girl," he said automatically, "or just help you hide 'em?"

She rewarded him with a laugh, but he heard the watery edge to it. "I know it's been a long time—like, *way* too long a time . . . ?"

Josh felt adrenaline starting to pump, fast and hard and fiery in his bloodstream, even as his mind went absolutely clear and time seemed to slow down. This was familiar. This was crisis mode.

This was Tam Doan, his best friend since middle school, the woman who'd helped him figure out his shit when he had melted down five years ago—and who, over the years, he'd let drift away as he buried himself in work and she distanced herself in her romantic relationship.

The woman who, per her code word, needed his help.

First things first. "Doesn't matter, we're good. What's going on? What can I do?"

He heard a long, low sigh. "And this is why I called you," she said in a tiny voice. "You don't judge. You just ask me how you can help."

Guilt assailed him. It well and truly sucked that the only person she could think of to rely on was a guy she hadn't spoken to in years, even if he still considered her his best friend. "And you still haven't told me," he pointed out.

Another ragged breath. "My life is the hottest mess in the history of hot messes. I'm not sure what you or anyone could do, actually, but . . ." She trailed off, sounding frustrated and sad.

"Where are you?" Last he'd heard, she was living with that tool boyfriend in Manhattan, the one who "didn't understand" how she could still be so close to her "nerdy" high school friends. "Still in New York?"

"Yeah. Right now, I'm in an all-night diner in Manhattan."

His eyes widened in alarm. "It's three in the morning there!" Which of course she knew. He winced at his stupidity even as his heart started to slam in his chest. "Are you all right?"

She chuckled humorlessly. "TL;DR, I hate my job with the passion of a thousand suns, I had the shittiest day on record, then came back to my apartment late to find my boyfriend—ex-boyfriend," she corrected herself, "in bed with another woman. And to cap it off, he threw out my emergency cheese."

"He threw out your cheese?" Anger rolled through him. Tam's relationship with cheese might seem silly, but to her, it was sacrosanct. The fact that the guy had taken Tam's possession and tossed it illustrated just how little he knew the woman he was supposed to be in love with.

Or simply showed that the guy didn't love Tam the way he should. He focused on the most pertinent part of that whole diatribe: cheating boyfriend. *Ex*-boyfriend. "Tell me you kicked his ass."

"Tempting," she said. "But no. I did tell him we were done, though, and stormed out. Unfortunately, that means I need to find a new place to live. Hell, I need to find a place to sleep tonight."

His mind started clicking through options, shifting into problem-solving mode. "Isn't Vinh in Manhattan too?"

"Yeah, but you know how he gets," Tam said, and he could hear the eye roll at the mention of her twin brother. "When *you* ask if I need help hiding a body, I know it's a joke. I can never tell if Vinh's joking."

Josh smirked. Vinh had never hurt anybody—not physically, anyway, that they knew of—but he could be kind of scary, especially when it came to family.

"Besides, last I heard, Vinh was traveling a lot for work, and I think he's probably out of town. I don't have the keys to his place. I don't even know if I'm on his emergency list to be let into his building—and his place is *swanky*."

Josh grimaced. Last she'd heard? Vinh was her twin brother. How did she not know?

What the hell had happened that Tam had gotten so disconnected from everyone she was close to? And why had he let it get this bad between them that this was coming as a surprise?

"Anyway, I figure I'll probably get a hotel room or something," she said. "I just decided to get some kind of comfort food in me before starting the search. And then I thought of you."

"I'm the human equivalent of a grilled cheese," he quipped, and smiled when she laughed.

"You really are," she replied. "How are you? I'm so sorry I haven't—"

"Nope, nope, no," he cut her off quickly. "You're not doing that."

"Not doing what?"

"Deflecting," he said. "You said *goldfish*. Don't worry about asking about my life, like nothing's wrong and we're just catching up. Right now, all I care about is *you*."

Another tiny sigh. "I know."

"Then level with me, and let's get this sorted out," Josh said. "Otherwise, so help me, I will jump on the next flight to New York."

"The funny thing is, I know you would," she said, and he could hear the smile in her voice.

"You said you had a shitty day even before all the cheating drama. What happened?"

With that, he proceeded to listen to her talk about what had happened with her job, getting hosed out of her promised time off, and then all the bullshit with her thankfully now-ex.

"Can't you force him to move out?" he finally asked when she wrapped up her tale of woe.

"The apartment's in his name. Even if it wasn't, though, I told him I was leaving, because there's no way I want to stay, and I don't want the knockdown, drag-out fight it'd take to keep it—like I could even afford to keep it." She paused. "We've fought before, even broken up before. I don't know if I was stupid enough to think it would somehow get better, or I was just too tired to fight, but I usually went back. I don't want to go back this time."

Deep down, Josh felt like growling, or hitting something. But he didn't voice that. It wasn't the time. Instead, he kept himself in cold, logical solution-finding mode and squelched the visions of hunting that dickhead down and pounding him to a pulp.

"You don't have to go back," Josh said with finality, an idea slowly starting to take shape. He opened the van and climbed into the driver's seat. "You've got a few days off of work, right?"

"I've got an inadvertent three-day weekend," she acknowledged before laughing bitterly, "although ten bucks says they try to call me in for something."

"Shut your phone off, then," Josh said, "and come out here to visit. Take a real vacation."

The phone went silent, and Josh glanced at his phone display, wondering for a second if she'd hung up on him.

"Go to Ponto Beach?" she finally answered. She sounded bewildered. "Dude, that's ridiculous. I can't just do a three-day turn-and-burn. Most of the time I'd be in the air anyway."

Thankfully, he had his tablet in the van and was already looking at travel sites. "There's a flight that lands in San Diego late morning, if you can make it to JFK by seven a.m.," he said. "I'll even pay for it. And I'll pick you up."

"You've got to be kidding!"

"Really not," he said as he typed. "There. Sent to your email. Totally up to you—but c'mon. You've got a bag right there, from the sounds of it, no work, and no place to crash. So why not?"

"This is like when we did that spontaneous road trip to Disneyland," she said, but at least she sounded amused. "How do you always talk me into these things?"

But there was a smile in her voice. And he grinned back, even though she couldn't see it. "Years of practice," he said. "See you soon, okay?"

"This is crazy, but . . . okay," she said, and he pumped a fist in triumph. "I'll catch that flight, and see you soon. Love you."

It was offhand, something they'd said to each other forever. Something he hadn't heard from her, at least not over the phone or in person, in far too long.

"Love you too," he replied, his throat scratchy. Then he hung up.

It had been five years since he'd seen Tam. The last time she'd seen him, he was the one who was in trouble: no job, no girlfriend, no home, no family. He'd hit rock bottom, and she'd dropped everything and come to help him find a way out. She'd cared enough about him to show him that all wasn't lost, and believed in him enough to boost him into action. And she probably had no idea just how much all that support meant to him—possibly because he'd plunged headfirst into fixing his life, losing sight of the woman who'd shown him the way.

He'd known on some level that he'd missed her, but it wasn't until he talked to her tonight that all those feelings came flooding back—along with over a decade's worth of memories. She was the closest person in his life—closer than his own family, closer even than the Nerd Herd friends he saw on a semiregular basis. His chest ached with it, and guilt burned in his stomach as he realized he'd let her help him . . . and then, he'd essentially let her drift away to deal with these demons alone.

By God, he was going to do whatever he could to help her fix her life. No matter how much his business meant to him, she was his girl, and he wasn't going to let her drift away again.

CHAPTER 3

"Ladies and gentlemen, we've just touched down in San Diego. Local time is 10:23, and the temperature is seventy-three degrees. For your safety and comfort, please remain seated with your seat belt fastened . . ."

Tam barely listened to the attendant's chipper voice as the plane taxied around the runway, headed for the gate. She rubbed at her eyes. Miraculously, she'd been able to fall asleep on the ride even though she was notoriously bad at flying. It probably had more to do with the fact that she'd been upright for something like twenty-six hours by the time she boarded. Now, she was awake, groggy . . . and almost immediately slammed with the thought that she had made a really, really bad error in judgment.

Why the hell did I let Josh talk me into this?

She hadn't been back in Ponto Beach in five years. In fact, the last time she'd been out here was a reverse of the current situation, sort of. Josh had been in dire straits, and she'd basically pretended she had pneumonia, called in to work, then maxed out a credit card getting a plane ticket so she could help him. Something that had gone over with Brent like a lead balloon, incidentally.

She frowned. Now that she thought of it, that was when Brent had started being harder on her connection to the Nerd Herd. He'd called it "immature" and claimed that nobody stayed friends with their high school classmates. He'd felt insulted that she hadn't invited him to her "visits" even though she'd known that he would have had a miserable time—and would have made her miserable. And he'd certainly gotten jealous when it came to Josh, wanting to read their weekly text exchanges and emails.

Hello, red flag. But instead, she'd just wanted to be extra reassuring, extra supportive. She'd wanted to *prove* that Josh was just her friend.

"C'mon. You must have had sex at some point," Brent had pressed. "Men and women aren't friends like that. There are a million movies that make that argument. And you literally called in sick to work and flew across country because he said he was sad, for Christ's sake!"

He'd never really believed her when she'd pointed out that she'd never so much as kissed Josh, and at the time, she hadn't blamed Brent. Even the Herd had teased about their closeness from time to time, although knowing Josh's nightmare homelife and her parents' temper tantrums, they'd seemed to get that Josh was her person, her rock. For anyone who didn't know the difficult dynamics of their childhoods, her friendship with Josh was hard to explain.

Now, she realized that Brent wouldn't understand the concept of fidelity—and that he knew how easy it would've been for her to cheat too. She wondered if Brent had cheated with others, beyond Daphne, and the thought made her feel sick. Not just because she'd loved this man, once upon a time, but because she'd been *so damned stupid.* She'd wasted six years of her life and gradually ghosted not only Josh but all her friends, because of that . . . that *shitbag.* She'd contented herself with the occasional social media connection, liking a post or video here and there, but she hadn't even posted on the Slack channel, telling herself she was too busy.

At this point, she could see she wasn't just toeing the line, pulling away because Brent disapproved. She had pulled away because she didn't want them to see how far she'd fallen, and she hadn't even realized it.

God, I hope they don't hate me.

The flight attendant told them that they could turn on their cell phones, and she saw most of the passengers pulling them out. She followed suit since she'd planned on texting Josh to let him know she'd landed.

Or maybe you could just turn around, get another plane ticket, and fly back.

It was cowardly, yes. She knew it sucked, but the last thing she wanted was to face the music for all her bad decisions.

But Josh had actually bought her ticket. This was his idea. He wouldn't hate her, and he wouldn't turn his back on her. She hung on to that thought, even as anxiety fluttered through her like poisonous butterflies.

As soon as she turned on her phone, she saw that she had incoming texts. She glanced at them, wincing.

As predicted, she'd gotten several from Lydia.

LYDIA: I know I said you could have the day off, but we need some sales data. Could you run into the office, log on to my computer, and then email them? I can't get Dropbox to work on my laptop.

LYDIA: The office manager said that they were delivering my new office furniture. As long as you're in the office, could you make sure they don't break or scuff anything? You know how they are.

LYDIA: You aren't replying.

LYDIA: Listen, I know you're upset, but this isn't acceptable.

LYDIA: Tam, call me as soon as you get this.

She winced. Ordinarily, there would be a Pavlovian response to Lydia's demands—do what needed to be done. Her heart rate accelerated a little. But Lydia had said that she had today off, and damn it, she wasn't paid to be on call. Perhaps it was petty, and perhaps foolish when she was going to have to find a new place to live—which meant an employment verification, no doubt. But the agency had taken advantage of Tam's willingness to go above and beyond for too long, and much as she hated to admit it, Brent had a point: the job had expanded past reasonable hours and was tapping her energy as well, affecting their relationship. She had to send up some kind of flare and let Lydia know that she needed better boundaries.

She grimaced. Speaking of Brent, he'd been texting her continuously since she'd left the apartment, from the looks of it.

BRENT: Where are you?

BRENT: We need to talk this out. You've got to let me explain.

BRENT: I'm sorry. It was a stupid mistake, and I promise it won't happen again.

BRENT: I know this isn't about the cheese. I'm not an idiot. Of course you'd be hurt.

BRENT: We need to talk.

BRENT: Okay, now you're just being childish.

BRENT: Goddamnit, where are you?

She deleted all his messages, then blocked his number. Then she took a picture of the brilliant Southern California sunshine outside the plane window, the sky an almost unreal turquoise. *Welcome back,* she added to the post, along with the tags: *#NoSleepTilPonto #SleepIsForTheWeak #DidIJustDoThis #HelloSoCal.* For just a second, she felt . . . vindicated? Comforted?

Finally, she texted Josh.

TAM: Just landed.

She waited a second, then saw the response.

JOSH: I know. Will see you outside the security area. I'll be the guy with the mariachi band.

She couldn't help it—she grinned. Josh had always made her smile, no matter what the situation.

She managed to pull her roller bag down from the overhead compartment and then slowly made her way through the lemming-crowd of people, all shuffling toward the exits. By the time she made it to the corridor and past the bored-looking TSA agent who manned the "no reentry beyond this point" doors, she was certain she was going to puke. Or pass out. Or both.

God, what had she been thinking?

No, that was the problem. She *hadn't* been thinking. She'd reacted purely on instinct and too little sleep. Ordinarily, she was never impulsive. She hated change and unexpected detours. She'd cried when their nearby bodega had closed, and despite her somewhat erratic work history on paper, it always took a metaphorical gun to her head to get her to change jobs. Most of the shifts in her life were things she'd been driven to. Not things she'd enacted.

If her life hadn't gone so unbelievably wrong, especially in the last few days, there was no way she'd be here.

At least it'll just be Josh, she told herself. And it was only for a few days. She'd have to fly back on Sunday and face the wreckage of her life, but at least for a few days, she could just . . . unplug. *Relax* was probably a bridge too far, but for forty-eight hours or so, she could at least pretend she wasn't the starring performer in a shit show of blockbuster proportions.

She thought about what little free space remained on her credit cards and bit her lip. Maybe she could get a little dinky hotel room, hang out with Josh a little. Get a decent night's sleep or two if she was lucky.

You're trying to hide.

She frowned. She was starting not to like this little internal voice she had going.

She scanned the crowd as she emerged. San Diego's airport hadn't changed too much in the years she'd been gone—still the same restaurants and coffee shops and bookstore, from the looks of it. There were still people crowded, waiting for their relatives, friends, and significant others to arrive. Tam surreptitiously wiped her sweating palm on the bottom of her T-shirt and readjusted her grip on her roller bag. She hadn't seen Josh in years, and in her head, she still pictured the high school version of him: worn clothes, scraggly, windblown bronze-blond hair, ice-blue eyes, too-thin build, wickedly wry smile.

She wondered absently at her own appearance. She'd been expecting to be at the conference, so she was wearing business-casual slacks and a plain T-shirt, but she was rumpled as hell, and her hair probably looked like she'd stuck a fork in a toaster.

Well. He'd never been friends with her because of her looks, at least.

She stopped suddenly as she took in a huge, obviously handwritten sign.

TAM. I'M PREGNANT, AND YOU'RE THE MOTHER.

People were snickering at it, and the man holding it, who was staring at her wearing a broad grin. A bit more scruff on his jawline, a touch more sculpture to the planes of his face, some crinkles at the corners of his eyes. Same ice-blue eyes, though now twinkling with humor.

She couldn't help it. She grinned back.

"I demand a maternity test!" she called out.

He let out a loud laugh, then dropped his sign and, before she could move, took a step and swept her up in his arms, hugging her tight. "Consider yourself lucky. I almost had Tobin loan me his inflatable T. rex costume to greet you." He pressed a kiss on the top of her head.

She could feel his chuckles rumble through the chest muscles under her cheek. She pulled away. "Dude, I haven't showered in, like . . . I don't know, I can't math right now. You might want to hold off on the hugging. I smell like plane and yuck."

"Shut up, you're fine," he scoffed . . . and then to her shock, he nuzzled into the juncture of her neck and her shoulder, breathing deeply, tickling her skin with the soft hair of his stubble. It felt like it had been ages since she'd been hugged, much less by him, and she wasn't ready for the confused response of her body, which was tingling and sparking like a campfire.

This . . . is Josh, she reminded herself.

He released her, grinning. "You're right. You smell like plane."

She smacked him gently on the arm, and he laughed, the sound warming her, starting from her chest before moving out to every part of her. He folded up the sign and tossed it in the trash, then took her roller bag.

"C'mon, let's get you home."

God. When was the last time she'd felt like someplace was really, truly *home*? Brent's place was always that: *his* place. New York had been somewhere she'd lived, but she'd been ground down by it. Her own parents had divorced, her father going back to Saigon, her mother moving to San Clemente and remarrying.

Did she even *have* a home?

She felt tears welling in her eyes, and she quickly brushed them away, but not before Josh noticed. They'd been walking to his car, and he stopped on the sidewalk leading to the parking lot. "Shhh, it's okay," he said, pulling her into another hug.

No matter what I smell like, he smells good, she thought absently, letting him soothe her. They'd never really shied away from physical contact—they were both snuggle bugs, even if they'd never gone further than that, for a variety of reasons. But it felt like it had been so long since she'd had someone just *hug* her, comforting her, that the tears went from welling to downright *falling*, pouring out of her like water from a pitcher.

"I . . . I'm . . . sorry," she hiccupped. "I feel like an idiot."

He stroked her hair. "You've been through a lot," he said. "It's understandable."

"I think I'm just tired."

He pulled back, giving her a gentle smile. "*Annnnnd* we both know that's bullshit."

Surprised, she let out a short gasp of laughter.

"But it doesn't matter," he added, chucking her chin. "Since I'm sure you're tired too. Let's get you back to my place, and you can crash for a bit if you want. Unless you're hungry. You hungry?"

Her stomach took that moment to growl. "I could eat," she said, embarrassed. Then she frowned. "Wait. Your place? I was thinking maybe a motel or . . ."

He stopped again, his eyebrow arching. "Tell me you're kidding right now."

She grimaced. "Well, I don't know," she muttered. Then a thought struck her—one that she probably should have considered before she accepted the ticket. "Do you, um, have a girlfriend?"

His eyes widened. "No. Why?"

"Having recently discovered another woman with my boyfriend, the last thing I want to do is freak someone else out because a strange woman is in her house." She grimaced as another fact occurred to her. "Also, your girlfriends tend to, erm, hate me? Historically?" Of course, he tended to date women who were jealous, and (if she was being uncharitable) paranoid, and a teeny bit high strung.

Okay, very high strung.

"Were you planning on sleeping with me naked?" he asked.

At first she was startled, but then she saw his lips quirk with amusement. "Well, maybe just the once," she deadpanned.

"Then it wouldn't have been a problem anyway," he said. "I'm drama-free now."

She shot him a skeptical look.

He caught it and laughed. "Any woman I'm with has to accept you are my best friend for life. The ones that wound up hating you never lasted long, anyway."

Tam processed that. He was . . . kind of right. Now that she thought about it.

"Besides, I've got the spare room all set up for you, all right?" he finished. "And we've shared everything from hotel rooms to tents to the world's stupidest air mattress—that popped in the middle of the night—so I think you can manage sharing a house with me for a weekend."

"Oh my God, the air mattress," she said with a giggle. "I'd forgotten about that."

She felt relief course through her. She could trust Josh not to make things awkward. Of all the people she knew—and she included her own brother in this—Josh was the one who she counted on to help her feel better. Even if it was short lived, she was going to hold on to this peace with both hands until she had to get back on a plane to New York.

They got to his car, or rather, his van. It had "Ghost Kitchens Unlimited" printed on one side, with a cute ghost chef logo on the other. He put her bag in the back, and then they climbed into the cab. Then he gestured to a cooler between the seats, making a big "ta-da!" motion.

"Congratulations, it's a cooler," she said, shaking her head. "Looks like you have other ones in the back. I like your delivery van."

"Thanks, but *this* cooler is just for you," he said, smugly grinning from ear to ear.

She tilted her head, confused.

"Open it," he prompted.

She humored him, lifting the lid. Then she stared, swallowing hard.

It was cheese. Lots of cheese. She carefully sifted through the contents. All of it was Cloud City Creamery, from the looks of it. Triple-cream brie, sharp aged cheddar, their imported firm Manchego and blue-veined Stilton. Even their silly specialty cheeses, Fifty Shades of Gruyère and Gouda Friends Forever. And when she saw that he had a sheep's milk Signature Sensation to replace the one Brent had thrown out, she felt her breath catch in her chest.

He knew what she liked, and he gave it to her. No questions asked. Just to make her happy.

"You can shower, even nap if you want," he said, starting the van, oblivious to her flood of emotions. "And I'll feed you. Then tonight, you'll get to hang out with the gang."

She was sighing, settling into the seat and fighting against tears of gratitude, when his words sank in. "The gang?"

"The Nerd Herd," he said. "I put out the 'Townies assemble' call this morning, and they can't wait to see you."

Just like that, she went tense as piano wire.

Seeing the people she'd essentially blown off? For years? After all the crap she'd just been through in the past forty-eight hours?

Shit. This was going to be hard.

She glanced back at the cooler, and then to Josh, who was smiling softly and sending small, contented looks in her direction, like he couldn't be happier that she was sitting there.

Well . . . as long as he was there, maybe it would be okay, she told herself, and leaned back against the seat.

CHAPTER 4

An hour later, they were at his house, a three-bedroom in the Ponto bluffs with a tangential view of the ocean—like "stand in the far corner and tilt your head the right way" tangential. Still, it was a hell of a long way from the small one-bedroom his grandparents had left his mother, where he'd slept on a sofa in the living room and listened to the train at night. Or, worse, startled awake by his mother stumbling in late, either with her latest "boyfriend" or alone, wasted . . . sometimes happy, sometimes crying, sometimes angry. And it was further still from his couch-surfing days with the Herd after his mother ghosted him to move to Florida.

He'd been living in this house for a few years now, but every now and then, he still woke up in his king-size bed, wondering where the hell he was.

Despite sleeping on the plane, Tam was obviously exhausted, both physically and emotionally. She'd probably want a nap. Still, he knew she was hungry, and she shouldn't just dive headfirst into the pounds of cheese he'd impulsively bought to replace the cheese that jackass had tossed. He let her get settled in the guest room, heard the shower start running. Then he called Amber.

"Hey, could you send a selection of stuff from all the restaurants, please?" he asked, without preamble, picking a bunch of dishes he thought Tam might be interested in. "Rush if possible."

Amber paused. “This tied to that emergency you called me about?”

“Yeah. I’ll explain more soon, promise. And I’ll be in tomorrow, although I can’t promise the whole day.”

“It’s cute,” Amber replied, her voice rich with amusement, “that you think that I actually need your bony butt here to keep things running.”

Which was absolutely true, and he knew it. Still, it felt weird not to go to the office in the large commercial kitchen.

That said, he had a mission.

He was going to ply Tam with food, let her rest, whatever it took to get her settled. Then, he was going to sit her down and help her figure out how to make her life better, instead of “not quite so hellish but essentially the same.”

As far as he could tell, when she’d left for New York for college, her life had jumped the rails and just gotten progressively worse. She’d become isolated, and miserable. If he was being honest with himself, he’d been too preoccupied with his own shit to realize just how far afield his best friend was going—and by the time he’d pulled his head out of his ass, it was too late.

Even worse: she was the one responsible for his life changing for the better.

Well, this time, it was his turn, and he was not going to fuck it up.

Tam padded out in fuzzy socks. “Hope you don’t mind,” she said shyly, gesturing to her outfit. “I only had business casual packed, and cheese T-shirts, and . . . ugh. I wanted to be comfy. Found these in the dresser?”

He smirked. She was swimming in a pair of his old gray sweats and a T-shirt with a cartoon cheese wedge wearing a pope hat, emblazoned with the text “Gouda Bless.” Her hair was damp from the shower, tumbling in dark waves, obscuring her face until she tucked them behind her ears. She had on her glasses, which were smudged and skewed slightly on her face. She pushed them up the bridge of her nose by pressing the back of her knuckles against the edge, the small gesture so familiar it made his chest ache.

He almost hadn't recognized her at the airport. Not that she'd changed that much physically: she still had that shoulder-length dark-walnut hair, those full dark-pink lips, the long-lashed, warm brown eyes. But now those eyes were shadowed, and he didn't think it was just from her being awake for thirty-whatever hours. Normally they sparkled with humor and cheer. Now, it was like seeing someone who had been in prison. Her skin, which used to be tanned by the Southern California sun, was pale. Where she used to have a slight bounce in her step, now she seemed hunched in on herself, so unsure it broke his heart.

"C'mere," he said, holding out his arms, and she stepped into them like she always did. He cuddled her, rocking slightly. "Feel better?"

"God, so much," she groaned. "Really needed that. Nice guest bath, by the way."

He grinned, even as his body tightened slightly. Which, he had to admit, wasn't surprising. He'd been pretty busy, and it'd been a while since the last time he'd been with anyone, sexually speaking.

Still, this was *Tam*. Which made it . . . odd.

He nuzzled her head, giving her one last squeeze, then backing off before his body got any more bright ideas. "Food's on the way," he said, then opened the fridge. "Can I get you something to drink? I've got sodas . . . um, sparkling limeade . . . ice water? I've got harder stuff too."

"It's barely noon, and I rarely drink, so maybe not the hard stuff," she said wryly, sitting at his kitchen island. "Besides, you had me at limeade."

He quickly fetched her a glass, then turned to serve her. He noticed she was looking around curiously. He found himself a little nervous.

"Josh, this place is amazing," she said, taking in his living room, with its huge brown sectional and built-in bookcases and big-screen TV. Then she turned her attention to the kitchen, where there was a commercial-grade stove and ovens, as well as a big fridge/freezer. He'd about had a heart attack when he signed all the mortgage paperwork, but it had been worth it. He felt like he'd needed to prove something to everyone who had ever doubted him.

"I knew you could do it," Tam said, and for the first time since he'd picked her up from the airport, her dark eyes shone and her expression was brighter than the sun. "I am *so* frickin' proud of you."

He felt a weird mash-up of embarrassment and accomplishment in his chest. "Wouldn't have happened without you," he found himself muttering.

"That's not true and you know it."

Her unshakeable conviction only amplified his cocktail of emotions. Thankfully, that's when his doorbell rang. "That'll be lunch," he said quickly, moving to the door. He opened it to find Robbie, one of the daytime drivers.

"I got more in the car," Robbie said after handing him several bags. Robbie was all of twenty and a little surly, but he had a sixth sense when it came to avoiding delays, drove like a demon but never got tickets, and was one of their best delivery people.

"I'll help you," Josh said. He put the food that Robbie handed to him on the counter, then followed Robbie to his VW hatchback. Robbie rolled his eyes, handing him three more bags. "I'll give you the usual five star and tip."

Robbie nodded. "You havin' a party or something?" he asked, his voice too monotone to be curious. "'Cause that's a lot of food."

Josh winced. *I wanted to give Tam a wide variety*, he told himself as he watched Robbie pull out of the driveway, then turned back to the house with his spoils. He wasn't even sure what Tam ate these days, what was her favorite.

Sure. And the idea of showing off all the ghost kitchen restaurants wasn't on your mind at all.

After letting out a long sigh, he went back in the house, shutting the door behind him. Tam's eyes widened as she saw him put the rest of the bags on the counter.

"How many people are we feeding here?" she asked, bewildered.

He felt his cheeks heat. "I wasn't sure what you'd want," he muttered. "Figured I'd cover my bases."

He started pulling out take-out containers from the five various bags, rattling off what he saw.

"Let's see . . . we've got some onion soup, a bacon-and-gruyère quiche, endive salad, and some chocolate croissants, covering breakfast and lunch bases," he said. "Those are from French Bistro. Got a cubano from Monster Sandwich, or a buffalo chicken sandwich with blue cheese. You still like blue cheese, I assume?"

She rolled her eyes. "If it's cheese, I like it."

"Some spring rolls and a spicy black bean burger from Healthy Bites. Some kick-ass barbacoa street tacos from our Oaxacan restaurant . . . and, um, some pierogies. They're from the restaurant that rents one of our kitchens—I haven't really tried much there."

Tam's stomach growled again. "Oh my God, I'm starving."

He grinned. Tam shared his love of food, which he appreciated.

Tam cooed over the packaging. "I love the graphic design. Everything's clean and simple, but stylish, and it all just *fits*. Did Asad do all of this?"

"Yup. He's good," Josh said. "I'm one of his biggest customers at this point. And Joel helped me with some new packaging—it's custom, so it's a little pricier, but it's still sustainable, and it keeps the food from getting squished or cold . . . although some of it probably needs reheating, depending . . ."

Shut up, you idiot. This isn't about you. This is about her. He frowned at himself.

"Look at you go," she said with a happy grin. "I *knew* you'd kick ass at this." She whipped out her phone, quickly turning it on and taking photos. "These are going on social media," she said. "I kinda want all of it."

She typed on her cell phone, then showed him the post. She'd gotten good at photos, he'd noticed—her pictures of the food were better than any he'd managed. He read the caption: *Bacon and gruyère quiche? Chocolate croissants? Cubano? Barbacoa tacos? HOW DO I CHOOSE? Answer: I'm not! #EatingChallenge #EnvyMe #FindSomeoneWhoWillFeedYou.*

He laughed, pulling out plates and then giving her a sampler of just about everything. They dug in with gusto.

"Soooo good," she said around a mouthful of food, covering her mouth with her hand. After she swallowed, she looked bright and happy.

Her phone buzzed, and she winced, quickly shutting it off again.

"Ex-boyfriend?" he asked, and his words had an edge to them. He still wanted to pummel that guy.

"Work," she said, sighing. "My boss is pretty pissed."

"Didn't she say you could have today off?"

"She always says that." Tam's expression dimmed. She tore up a croissant into small bites before nibbling each.

"Well, fuck her," he said. "You deserve a break. You work for her. You don't *serve* her. She's not a feudal lord, for Christ's sake."

Tam sank lower on the barstool pulled up to the kitchen island. Josh sighed.

"And you don't need to hear that from me right now," he said ruefully.

"No, I know you're right." She took a deep breath. "I know that they rely on me way too much. Still, they'll say, 'Nobody takes care of us like you' or, 'You do the work of five people' or, 'We've never had an assistant as good as you.' And that feels nice."

He grimaced. *Do they give you the pay of five people, though?*

They ate for a few minutes in silence. She sighed around a bite of quiche. "But it meant really long hours," she finally admitted. "Which might've contributed to the Brent-cheating thing."

"Do *not* let him off the hook," Josh growled. "That's not your fault."

"Problems in relationships are fifty-fifty, I hear."

"Relationships falling apart might have some joint culpability," Josh clarified. "Fucking around is *not* fifty-fifty."

"I know that," she shot back, then huffed in exasperation. "I mean, logically I know that. Look, I'm not proud of all this, okay?"

He sighed. "I know," he said. "I'm sorry. I don't mean to push. I just hate seeing you so unhappy."

"Not really a picnic from this side," Tam muttered.

Josh forced himself to calm down. This was about helping Tam, not making her feel like shit for being in this position. *Problem solve, you dipshit.*

"You don't have to be stuck there," he said slowly. "You've got options."

She chuffed out a humorless laugh.

"Seriously. I thought my life was a dumpster fire, remember?" he prompted. "When I was working for Sergio's, and I quit." He paused. "After Mom . . . left, and that whole fiasco?"

She looked sympathetic—and obstinate. "That was different, though."

"How?" he pressed. "I thought I was screwed. That every place I worked was going to suck, that no one was going to love me, that my life was just a big dead end. And you helped me figure out a path I never would've expected on my own." He paused for emphasis. "You could do that too. You could find something better, something you actually love, a place you feel you belong, with someone who treats you right."

And I could help you.

"Okay, this is way too heavy," she said with the small, firm nod of her head that told him she was done with that portion of the conversation. "You brought me out here to put that away for a while. So let's just . . . just gorge on this utterly amazing food, all right? And then maybe . . . wait, when does the Herd get here?"

"I told them to come by whenever. I imagine they'll start heading over around six?"

"Okay. So about six hours." She looked at the ceiling. "I could go for binge-watching and maybe some napping. Something fun? I'll even let you pick it out."

He sighed, frowning, but still nodded. He loved her, but damn, she was stubborn. She loved being the help-*er*, not the help-*ee*. He didn't know if it was because she felt validated by helping other people, or if she felt like she didn't deserve help, or what.

Well, tough shit. He was going to help her, damn it. Because she was valid no matter what she did, and she deserved all the help in the world and then some.

He just needed to get her to see that. Unfortunately, he only had about forty-eight hours to do so.

CHAPTER 5

You could find something better, something you actually love, a place you feel you belong, with someone who treats you right.

Tam spent the rest of the afternoon on Josh's way-too-comfortable couch, snuggled against him as they watched cheesy action movies with lots of explosions, intermittently napping. The problem was, she couldn't stop hearing Josh's words. She'd just meant for this weekend to be a little breather. Yes, work sucked—that's why they called it work. And the Brent thing hurt, but if she was honest, they'd been having problems for some time, and she probably should've seen it coming. She needed to fix a few things, but what Josh was talking about was a complete overhaul. It sounded exhausting and unnecessary.

It sounds terrifying.

The Herd arrived—or at least, those who had remained in town—at around six, as predicted. First on the scene was their friend Asad, with a companion. He hadn't changed much, although his clothes were a bit more dashing and his black curls had been tousled by a professional. He gave her a big hug, wearing a broad grin. "I don't know if you remember meeting him," Asad said, "but this is my boyfriend, Freddie."

He said *boyfriend* the way most people would say *soul mate*, and the glow in his eyes backed it up. There was so much love in his expression that Tam grinned back. "I recognize you from Asad's Insta," she said. "Caterer, right?"

Despite looking like a huge, red-bearded lumberjack, Freddie smiled shyly, his cheeks blushing a little. "That's right."

"Your food looks amazing." For her, that was a high compliment.

"You should taste it," Asad enthused, then winked. "Which you can, actually. We brought stuff."

She smiled back at both of them, then turned to Josh. "We should—"

"Already on it." He gestured to the cheese he'd bought for her, which he'd removed from the fridge and now had out on the counter, along with a decorative cutting board. "I'll just—"

"Perfect," she said with a grateful smile. "I shouldn't eat it all myself, and it would—"

"The plane," he agreed sagely. "That's a lot to carry. And you're still figuring out—"

"Right." She didn't want to talk about not knowing where she was going to be sleeping when she got back to New York, so she cut him off.

"Are you two starting with that already?" Asad said, shaking his head and smiling with amusement. "She hasn't been back twenty-four hours and you're already sharing a brain."

Josh winked at her, and she smirked. It had been a running joke, back in the day. They weren't mistaken for a couple so much as two halves of one sentient being . . . *Jam.*

"What brings you back to Ponto Beach? It's been ages. We've missed you!"

She grimaced. *Well, my life's a dumpster fire, Asad, so I figured I'd hide out for a weekend.*

It was bad enough that she'd gradually ghosted them. Finally revealing what she'd hoped to fix, to *hide*, before speaking with them again . . .

Insult. To. Injury. *Blech.*

Before she was forced to confess the magnitude of her current mess, their friend Hayden knocked before letting himself in the unlocked front door. "There's our girl!"

She let out a squeak as he gave her a huge hug, to the point where she felt engulfed—a neat trick, since he was the human embodiment of Shaggy from *Scooby Doo*, a gangly, long-haired, scraggly-bearded beanpole of pointy elbows and knobby knees. He squeezed her with enthusiasm.

"Hard to breathe," she said in a strained voice.

He kept hugging her, stroking her hair. "Shhhh," he murmured. "It's only weird if we *make* it weird."

She burst out laughing, shoving him off her. "*You're* weird."

He laughed, not insulted in the slightest. "Don't judge me!"

From there, Josh ushered in a . . . well, a Herd of townies. Keith, Melanie, Juanita. They hadn't changed that much, but at the same time, five years apart and a decade of aging had made their mark. Juanita's long black hair was now cut in a blunt bob at her chin line, chic and stylish, while Melanie's normally shoulder-length platinum-blonde hair was almost to her waist. Keith's darkly tanned skin and strong physique suggested he was still surfing, but his clothes screamed office work—must've come straight from his job, whatever that was. Hayden, on the other hand, was wearing a shirt she was pretty sure he wore in high school, with the Big Lebowski raising a glass and the words THE DUDE ABIDES emblazoned across the bottom.

They wound up settling in around Josh's patio. It wasn't quite cool enough for the firepit, but he had it set up for when the sun set. He was right: his house did have an ocean view, even if he did joke that you had to "tilt your head and stand up on your tiptoes" to get a look at it. She could see the waves off in the distance.

She'd told him he was going to succeed, and with a tired, smart-ass smile, he'd said, "Okay, I'll buy a house with an ocean view when I do."

He really had made it, more than he'd let himself dream. She felt a quiet sense of affection and pride at just how far her bestie had come in the five years since she'd last been in Ponto Beach.

Freddie and Asad put out all kinds of deliciousness, including a charcuterie setup showcasing cheese that made her want to weep, bite-size beef wellingtons, bacon-wrapped, chèvre-filled dates, and wild-mushroom-gruyère-stuffed puff pastries. She couldn't help cooing over everything. Josh kept her plied with virgin drinks and soda. He hovered just on the periphery, giving her plenty of time to reconnect with their friends while making sure she was feeling okay. It was weird, having someone watching out for her this way.

She hated to admit it: it was nice.

She found out that Melanie was now expecting her first child with her husband—a wedding that Tam had missed, making her squirm with guilt despite Melanie's assurances that it wasn't a big deal. "We knew you were busy," she said without rancor. It made it worse. She also found out that Keith was now a software engineer with a nearby cell phone manufacturer (which didn't surprise her), that Juanita owned a coffee shop (which *did* surprise her), and that Hayden was apparently a part-time DJ, freelance photographer and videographer, house sitter, dog sitter, and all-around bon vivant (which made an odd sort of sense when she thought about it).

"And you're telling me that Lily and Tobin finally got *together*?" she asked, holding her sides from laughing.

"I shit you not," Hayden pronounced, dragging his finger in an X across his chest. "They've been at it like bunnies. It's kind of disturbing."

"It was weird," a new voice chimed in. "You should've seen them at the ten-year reunion last month. Of course, they sort of had a hiccup after that, but it's all smoothed out now. They're still out of the country. Lily texted me this afternoon."

Tam looked up to see Emily—one of her childhood best friends, and her brother's ex. Emily looked older, although that might've had to do with the dark shadows beneath her eyes—and in them, if she was being honest. She looked as exhausted as Tam felt. Her blonde hair was a little darker, more toffee colored, less sun streaked. Still, she was as pretty as Tam remembered, even if her smile was weary.

The way Emily's relationship with her twin had splintered was a big part of why Tam had avoided Ponto, truth be told. She hated how Vinh had hurt the woman who loved him so much. Especially when she knew just how much Vinh had loved her—and still loved her, if he'd just be honest with himself. Tam knew why her brother had the issues he had, but she hated seeing it in play, and she'd never known how to explain it to Emily, or if it was even her place.

"I missed you," Emily said, holding her arms out and giving her a hug that, while much gentler, was no less enthusiastic than Hayden's. Tam sighed, hugging back and fighting tears. "Not that I'm blaming you. We all have stuff we have to handle sometimes, I totally get it. Just . . . really missed you. How long are you back for?"

"Just the weekend," Tam said, and in that moment, she wished that she could stay longer. She hadn't realized just how much she'd missed all these people until she saw them again, and it crashed over her like a wave. "How was the reunion, anyway?"

"Your brother showed up," Keith interjected. "Did not see that coming."

Tam gasped. "*Vinh* was here? He never said a thing!"

"Your brother not being communicative?" Emily said with a tiny, sarcastic smile. "Shocker."

Tam winced.

"Hey, don't worry about it," Emily said with a dismissive wave of her hand. "He just popped in to say hi, didn't stay. You know how he is."

Judging by the curious looks on the faces of the other townies, she got the feeling that they had more to say, but out of respect for Emily, they didn't. She'd ask Josh about it later. Maybe even ask Vinh.

"I never got the chance to tell you before, but whatever happened between your brother and me, it has nothing to do with us," Emily said firmly. "Which means no more going dark, okay? Even if it's just texting me goofy GIFs and memes. I missed you, and I don't want to lose a friend over a relationship. Even if it was with your twin. Deal?"

Tam swallowed against the sudden lump in her throat. "Deal."

"Good. Now tell me everything. How's life in New York treating you?"

Tam sighed as all the townies fell silent, giving her smiles of encouragement. She hated to be the center of attention like this, but they were right: she'd disappeared on them and been a shitty friend. She needed to do better.

"New York . . . sucks," she admitted. "Caught my boyfriend cheating, hate my job, need to find a new place to live."

They stared at her, as if waiting for the punch line. She chuckled bitterly at herself.

"On the plus side: vacay with friends!" She raised her virgin moscow mule in toast.

Josh scooted her over on the patio love seat, sitting next to her and putting an arm around her shoulders. "But she doesn't have to keep living that way," he said, squeezing gently. "And we're gonna figure out something better."

"So when are we wheels up to kick the shit out of this guy?" Hayden asked. "'Cause these hands are rated 'E' for everyone, and I have no problem showing him that."

"Same," Juanita said, her dark eyes glinting.

"What sort of job are you looking for?" gentle Melanie interjected, even as Hayden and Juanita plotted vengeance.

"Not sure, honestly. I can always go back to temping . . ."

"That's what got you into this job, though, right?" Josh protested. "Maybe it's better to think about what you *want*, rather than just what you feel you can plug into quickly."

She frowned at him. Much as she hated to admit it, he had a point.

"I'll certainly think about it," she lied.

Asad showed up at her side, handing her a plate laden with food. "Sorry you're going through it, babe," he said. "Here."

She glanced down at his offering, then grinned. "Thank you. Cheese is my love language."

"I know." He chuckled. "Hey! Maybe you can get a job where you get to eat cheese all day."

"From your mouth to God's ear," she joked, then nibbled at a crostini with a truffled brie. "A girl's gotta dream."

"Yes," Josh said, stroking her shoulder. "She really does. Remember you told me to aim higher? Dream bigger?"

"How dare you hold me accountable for my own advice?" she scolded, then nudged him. Pulling out her phone, she snapped a picture of the two of them, with Asad, Emily, and Hayden grinning and mugging behind them. She was smiling, brighter than she could remember smiling in a long time.

Back where I belong, she captioned. *With the best people on earth. Love you guys. #BFFs #NerdHerdForLife #PontoBeach.*

"Eat your cheese," Josh prompted, nudging her. "We're still talking about this later, by the way."

She arched an eyebrow at him, and he smiled—the smile of a man who knew that he wasn't going to let her bullshit slide.

"Damn it," she muttered, then viciously crunched her crostini.

CHAPTER 6

"I just have to stop in to work for a second," Josh said the following morning. He'd planned on letting Tam sleep in, but she was still on East Coast time, so she was up relatively early, and hungry. He'd taken her to a restaurant that served a fantastic breakfast. He'd ordered the spicy rancheros chilaquiles, one of his favorite dishes, and now was watching her wiggle a "yummy dance" in her seat as she took a picture of her stuffed peanut-butter-and-strawberry french toast. She looked up to see his expression, and smiled back.

"I really don't mind. I've been dying to see what your setup's like," Tam answered. "Until you talked about it, all those years ago, I had no idea what a ghost kitchen even was. It'll be neat to see how it's laid out. And you know I like restaurants . . . and food."

His smile broadened. "Honestly, my executive chef is able to keep all the restaurants in line, and I'm sure she can handle stuff, sometimes better than I can. But I want to make sure that some of the administrative details get captured. One of our suppliers has been inconsistent, and sending wrong ingredients, and I told him if they continued, we would be having words."

She grinned, slicing into the toast. "Look at you, scary businessman," she said before taking a bite. She wiggled her eyebrows.

What he didn't say was: he wanted to show off. It was embarrassing, but there it was. He wanted to impress the woman he felt was so responsible for his success.

"And if I know you," Tam continued, "I'll bet you feel better when you're at the helm, knowing what all is going on."

He squirmed, sending her a sheepish half smile. "You know me."

"Don't I." They tucked in. When she'd gotten halfway through her plate, she glanced at him expectantly.

"These are really good," he pointed out, "and you ordered a breakfast *dessert*."

"Shut up. You've been eyeing my french toast since it hit the table," she said, and, well, she wasn't wrong. "Besides, this is what we do, dude."

"Just messing with you." They traded plates, per tradition. And she was right. The french toast was delicious. "What do you think?"

She tasted the tortilla-chip-and-enchilada-sauce-laden dish. "I think I'm glad you saved me an egg," she said. "This is really good. Needs more spice, but really good." She grabbed the bottle of Cholula from the table and liberally doused it.

"Good thing I was done with that," he noted. "I'm sweating just looking at it."

She sent him a pitying look. "You've got heat issues," she said. "As in: you can't handle any."

"I've got testimonials that counter that," he joked. "Plenty of women say I can bring the heat."

"There's spice, and then there's Vietnamese spice," she pointed out. "I am fifty percent asbestos. Trust me, I can handle heat. And as for bringing it?" She rolled her eyes. "Don't come at me with that 'I can handle heat' when you've essentially been playing with cottage cheese."

He choked on a bite of strawberry, then took a bracing gulp of coffee to wash it down as she laughed. Then he joined her, snickering. "I should know better," he admitted.

"You try," she agreed. "It's cute."

Humbled and grumbling, he drove her to Ghost Kitchens Unlimited. "We call it the Tombs," he said. "Because . . . ghosts, you know?"

"I see what you did there." She tilted her head, taking in the building. "It looks like an office building. A nice one," she quickly added. "But I don't see any signage, and it seems surprisingly plain."

"It's supposed to," he said. "We're not a restaurant, and we don't want customers trying to drive up."

He hated how nervous he felt. He'd taken plenty of the Herd to see it. Asad had been to his office to help him develop branding and work out designs for the various restaurants, for instance. Tobin had done a mukbang video—technically a "cookbang" show, where the YouTuber both cooked as well as ate the food—with Josh, assembling and then bringing home the entire Oaxacan menu to devour on camera. But this was the first time Tam had seen it . . . and her opinion meant the world to him.

He guided her inside, holding the door open for her, then walked down the hallway. By this point, the kitchens were in the groove: getting any prep that wasn't done the night before ready for the lunch rush, setting up the "meez," or mise en place, at various stations. He could hear the clang of utensils, smell the savory scents of onions and garlic, various seasonings. Beefy onion soup broth simmered over at French Bistro, and fresh tortilla chips were being fried over at Oaxaca. It was home, more even than his big house on the bluff.

I really hope she likes it.

He glanced down to see her eyes widen as she took in the bustling kitchens, with their shiny stainless appliances, spotless white tile. The cooks were moving easily, wearing black-checked pants and white chef's coats with rolled-up sleeves. They joked with each other in Spanish and English.

"Well, look who decided to show up," Amber said, wiping her hands on her apron as she walked up to him. "Don't tell me. She's the emergency."

Josh glowered at her, but Tam laughed. "I'm Tam," she said as they shook hands.

"She's my best friend," Josh added.

"You have to understand," Amber continued, ignoring him, "this guy *never* takes a day off. I figured he was either having surgery, or helping smuggle someone out of the country."

"We're on our way to Mexico," Tam said. "I'm wanted for murder in seven states."

Amber's grin was wide. "I like this one," she said. "You should keep her."

Josh chose to ignore that. "Tam, this is Amber, my executive chef," he said instead. "She keeps us running and in the black. She's awesome."

"And he," Amber said, beaming, "is too kind."

"But not wrong."

"No, not wrong," Amber accepted, eyes gleaming. "In fact, you really don't need to stay. I told you, I got this."

Josh felt itchy in his own skin. "I wasn't planning on staying that long, though," he said. "I mean, the temp logs . . . and I was expecting those deliveries from Samson's and Gianetti's . . ."

Amber looked at him, arms crossed. "You're right. It would be impossible for me to monitor something *we do every day*."

He cleared his throat. "I, um, wanted to crunch some numbers too," he said. "And there's still the pivot for Healthy Bites to consider."

"You, my friend, are a control freak."

He shot Amber a flat look. "I prefer the term *attentive to detail*," he said loftily, "but I'll accept *tyrant* or even *despot* in a pinch."

Tam grinned, biting the inside of her cheek. "You have that dashing authoritarian look about you."

"Well then, boss," Amber said, "why don't you pop on over to your office, crunch your numbers, and then get out of my hair? Let me show you why you're paying me the big bucks."

Josh grinned. "All right."

Amber took a step closer to him, dropping her voice. "Heads up," she murmured. "Heidi's in house today."

Josh bit back a curse. "Thanks," he said, hustling Tam into his office and shutting the door.

"Who's Heidi?" Tam asked.

He sighed. "She's the owner of the only restaurant space I rent out here, Pierogi Princess," he said. "She and her husband signed a lease with me a few years back, when I was still getting my bearings. Just before the French Bistro deal. I had a few renters back then because it was steady money. Now, I'm just waiting for her lease to run out so I can replace it with another one of my own restaurants, or another agreement with a larger chain or something."

Don't ask me why. Please don't ask . . .

"Why?" Tam asked.

Dammit.

"Well . . ."

"Yoo-hoo! Knock knock!" a woman's voice with a heavy Texas twang rang out as the door opened. He probably should've locked it. "Josh! Darlin', I really need to talk to you."

He grimaced. Tam's eyes went as wide as an anime girl's, and she turned from him to Heidi, who had framed herself artfully in the doorframe. She was wearing a pair of Daisy Duke cutoff denim jeans, mile-high wedge heels that had no place in a commercial kitchen, and a tiny tank top that showed off her voluptuous figure. Her chocolate-brown hair tumbled around her in huge curls, boosted by what had to be a fire hazard's worth of hair spray. Not that he had any problem with the outfit, per se. He was a firm believer that a woman could wear what she wanted. Nonetheless, he could almost hear his instructors from culinary school railing against her ensemble, and he winced at the thought of the boiling liquids and spattering oils that she exposed herself to daily. Not to mention the stuff that would probably light her hair on fire.

"Oh. I didn't know you were with anyone," Heidi said, her green eyes narrowing as she took in Tam. Tam still looked stunned. "And you weren't here at *all* yesterday! I was starting to worry!"

Tam tilted her head, looking at him. He could tell she was trying desperately not to laugh.

Forgive me for this one, Tam.

He took a deep breath, then fitted Tam against his front and rested his chin on the crown of her head, wrapping his arms around her. "I've been busy," he said. "My best girl's in town, and I want to spend as much time with her as possible." Which wasn't a lie. Misleading, maybe, but not a lie.

Heidi took in their affectionate posture, looking shocked. Then her smile turned brittle, her green-eyed gaze sharp. "Oh! I'm so sorry, honey. I didn't see you there. You're just tiny, aren't you? Like a little doll! Who are you, again?"

"I'm Tam."

"Tam. That's an odd name," Heidi said, in her best "bless your heart" tone. "I just want to have a talk with Josh here, won't take but a second."

He didn't release Tam, which made Heidi look more frustrated.

"In private?" Heidi finally said.

"Actually, we were just leaving," he said, deciding in that instant that Amber was right—she could handle the Tombs. Any brainstorming or number crunching he wanted to do he could just as easily do from his home office. Besides, he didn't have much time left to help Tam figure out her problem, and that was the most pressing issue. "Sorry."

Heidi pulled her lips into a taut, unhappy line before forcing a smile. "It's just I wanted to talk to you about Pierogi Princess," she said in a cross between a purr and a whine. "I just know my restaurant could be doing a whole hell of a lot better, and you said before that you'd be happy to help me. Remember?"

Now who's being misleading?

He sighed, holding Tam tighter. He had made that offer, early on in the lease when Pierogi Princess was floundering, but her husband didn't seem to mind pouring cash in, and Heidi basically treated the place like a hobby. When they'd divorced nine months ago, he'd noticed that she hadn't had the same kind of cash to burn. He'd heard she'd stiffed her employees, and now she was down to one working cook—not that there was enough business from the restaurant to keep the guy busy. Heidi had finally asked for advice, but once he tried to talk to her, it became clear that what she really wanted wasn't a lesson he wanted to give. She was looking for a sugar daddy replacement for her rich ex-husband, and she'd decided he'd do nicely. He'd been dodging her ever since.

Heidi arched her back a little, putting her boobs out like a platter of appetizers. "It's just you've got the Midas touch when it comes to restaurants," she said breathlessly. "So I thought: how can I get this guy to touch *me*?"

He felt more than heard Tam choke, a low, surprised snicker emerging.

"I don't think that's a good idea," he said as diplomatically as possible. "I, um, don't know anything about pierogies."

Heidi unfurled a slow smile. Seductively, he had to assume. "I'm sure we could teach each other a few things, then," she said.

"Standin' right here," Tam muttered.

"Maybe you could come by my place, and we could . . . come up with something?" Heidi plowed forward like a wrecking ball.

"Like I said, I need to spend time with Tam."

Heidi looked like she'd just sucked on a lemon. "Because you're in town," she repeated. "Where are you from, sweetie?"

"New York."

"Oh." Heidi's smile was poisonous. "Staying long?"

"No," Tam said, and Josh winced as Heidi brightened.

"But I'm doing what I can to convince her to stay," Josh tacked on.

"Guess I can be patient," Heidi said, and he didn't like the predatory gleam in her eyes. "I'll make sure your Josh isn't lonely while you're gone, Tam, don't you worry. He'll be well taken care of."

Before he could answer, Tam leaned forward. "I'm so sorry. We've got to go," she said, her voice sounding amazingly apologetic.

"Oh?"

"He's going to be busy taking me home, stripping off my clothes, and pounding me through a mattress."

He goggled. She'd delivered the line as calmly as a news announcer. *Tonight's forecast: light showers, with a chance of wall-banging sex.*

His body tightened. He knew she was kidding—acting as a shield, protecting him. His dick seemed to have a problem making that distinction.

Whoa. Stand down! False alarm!

Tam turned in his arms, her eyes dancing with mischievous delight as she surveyed a slack-jawed Heidi. "You ready?" she asked him, stroking his chest. "Got whatever stuff you needed to pick up? Grabbed your vitamin E?"

He burst out laughing, then nuzzled her. "You," he whispered in her ear, "are a menace."

Tam looked at Heidi over her shoulder. "Nice to meet you!" she called out.

Heidi turned an unpleasant shade of red. She turned on her heel and literally stomped out.

"Holy shit," Tam breathed. "Was she for real? Seriously. It was like a bad Jessica Rabbit audition. Who *does* that?"

"She does, unfortunately," he said. "Come on. Let's get out of here before she strikes again." Still chuckling, they made a break for the van.

There was one thing that he couldn't stop thinking about, though.

"I'm doing what I can to convince her to stay."

That . . . was actually a good idea.

CHAPTER 7

Tam hadn't looked forward to going back to New York that Sunday morning. She'd had an amazing time with Josh. She'd actually gotten rest for a change, and feeling like she'd patched things up with the Herd had been more of a relief than she'd realized. She didn't feel so alone, even if she was heading back to a city where she had few friends . . . and several of them were people she only knew through Brent. Besides that, she still needed to figure out a place to stay.

That said, she hadn't actually anticipated *not being able to return.*

She'd woken up to a call at four thirty in the morning—it was still dark, for God's sake—telling her that her flight was postponed indefinitely. That's when the panic set in. If she'd made her original flight at seven, she would be back in New York by three-thirty in the afternoon. Plenty of time to get a crappy hotel room and at least eat something, then get a night of sleep under her belt before Lydia gave her shit on Monday. But now, it didn't look like she was getting into New York at all today. At this rate, Monday wasn't looking good either. She'd tried all the even somewhat nearby airports: Orange County's John Wayne, Burbank, Ontario, LAX. According to the (numerous) airlines she'd called, and the news sites she'd googled, there was a massive DDoS attack that had essentially shut down the air control grid in the Southwest.

If you wanted to escape from So Cal, you'd better be driving.

By ten, she'd moved from frantic to nauseated. The news was saying that it was the work of a hacker, a kid who hadn't quite meant to do as much damage as he had, so at least it wasn't a terrorist. But because of safety protocols after 9/11, the grid was going to take a while to get back online, or something. And then there was all the squabbling of how to get onto a flight, since there were more people who wanted to fly than there were planes, thanks to the giant fubar.

She didn't have a choice. She needed to email Lydia and let her know there was a good chance she wasn't showing up on Monday. Anxiety twisted her like a damp rag.

Sitting on the guest bed—which she'd really, *really* love to just dive into and nap the anxiety away—she then quickly typed out a note, explaining the situation. Despite it being Sunday, she wasn't shocked when Lydia's name flashed on her incoming call screen. Steeling herself, she accepted it.

"Lydia, I—"

"What do you mean, you can't make it into the office on Monday?" Lydia demanded, running her over verbally. "And what the *hell* are you doing in California? How is that possible?"

"I'm not on parole or anything," she said, feeling dazed, then giggled. "I didn't know I wasn't supposed to cross state lines?"

Lydia didn't find it as funny. "You were needed in the office on Friday," she said, her voice glacial.

"You gave me Friday off," Tam reminded her.

"Yes, but you were *needed*," Lydia said sharply. Like that should have superseded any prior agreements. She sounded even more annoyed that Tam had pointed out the earlier promise, and the fact that she'd reneged—not that Lydia felt guilty, but that it was gauche of Tam to bring it up. "You didn't tell me you were going to traipse three thousand miles away!"

"I didn't need to," Tam replied with some sharpness of her own, and Lydia fell silent.

Tam didn't raise her voice to her bosses, ever. Part of it was because she felt like her mother would somehow materialize and smack her for being rude to a superior, and part of it was because she had this innate need to people-please—and people didn't like being yelled at. Considering Lydia's default crisis voice could be called "a little curt" at best, Tam usually tried to provide a counterpoint of calm.

Today, she was all out of calm.

Lydia tried to wrangle her back into submission. "If you're going to do anything that makes it difficult for us to get ahold of you, when you're needed, then you're damned right you need to clear it with me!"

Tam took a second to stare at the phone. "I'm sorry?"

"You should be!" Lydia snapped. "And now this? I know that you're upset, but this is just . . . just petty!"

"I didn't ground the planes, Lydia!" Tam protested.

"Figure it out." Lydia's voice brooked no argument. "Get another flight."

"I really can't," Tam interrupted. "Every flight in Southern California is grounded, and all the airports are essentially shut down. Even private planes." Not that she could afford one, but she could see Lydia trying to make the argument.

"So go to Los Angeles!"

"They're grounded too!" Tam said, feeling her own voice start to rise. "Trust me. I've looked at everything."

"Then go to San Francisco!"

Tam goggled. *Do you even geography, lady?* "That's, like, seven hours away. You can't be serious!"

"Trust me, I'm serious," Lydia said, and she was definitely using the "I'm super pissed" deadly serious voice she trotted out when she wasn't getting what she wanted. It usually made account managers scurry and the people in Creative threaten her with voodoo dolls behind her back. "I know you're upset. But stronger people than you have tried to fuck with me and make some kind of passive-aggressive power play, and I'll tell you what I told them. I won't stand for it, and you'll be on unemployment before you can blink. Do you understand?"

Tam stayed silent for a long second as her brain processed Lydia's threat. She didn't use it on Tam, ever. She didn't need to. But she had done variants, in one form or another, with other assistants, and junior execs.

And now Lydia was threatening to *fire* Tam? After all the shenaniganry of the off site? After . . . after everything?

"And if I can't figure out a way to get to New York and in to work on Monday?"

"Not late either," Lydia added. "I know this kind of shit. The last thing I need is for you to start skulking in late to show how mistreated you are. We're in New York, dear. Believe me when I say that in Manhattan, in this economy? I could have you replaced by someone cheaper, younger, and smarter in half an hour."

The words were like a punch in the chest.

All the times she'd been told "you're the best assistant we've ever had" before she had to tackle something impossible. Or, rather, after she'd *accomplished* something that was impossible. That whole "you do the work of five people" business?

Yeah, she did. And it still wasn't enough if she didn't keep doing it at her same rate of pay.

They didn't value her. They complimented her because that was how to keep her going. And worse: she'd trained them to expect the miraculous from her, to the point where she felt guilty if she somehow wasn't able to pull it off.

A little part of her soul crumpled.

"So?" Lydia's voice was stern. "You'll be here at seven thirty on Monday morning, and maybe we can move past this."

"No."

Now it was Lydia's turn to pause. "I beg your pardon?"

You damned well should, Tam wanted to echo.

"I said *no*. I'm not going to make it by seven thirty tomorrow," she said, her voice strangely calm despite the quaking inside her stomach.

"I see." Lydia's voice was like a razor. "So . . . what? You think you're going to show me how invaluable you are? You honestly think that you've got anything special?"

"I think that you'd better start your timer," Tam said instead. "Half an hour, to find my replacement. Because I quit."

Lydia's strangled noise was pure fury. "Fine. *Fine.* Don't bother coming in again, or I'll have security escort you out."

"Fine." She hadn't planned on going back in anyway. They didn't let her keep personal items there—Lydia thought it was too cluttered—and while she loathed the idea of not giving notice, this was the nuclear option. She was salting the earth at this point.

"Good luck getting a recommendation," Lydia said, her teeth obviously gritted. "We'll just see—"

Tam hung up on her. Then she stared at her phone again, like it was some weird piece of alien technology.

What did I just do?

She swallowed. She'd done what she needed to do. She thought about Josh, back when he'd hit the perfect shitstorm, five years ago. He'd ended up at rock bottom, asking himself why he was bothering, putting up with restaurants that screwed him over, a mother who berated him, girlfriends who made jumping through hoops seem like the price of admission. How long did he need to be abused and torn up before realizing he didn't need any of it? That he could find something better?

In the same dazed, dreamlike state, she went to her messenger bag and pulled out her laptop. Thankfully it was hers, not the agency's. Methodically, she typed out a terse resignation for HR and copied Lydia. After proofreading it eight times, she sent it, then tucked her computer back in her bag.

And just like that, she was free.

She wasn't quite sure how long she'd stayed curled up in a fetal ball in the guest bedroom, but there was a quiet, tentative knock.

"Tam? You okay?"

It was Josh. She nodded, then realized he couldn't see her through the door. "Come in," she croaked.

He opened the door. "It's not looking good for flights," he said. "Might be able to really punch it and get to Vegas. I think they've still got flights going out. Maybe with a red-eye . . . hey," he interrupted himself, as he took in her face. "What? What happened?"

"Remember the cheese thing?" she murmured. "And the . . . the Brent thing? Moving out?"

He nodded, still looking puzzled. "Yeah?"

"Apparently I couldn't stop there," she said, before giving in to hysteria-tinged giggles. "I went for the hat trick and just . . . quit."

CHAPTER 8

As much as he wanted Tam to stay, he knew that the situation with the airport was freaking her out. He'd gotten up early, fully intending to drive her to the airport and savor at least his last few face-to-face moments with his friend before she flew off for God knew how long. But instead, he was faced with her in a complete tailspin.

"They've grounded all the planes, Josh," she said, her eyes frantic. "I can't get back to New York. I can't get back in time!"

He felt a little ping of happiness, which he quickly stomped out in the face of her obvious *un*happiness. "We'll figure something out," he said instead, nodding resolutely. "Don't worry."

That is, until he'd found out that it was a complete air control shutdown. It sounded like they were sorting things out as quickly as possible, but getting her to New York in time for work on Monday was going to be a stretch. He hoped that hideous boss of hers didn't give Tam too hard a time. Tam had been through enough.

After some brainstorming and some Google researching, he finally came up with a few different options. Tam was doing the same thing, making distraught-sounding calls and trying to get something worked out on her laptop in the guest bedroom. But she'd been quiet, and he had a possibility here he wanted to run by her.

He knocked gingerly. She didn't seem to be talking. Maybe she had good news, but he'd give it a shot.

"Tam?" He knocked gently, and she answered, ushering him in. He opened the door. "It's not looking good for flights," he said. "Might be able to really punch it and get to Vegas . . . I think they've still got flights going out. Maybe with a red-eye . . . hey." Her expression was one of exhausted horror, and he stopped abruptly. "What? What happened?"

"Remember the cheese thing?" she murmured. "And the . . . the Brent thing? Moving out?"

He nodded, still looking puzzled. "Yeah?"

"Apparently I couldn't stop there," she said, before giving in to hysteria-tinged giggles. "I went for the hat trick and just . . . quit."

He felt a bubble of sheer, unfiltered joy expand in his chest.

YES!

Her voice, her entire composure, seemed numb—like she was just coming out of anesthesia. Or maybe just going under it. She stared at him.

"Oh my God, Josh. What is *wrong* with me?"

The bubble popped as he saw she was truly panicked. "Whoa! Now, wait a minute," he said, crossing the room and then sitting next to her on the king-size bed. He put an arm around her shoulders. "There is absolutely *nothing* wrong with you."

"I dumped my boyfriend . . ."

"Who was cheating on you," Josh pointed out.

"And just walked out of the only housing I had . . ."

"We can figure out something else."

"I *quit my job*, Josh!"

He didn't miss a beat. "Because they were emotionally abusive fuckwits who took advantage of you and tried to make you feel grateful for it," he growled. "I would've done more than quit. I would've trashed the place."

She shook her head. "No, you wouldn't," she said, although a tiny bit of a smile tugged at the corners of her lips. She took a deep breath.

"But I fantasized about it, I admit. Like taking out cubicle walls with a sledgehammer. I was tempted to quit way before now, but I needed the money."

"To pay for rent you no longer have," he said, his voice gentle. "Staying with a guy you're no longer with."

She rubbed her face with her hands. "So, essentially, I have nothing."

That's not the point at all! He wanted to shake her. "*No.* Not nothing. You have a fresh start."

"I hate change," she said, the words muffled from behind her hands until he tugged them away. She looked teary eyed. "Why am I like this? God. I feel like *such* a fuckup."

"None of that either," he said. "That's your parents talking, not you. Maybe even Vinh."

"I am homeless, unemployed, and got cheated on," she said. "Hashtag: *winning*."

She was backsliding into a downward spiral, and fast. Unfortunately, when she got into this frame of mind, being sweet didn't help—it wasn't what she grew up with. He sighed.

"Is this pity party gonna last for a while?" he finally said, even as he internally winced at the tactic. "Because I'll make tea."

She glowered at him.

"I could throw in some cookies," he added. "Order a pizza?"

Finally, she reluctantly smiled, and he realized she was at least out of the tailspin. He stroked her cheek.

"Look. I know you," he said, hoping that he could get it out without scaring her off. "Even bad stuff is still familiar. But this could be the Universe's way of telling you—time to give up that shit and do something better for you."

"You believe in the Universe? Capitalized?" She still sounded sad, but at least she was rallying.

"Are you kidding? I am a walking infomercial for the Universe," he said with pomp, and was rewarded with a giggle. He pressed a kiss to her temple. It was so easy to shift back into cuddling her, being physically affectionate. He missed it. There just wasn't a lot of time or opportunity for cuddling in his life right now.

He took a deep breath of her scent as she settled into the crook of his arm, resting her head on his shoulder. She smelled like coconut or something tropical, probably from her shampoo, but she also just smelled like Tam, a subtle spice that was as familiar to him as breathing, even after all this time.

"I don't know what to do, and I hate that," Tam said finally, nuzzling against him. "If the Universe wanted me to make changes, it could've done something a little less dramatic."

"In my experience, it probably did give you plenty of messages that were less dramatic," he said, feeling a little bit like a tool. "But you kept ignoring them. So the messages got a little bigger. Finally, it gets kind of sick of you not paying attention and it just . . . well, clubs you. Metaphorically speaking."

She pulled away, studying him. "That . . . makes a frightening amount of sense," she admitted. "Although I never took you for a fatalist."

"I'm not. Exactly." He shrugged. "I was just really hopeless there for a long time, and I thought that my life couldn't get better. Then you slapped some sense into me . . ."

"*Slap* is a strong term."

"And here I am. I have a multimillion-dollar business, a house with an ocean view, and a happier life than I ever thought possible."

She smiled. "Love that for you," she said, and he could hear the warmth in her voice.

"What I don't get is, Why did you believe I was capable of all this, yet somehow think that you're not?"

She took a deep breath, then tugged away from him, throwing herself down bodily on the bed and yelling into a pillow. He gave her a second to regain her composure.

"All right. You might—*might*—have a point," she finally conceded after removing the pillow from her face. "I think I just feel overwhelmed. It's like everything in my life just imploded in one fell swoop in one long weekend, and now I am just free-falling. You know?"

He nodded. Here is where it would get tricky. But worth it.

"What did we do when I was in this position?" he said. "I wasn't going to have a place to live. Sergio had just shitcanned me for being too ambitious and for 'trying to tell him how to run his restaurant.' And Callie and I were still on the emotional roller coaster. What did you have me do?"

She grimaced. "I had you read that life design book by that guy from Stanford while I was flying out here."

"Then what?"

"Then we wrote down everything you liked doing, everything you were good at. And did some pros-and-cons lists for what was happening," she grumbled.

He grinned. "And then?"

"Then we did Jäger shots," she said, making a face. "Even though Jäger tastes like if you put a gun to a licorice plant and threatened it until it peed."

He barked out a laugh, and she shot him a reluctant grin.

"It was all I had. Anyway, once the hangover wore off, when we woke up the next morning," he continued, "you had a plan for me. I wound up renting a room with Hayden." He suppressed a shudder, because as much as he liked the guy, he was hard to room with, gnashing his teeth and making weird whining and whooping noises in his sleep. "I stuck to the plan and saved a lot of cash that year, fixing my credit, doing my research. Worked out the software and got all the pricing. Then I started approaching VCs to implement my plan, and stuck with it until I got funding. I broke up with Callie—"

"Whoa, that was never something we brainstormed," Tam interjected. "That was all you."

"I know. But I know how you felt about her."

Tam bit her lip. "Hey. I don't judge your love life."

Which made *him* feel bad, because even before she'd dumped the guy, he'd sure as hell judged hers. "I appreciate that," he said instead, "but you honestly should have. I think I just kept getting sucked into these relationships with women who . . ." He paused, grimacing, trying to find the diplomatic way to put it.

"Women who needed you to put them at the very center of your life?" Tam supplied. "And who liked it when you proved how much you cared for them by putting up with their crappy behavior? And who would *test* how much you cared about them by teasing you with their exes, or making scenes at your place of work, or keying your car?"

He stared down at where Tam lay on the bed. "This is you not judging my love life?"

"Well, it's apparently not your love life anymore, right?" She grinned impishly. "You're drama-free. Actually, that sounds nice. I could do with some drama-free, myself."

"The *point* is," he said, grinning back, "we came up with a plan. And it turned my life around. There is absolutely no reason why you can't do the same."

She sighed. "You make it all sound so reasonable. And logical. And easy." She sounded wary. "How are you so cool about all this?"

"It's like that joke," he said. "The one on *The West Wing*, where the guy was stuck in a hole and was asking for help, and another guy jumped in, and when the first guy was like, 'What the hell did you do that for? Now we're both stuck!' he said—"

"He said, 'Yeah, but I've been here before, and I know the way out,'" Tam finished. She rolled to her side, propping her head up with her arm.

"So." He stretched out next to her, looking deep into her eyes to make sure she wasn't just humoring him. "You gonna let me help you get out of here, or what?"

She smirked.

"The least I could do is let you try."

He smirked back. "Come into my office, then, and let me work some magic."

CHAPTER 9

Tam felt like she'd been cudgeled by a gang of gnomes or something . . . just a bunch of small punches that added up to one big wallop. If the Universe was trying to get her attention, it'd done that and then some.

On the plus side, having Josh volunteer to be her jungle guide to help her machete her way out of the wild mess of her life wasn't like her parents' version of "guidance." They wanted her to change her life because they disapproved of her seeming inability to get her act together despite her degree and her work ethic. Josh also wasn't like Vinh, who treated life like a war he waged with viperlike cunning and absolutely ruthless determination. Josh genuinely wanted to see her happy, no matter what that looked like.

Really, the least she could do was listen, even if she felt like a popped balloon. She just wanted to curl up in a ball and cry, only stopping for bathroom breaks and the occasional cheese indulgence.

Josh stood up, and to her surprise, he started pacing. "I should've made a PowerPoint," he said, and she chuckled, making him jolt with surprise. "Actually . . . come with me."

He took her hands, gently tugging her off the bed and guiding her to his home office. It was basically a spare bedroom, except for the really snappy computer setup and an immense whiteboard on one side of the room with words like POSSIBLE NEW CONCEPTS and then a bunch of different kinds of food listed around it, as well as doodles and lines. He snapped a quick picture with his phone, then erased it. He sat her in his office chair—a really comfy one, she couldn't help but notice—and then spun her to face him and the board. Then he grabbed a dry-erase marker, writing TAM'S LIFE in big letters at the top.

"First things first," he said. "We need to figure out what you like doing, what you're good at, and look at the Venn diagram of where that overlaps."

She bit her cheek to stop from smirking. This was so *Josh*. When she'd helped him five years ago, she'd grabbed a notebook and an old ballpoint after they'd talked for a few hours, just to make sure they didn't forget anything. (This was before the great Jäger-shot experiment, thankfully.) He'd been like this in school, too: the kind of guy who would sink his teeth into a problem and not let go.

Of course, that was the rub. She didn't want to be a *problem*.

"I don't know what I like, though," she said. "And 'follow your bliss' sounds great until I have to figure out a place to stay in New York on whatever salary I manage to eke out."

"You could always live with Vinh." He pursed his lips like he'd just chomped on an unripe loquat. "Although . . . I mean, I like your brother, you know that. But I know the two of you, and . . ."

"It'd be a thing," she agreed. She loved her brother to the ends of the earth, and they'd often been a united front against their parents' craziness, temper tantrums, and infidelity. That said, it didn't mean that she wanted to *live* with her brother again, especially since despite their twin nature, they were polar opposites. "I think he'd let me stay if I asked, though, so it is an option."

"You know," Josh drawled, "you don't even have to stay in New York."

She started to laugh, then stopped. "I . . . guess I don't?"

It just seemed so set in stone. She worked at the ad agency. She lived with Brent. She lived in New York. All these things, just a given.

Why couldn't she live somewhere else?

"You could, say, move back here. To Ponto Beach," Josh pointed out.

She laughed, shaking her head. "Yeah, right."

Then he wrote NEW YORK on one side, and PONTO BEACH on the other. He even drew a little skyline on the left and palm trees and a beach on the right, making her smile. "So. Let's start with some simple pros/cons, okay? Pros of staying in New York," he said. Again with the loquat face. "Are there any?"

She couldn't stop the quick burst of laughter. "It's a great city," she chastised. "There are lots of beautiful buildings, and great food, and lots of energy." *If I'd had him come visit me, he'd know,* she thought.

Yeah. Brent would've loved that. She scowled. *No more Brent thoughts,* she chastised herself.

"Hmm. Okay." Josh wrote down *buildings, food, energy* in a column in his neat handwriting. "As far as enjoying the buildings—do you go on a lot of sightseeing tours and such? For the architecture? Do you spend time enjoying your surroundings?"

"I've gone to Central Park sometimes," she said, but buckled when he stared at her, looking like a district attorney. "Fine. It's been a while."

"Define 'a while.'"

"A few years," she muttered.

"And the food," he said. "You said it's got great food. Eat out a lot?"

"Sort of," she said. "I get stuff when we order for meetings at work, sometimes. And the bodegas have some great sandwiches. There's great street food. We eat a lot of takeout." She frowned. "*Ate* a lot of takeout."

Dammit. She wanted everything Brent related to be past tense.

"People talk about the energy of the city," he pressed. "Does it amp you up? Do you like it?"

"Sometimes," she hedged. "Look. I know where you're going with this."

"I'm just data gathering at this point," Josh said, and she rolled her eyes. "Okay, cons." He looked at her expectantly.

"Expense," she said. "Although let's face it, it's not like North County is cheap."

"It's cheaper than Manhattan, but point taken," Josh said smoothly. Maybe too smoothly. "Job market is fairly tight, from what you've told me. So that's a con, right?"

"I don't know how much better it'd be here," she tried, but sighed. "Yeah. It's pretty bad."

"And the dating scene?"

"I don't know. I haven't dated in six years." She grimaced. She'd hated dating, actually. She was single for almost a year between Collin and Brent, and while she'd gone out on the rare occasion with some of her old friends from Vassar when they'd come to the city, she couldn't help feeling that whatever guy she was talking to was looking around, sizing up whoever walked in to see if he could trade up and do better. Even Brent had that expression from time to time when they'd gone out to eat, she suddenly realized.

Well, fuck Brent.

Or rather, don't fuck Brent.

Someone else could fuck Brent.

Someone else *did* fuck Brent.

She shook her head at herself. *Focus.*

"Now let's look at Ponto Beach," he said, grabbing a green marker this time. She noticed that he'd written *New York* in red. Subliminal, she supposed, but she could still see what he was trying to do. "Pros: the Herd."

She smiled broadly, even as her chest warmed. "That is a pretty big pro."

"You've got plenty of friends here, people who love you," he pointed out. "I don't know what your support network was like in New York, so maybe I'm speaking out of turn here, but . . . are you leaving a lot of friends behind in New York?"

She bit her lip, hard enough to sting. Was she? No. Her college friends had scattered across the country, and the ones who had stayed in the state were either upstate, where she rarely ventured, or working hellish hours of their own in their respective careers. She couldn't remember the last time she'd gone out for drinks or a meal with any of them. She knew some of her coworkers, but not enough to go out with them after work, she now realized. She didn't even have personal phone numbers. She shared a few friends with Brent, but she wasn't sure how that was going to turn out, and they weren't anybody she felt comfortable socializing with when she wasn't with Brent. Not that she'd done a lot of socializing. She basically went to work, then came home. Her life was a smaller bubble than she'd realized.

She was largely cut off, if she was being honest. She frowned again.

"Tam?" Josh asked, sounding concerned.

"Sorry. No. I'm not leaving a lot of friends behind," she finally answered.

"It's beautiful here," he added, writing WEATHER with a doodle of a sun with sunglasses. "You used to really love the beach."

It was true. It had been years since she'd gone there, too, now that she thought about it.

"The food here is pretty damned good," he said. "And if it isn't, I can find you whatever food your heart could desire. It's kind of what I do." He winked.

She felt her heartbeat kick up a bit, but she shook her head. He was just being his usual charming self, and it had been too long since someone had taken this kind of care with her. "All right. Still doesn't change the cons," she said, trying to be practical. "I still don't have a place to live, it's still expensive here, I still don't have a job here and have no idea what kind of job market there is. And the dating thing . . ."

Ugh. She didn't want to think about the dating thing.

"Manhattan was hard enough," she finally said. "I don't want to think about trying to date in a world of suntanned blonde So Cal coeds. Blergh."

"You know," he said, drawing out his words slowly and carefully, "you might consider not dating for a while, until we pin down the other parts of this equation. Getting out of the dating scene was a game changer for me, as far as getting the Tombs off the ground. Too many moving parts, you know?"

"Absolutely no problem there." She shrugged. "Trust me, right now, the last thing I need or want is a boyfriend."

Although sex would've been nice. It had been a while since she'd actually had sex with Brent, due to a big project at work and (she was now realizing) his affair with Daphne, if not others. But the idea of making some guy feel like he was the best lover on earth while he barely noticed her body under him . . .

"We'll definitely take dating off the list," she agreed with resolve.

"Perfect."

She looked at his lists. "It looks like it doesn't matter where I am, geographically," she said, feeling like she was whining but at the moment not really caring, because Josh was someone she felt safe in being a little selfish, a little whiny with. Just for a second. Then she'd slap some sense into herself and snap out of it. "Whichever coast I'm on, no matter how great the city, the problem's me. I need a job and a place to live, and both places are too much to afford."

Josh erased the board again, quickly, as the gears in her brain spun relentlessly.

"I could get another assistant job," she muttered. "I have the experience, and they can't bad-mouth me, legally I mean. I can start temping. I can—"

"Now, hear me out," Josh said. "You've done that before. You get scared, and you grab the first thing you can, like you've just fallen off the *Titanic* and you're hanging on to a door."

She snickered. "Thank you for describing my desperation so cinematically."

"The thing is, maybe you shouldn't do that this time."

"Is this the Universe talking?"

He crossed his arms, and she was surprised to see he really was serious. "What you've been doing hasn't been working," he said. "Remember when you encouraged me to take a big risk? I was scared shitless, going to angel investors to raise money for the ghost kitchens—for a concept nobody had really heard of. But you told me I deserved to dream big." He paused. "So why don't you?"

She felt every muscle in her body tense. Why didn't she?

"I wouldn't even know how to start," she said, her voice thready.

"Let me help, then." He knelt down in front of her seat, resting his hands on the armrests, looking into her eyes. "I owe you, Tam Doan. More than you will probably ever know. So I don't want you to worry about making ends meet. I don't want you to stress about a place to live, or what you're going to be doing. I want *you* to be happy, for a change."

She was about to protest, but the words stuck in her throat.

His blue-gray eyes were sincere. "You can stay with me as long as you like," he said. "That guest room? It's all yours. And we'll figure the rest out. Okay?"

She shouldn't. It felt . . . weak. It felt like she was taking advantage.

On the other hand, he was her best friend, and right now, she felt like if she could be weak with anyone, it was him.

"All right," she heard herself say, and let him whoop, pulling her into a big hug as she hoped she wasn't making an even bigger mistake—which, for this week, was saying something.

CHAPTER 10

Josh went in to the Tombs the next day, on Monday morning. They worked on an abbreviated schedule on Sundays, thankfully, and Amber had yet again stepped up to the plate when he called in. He didn't want to leave Tam alone for too long, especially in her fragile mood. She was still kind of out of it from quitting her job. He knew there were going to be loose ends to be addressed—like getting her stuff back from Brent the Asshole, things like that—but for now, he convinced her to just rest. As much as he wanted to solve all her problems all at once, he knew it was unrealistic. Five years ago, she'd helped him see a way out, but they hadn't nailed everything down in the week she'd been out to visit. He couldn't expect her crap to dissipate overnight.

That's why he'd fixed her brunch, of sorts, since she hadn't eaten out of sheer stress all morning. Nothing fancy, just some poached eggs on sourdough toast, which he knew were her favorite, just like he knew she felt poached eggs were too much of a pain in the ass to make "just for herself." He'd make her eggs florentine sometime this week, he decided. She really loved that, and as much as Amber made fun of him for losing his touch in the kitchen, he could still cook when he wanted to.

He'd left Tam eating and watching his big-screen TV in one of his old Ghost Kitchens Unlimited T-shirts and a pair of sleep pants. He'd even made her a vanilla latte. He wanted to do everything he could to convince her that she'd made the right decision.

Now, after touching base with Amber and looking over the logs and administrative details for each separate restaurant (well, except Pierogi Princess, but as a renter she wasn't his problem), he had hunkered down in his office to double-check the numbers he'd been mulling over before Tam showed up. As he'd suspected, French Bistro was doing great, as was Oaxaca, and Monster Sandwich was holding its own. But Healthy Bites was riding the line of profitability and heading toward the red. He'd originally thought that the number of local families with two working parents would justify the restaurant, especially with the boost of meal kits that were selling in the area, but apparently the healthy menu wasn't clicking with them, for whatever reason. He could try to chase down the problem, or he could pivot.

Pivot made more sense. It was drastic, and risky, but he was used to that by now after taking the leap five years ago.

His phone buzzed, and he quickly checked it in case it was Tam. Instead, it was his venture capital angel, Darius Guest. "Darius, hi. What can I do for you?"

"Just touching base," Darius said, an amused rumble in his low voice. Finding Darius, and having Darius invest in his fledgling ghost kitchen concept five years ago when it was barely a real idea in the restaurant world, had saved Josh's life and made him the success he now was. While Tam had given him the idea, the faith, and the nudge, Darius had given him the money and the support. He owed more to Darius than anyone other than Tam, and he'd take a bullet for the guy. "How are things going?"

"Things are going well," Josh said. "Want me to send over some numbers? It's early yet for Q3, obviously, but I could—"

"Anything I should be concerned about?"

Josh thought about prevaricating a little but gritted his teeth. He trusted Darius—and he needed to be transparent, to ensure that Darius trusted *him*. "We're not seeing the kind of growth or income I want from Healthy Bites," Josh admitted. "I figure we need to pivot. Just on that concept, though."

He waited for a second to see if Darius was worried. Darius technically owned part of the company, after all. He had been an independent "angel" investor when Josh had nothing more than a heavily researched presentation and an ambitious pitch five years ago. He gave preseed funding because he believed in Josh, even though he had never invested in anything restaurant related before and his investment group wouldn't touch it, primarily because Darius was impressed with Josh's research, game plan, and proposal, which he'd pitched with a presentation similar to a Silicon Valley tech startup rather than a food venture. Josh was afraid Darius had looked at it as almost a hobby initially, to be honest. But when Josh had made the first ghost kitchens successful within the first two years, then expanded and signed a contract to be the outsourced kitchen for the wildly popular French Bistro chain, Darius had helped him secure seed funding, which had allowed him to expand. He was killing it, and Darius was reaping the benefit.

"I trust you," Darius said. "If you think you need to change a concept, then you should. That's how you sold me on the ghost kitchens anyway . . . you're out the sunk costs for packaging, but you can roll out a new marketing campaign and new branding relatively easily without front-of-house stuff to worry about, right?"

Josh nodded, feeling some relief. "Yeah. I've already got some concepts kicking around, but I need to get the research done. Fortunately, I already wrote the program to scrape data from the necessary resources, so it shouldn't take long at all." He would need to ask Asad what his calendar looked like, to make said changes. But Asad was one of his best friends, and he knew he could count on the guy to not only make time for him but make his product and websites look stunning.

"That all actually brings up a point," Darius said.

Josh braced himself. As much as he told Tam to think positive and the Universe would point her in the right direction, he'd grown up in chaos: utilities getting shut off, strangers showing up, his mother disappearing for weeks at a time. He had a lot more hope and was a lot more optimistic these days. Still, he wasn't naive enough to pretend that he didn't tense up, waiting for the other shoe to drop, out of sheer reflex.

He was used to bad things taking good things away.

"My investor group is meeting near the end of September," Darius continued. "I want to pitch them for your next round of funding—and look at truly expanding Ghost Kitchens Unlimited. Emphasis on *unlimited*, you know?" Then he let out his low laugh.

Josh felt his wariness get drowned out by a wave of excitement. "That would be awesome! What do you need from me?"

"I need you to present to them like you did to me," Darius said. "You give more information than anybody I've ever been pitched by, and in a clean, comprehensive format. You know the numbers. Show them it's profitable. As long as you're going to be pivoting, show them how easy it is to retool a space. And show them all the systems in place—including your own delivery team—that makes this whole thing worthwhile."

Josh nodded, then realized Darius couldn't see him over the phone. "Yeah. Sure!" Then he paused. "End of September, you say? So . . . like, a month?"

"Just about," Darius agreed. "That's not a problem, is it?"

Josh frowned, doing the mental math. Pulling together his presentation for Darius had taken half a year—but then, it had all been conjecture. This was more like pulling together stuff he could prove.

How hard could it be, right?

"No problem," he said quickly. That's how he'd become successful, after all—by rushing in with all the confidence he didn't quite feel. By taking the risk. That's how he'd get ahead.

"All right. I'll be in touch and run through what you've got. Let's say a week?"

"Okay."

"I'll meet you at that café you like, over in Ponto," Darius said. Then they hung up.

Josh felt excitement bubbling through him like celebratory champagne. Expansion! That could mean another set of kitchens, maybe somewhere with a larger market share. Maybe downtown? Of course, the kitchen concept could work just about anywhere, so that didn't matter. The bottom line was, he was getting the chance of a lifetime.

"YES!" he shouted, pumping his fist, letting the adrenaline flow.

Amber came in, knocking on his doorframe. "What's all the celebration?"

"Darius wants to do another round of funding," Josh said. "With his partners, this time."

Amber let out a low whistle. "Welcome to the show," she said.

"I know, right?" Josh said, still grinning foolishly. "This is gonna be my life for the next few weeks, that's for sure."

"Did your friend get off okay?"

His eyes narrowed. The way she said it was definitely suggestive, and paired with her waggling eyebrows, he knew what she was implying. "Long story," he said instead.

"You know, I thought that you didn't date because you were a monomaniacal workaholic, which frankly is pretty much the norm for restaurant owners," Amber said with a smirk. "Then I saw the way you look at her, and I thought—aha. The boy's been pining. It all became clear."

"Huh?" Josh sat back, stunned. "I do not *pine*. And certainly not for Tam!"

"Sure, buddy. Whatever you need to tell yourself," Amber said around a chuckle. "So you just merrily dropped her off at the . . . oh, wait." Amber's eyes widened. "The plane thing. I saw that on the news. Is she still *here*?"

"Yeah. Her flight got grounded." He cleared his throat. "So she's staying with me." He didn't add *for the foreseeable future*.

"Did you guys really never get together?" Amber asked. "In the past, I mean. You two seemed awfully close."

"Why does everyone ask that?" Josh grumbled, pacing his office. "No, we really didn't. She was my best friend. *Is* my best friend. I don't . . ."

He stopped himself.

There were some people he felt absolutely no spark with. Say, his friend Melanie, or even Amber herself. Even if Amber wasn't happily married, he wouldn't be attracted to her. There just wasn't a click.

With Tam . . . if he was being brutally honest, there wasn't just a click.

There was a *spark*.

But there were also more important things than sparks and clicks, and he and Tam were living proof of that.

"I dated a lot in high school," he said instead, frowning. "Tam was always my friend. Just my friend."

"So you were a man slut," Amber translated, "but you saw Tam as above all that? Little Madonna-whore complex thing?" She tutted. "Disappointed in you, my dude."

"No. That wasn't it at all," Josh protested. He sighed. "We had kind of a rough time in high school."

"What, like bullied or something?"

"My mom was a high-functioning alcoholic disaster magnet," Josh said, and watched as Amber's mouth snapped shut, her amusement disappearing. "And Tam's family . . . not really my place to talk, but she was dealing with her own shit over there."

"I'm sorry," Amber said, but he waved a hand.

"Don't be. It was rough, but we both got through it. The thing was, if she was ever in a jam—if her parents were having a screaming match or whatever, she'd call me up and say 'goldfish,' and I'd go get her," he said. "I was driving a terrible avocado-green Datsun B210 that we called Kermit, and I'd roll up and take her out to the beach or whatever. And if I got kicked out again, or whatever, I'd call her, and she'd smuggle me into her room and let me sleep on her floor."

"Jesus."

"It's not as bad as it sounds," Josh said, rubbing the back of his neck. "And we had plenty of fun, and lots of good friends who were better than either of our families. But it's what I mean when I say we didn't date."

Because what they had was more important than that. For some people, that was a platitude. For Tam and him, their friendship had literally been a lifeline. He knew better than to fuck up a survival hatch, for either of them.

"Yoo-hoo!"

Josh winced. After opening up about his past, something he rarely did outside of the Herd, the last thing he needed was Heidi. Amber gave him a sympathetic glance as Heidi waltzed in, wearing a short denim skirt this time and open-toed sandals, her hair looking like she'd stuck her head out the window to tousle it. Tease it to Jesus, indeed.

"Hey, darlin'," she said, sauntering over to the desk where he was leaning. "Wanted to brainstorm some new pierogi ideas with you. Remember?"

"Now's not a good time, Heidi." He glanced at Amber, silently begging her not to leave him alone with this woman.

Amber looked like she was suppressing her laughter. Barely. *At least she doesn't look sad about my revelations about my childhood anymore,* he thought. And she did stay. Small mercies.

Heidi ignored the admonishment. "Your friend went home, didn't she?" Heidi said, leaning forward, invading his personal space. He reflexively took a step away, skirting around her.

"You know," he said, "you shouldn't wear open-toed shoes, or heels, in the kitchens. It's against health codes, not to mention being a safety hazard because those soles aren't nonslip. And you need to wear a hair-net or a hat. What if an inspector showed up?"

She touched her hair, looking outraged for a second at the thought of somehow containing the towering mass. Then she smiled.

"If I can't cook here," she said, her eyes gleaming, "then I guess we'll just need to head back to my place? Ain't no health inspector popping up at my condo, and then we can . . . *experiment*."

Amber actually chuckled at that. He blanched. "That's not a good idea. I'm seeing someone," he blurted. "Tam. You met Tam."

"Tam's all the way in New York, honey," Heidi said. "And it's just two people enjoying each other's company and having something to eat. No harm there, huh?"

"Actually," he said, and prayed that Tam would forgive him for throwing her under the bus this way *again*, "Tam decided to stay here in Ponto Beach."

"She did?" Amber said, her eyebrows jumping to the ceiling.

"Oh, she did?" Heidi frowned, her eyes narrowing with suspicion. "That's not what she was saying yesterday. Thought she had a flight booked for this morning."

He considered explaining the whole airline control-tower/grid kerfuffle, then decided to cut to the chase. "I convinced her," Josh said. Which was technically true. "She's moving in with me." Also true.

"Well, I . . . *hmph*." With that, Heidi glared at him, then turned on her (high) heel and stomped out. Amber stared at him.

"How do you get into these positions?" she asked. "And did Tam really move in with you?"

"I have no idea, and yes," Josh answered.

Now, he just had to figure out how to pivot a restaurant and fix his best friend's situation.

This was going to take a lot of Post-it Notes. And possibly a second whiteboard.

CHAPTER 11

On Monday morning, Tam woke up late—in itself a rarity. She'd showered and come out to find Josh had cooked for her, one of her favorites: poached eggs and sourdough toast. He'd made her another latte with his fancy coffee machine before he went off to work at his ghost kitchens. He said that they'd brainstorm more about her future plans, which had made her muscles tense up a little, but he'd noticed and then given her a hug.

"Today, I have a homework assignment for you," he said, chucking her under her chin. "Relax. Seriously. When was the last time you had downtime?"

Granted, he had her there.

Which was how she found herself at eleven thirty in the morning, wrapped in a blanket on Josh's insanely comfy couch, drinking coffee and binge-watching *Warrior*. She didn't need the blanket for warmth, per se—it was late summer in San Diego County, after all—but the weight made her feel like she was cocooned. She could probably nap if she let herself.

If she was back in Manhattan, back at the agency, she'd be fielding calls, juggling appointments, duking it out with other assistants for the strangely overbooked meeting rooms. She'd be doing graphics and posting on the agency's social media accounts. She actually would miss that a bit—she was good at it, especially when it wasn't *her* social media accounts she had to worry about. She'd be filling supply orders and dealing with the office manager over Lydia's new furniture. She would be up to her eyeballs in other people's problems, ones they expected her to alleviate as rapidly as possible.

To just sit here and veg felt decadent. Strange. A little guilt inducing.

But she . . . liked it?

Speaking of social media . . . she opened her own accounts, realizing that she hadn't blocked Brent. Sure enough, he'd commented on the Instagram pictures she'd taken of the food Josh had brought over on Saturday. He'd sent her private messages, she noticed.

BRENTTHEMAN: Baby we need to talk.

She grimaced. He was right, actually . . . they did need to talk. They needed to discuss logistics, namely her grabbing her clothes and things. She doubted he'd be understanding enough to mail them to her, and she couldn't just make do with two business casual outfits, three T-shirts with cheese motifs on them, some pajamas, and whatever spare clothes Josh had lying around. Beyond that, she didn't have the money or the energy to get a whole new wardrobe.

Nonetheless, she was still in this weird "relax" mode, and Brent was anything but relaxing. She grimaced, then typed an answer.

TAMOZZARELLA: I'm not ready to talk to you yet. I will get in touch soon.

Unfortunately, he either had an alert on, or he was simply online.

BRENTTHEMAN: You owe me at least a conversation. We've been through too much, and this is cruel. It's not like you.

She bared her teeth, even as she felt guilt worm its way into her stomach. How was he able to do that so easily? And why did she let him get away with it so often?

BRENTTHEMAN: Just call me? I know you blocked my number.

BRENTTHEMAN: Where are you? Are you back in California?

She sighed.

TAMOZZARELLA: I will call you next week. I need space, and I need to think.

There was a moment's pause, then another rapid-fire message.

BRENTTHEMAN: You're with HIM, aren't you?

She rolled her eyes. How, exactly, did he think he had the moral high ground here?

Then she quickly blocked him on all her social media accounts. She was tired of his bullshit. He was harshing her binge-watching and coffee buzz.

When her phone vibrated, she thought for a second that he had somehow found a way around her block. Or that it was Lydia, asking for something ridiculous . . . insisting that she needed to post or asking for passwords or something. But it was equally surprising to find her brother on the other end of the line. "Hello?"

"Hey." Vinh's deep voice sounded tired. "What's up?"

"Why are you calling?" she asked.

"Can't a guy just call his sister?"

"Last time you called was . . ." She did the mental math. "Six months ago. So, yeah, little bit of a shock."

"I know, I suck," he said, the exhaustion coming through a little clearer.

"You calling for a specific reason?" she pressed, wondering if somehow he was aware of her situation. She wouldn't put it past him—when Vinh wanted to know something, he could find out. He just didn't usually turn that kind of observation on his family.

"I felt a disturbance in the force," he said wryly. "Thought I ought to call."

She blinked. They never had that whole "twin sense" that so many people talked about. "Really?"

"Nah. It's three thirty in the morning here in Tokyo, I'm jet lagged, but I'm awake. And I didn't want to watch a movie," he said with a short laugh. "Thought it was time I touched base."

She snickered. That sounded more like her brother. "Work, I assume?"

"Yeah. Just some negotiations that need wrangling," he said, and she could hear the shrug in his voice. She still was fuzzy on what exactly Vinh did for a living, but she knew that he was on track for being vice president and that whatever he did paid him a downright silly amount of money.

"You okay?" she asked.

"Yeah. Just kind of pushing hard," he said dismissively. "Lotta travel. Should make VP in a month or so, I'd say."

That sounded about right. She sighed. Vinh was driven, more than she was. It was part of what made him so successful. *And me not so successful.* She frowned.

"Hey, why didn't you tell me you were going to the reunion?" she said off the cuff, trying to derail that train of thought. "I would've tried to go, maybe, if I'd known you were going." Then remembered she probably wouldn't have been able to, because of work, and honestly, because of Brent. But she was curious that her workaholic brother had somehow carved out time in his busy schedule to go.

"How'd you know I went?" He sounded surprised.

"They told me."

"I wasn't there that long," he said, and to her shock, he sounded uncomfortable. Or maybe . . . guilty? "Didn't know you were still talking to the Herd, honestly. Was this on the Slack channel? I don't really check that out anymore. I don't even think I have my log-in."

She wondered if he'd avoided the Herd for the same reasons she had—guilt. Especially since he would have felt they would choose sides after he broke up with Emily. Not that he ever blamed Emily for their split. If anything, he shouldered the responsibility for the implosion.

"No." She took a deep breath. "I'm, erm, here. In Ponto Beach."

There was a long pause. "You're there? Now?" he repeated. "Did you take a vacation?"

"It started as a vacation." Now it was her turn to sidestep.

"I'm surprised you got the time off," Vinh said. "Seems like you work as many weekends as I do. Which reminds me: Have you asked them for a promotion yet? Because it's criminal that you've been working there for that long, and worked that hard, only to be kept in one place, sis."

She grimaced. "Yeah, that's not gonna be an option anymore," she said.

Another pause. "You quit, didn't you?" Vinh's voice was resigned. "Dammit, Tam."

"They were being dicks," she said. "And it had been a really, really shitty week. I just had enough."

"I know they were dicks," Vinh said, and his voice was more sympathetic. Despite the fact that he was five minutes older than she was, he acted like it was fifteen years. "I told you that job sucked, remember? I hated the way they treated you."

"I know . . ."

"And I'm glad you quit, believe it or not," Vinh said, more gently. "But . . . okay, I gotta ask. Do you have another job lined up?"

She sighed, feeling a headache starting to brew. "It was kind of sudden," she admitted.

He sighed back. "You lasted that long. You might've looked for another job while you were still there and waited to hand in your resignation until you had something else lined up, you know?"

"I know I *could* have," she said through gritted teeth. "I've done that before, remember? But this was . . . there were . . . circumstances," she finished, feeling foolish.

"You've got to rein in those impulses, is the thing," Vinh said. "That's how you get ahead. Don't let them push your buttons."

"We're not all machines like you," she snapped. "Jesus, Vinh. I know I screwed up, but you're not helping."

Vinh was quiet for a second. "I'm not trying to make you feel worse," he said. Then she could hear the sourness in his voice as he added, "How did Brent take it?"

"Thought you weren't trying to make me feel worse," she muttered, and she could hear him tsk over the phone. "Although, strangely enough, he doesn't know that I quit."

"You're just keeping it from him?" Vinh said, sounding stunned. Then he barked out a laugh. "Good idea. No way *that* could go wrong."

"As it happens, where I work, or anything else, really isn't his concern right now," she said, tight lipped.

Now Vinh sounded really stunned. "You broke up with Brent too?" He let out a low whistle. "God *damn*. Sounds like you had a week."

"More like a very intense weekend."

"Wait. You said you're in Ponto," Vinh said, finally connecting the dots. "Did you . . . what's going on? Where are you, exactly?"

"I'm staying with Josh," she said. "In his guest bedroom. And . . . I'm pretty sure I'm moving back here."

It took Vinh a long minute to process that. "How are your savings?" he asked. "I can help out if you need. For, like, a deposit or whatever. But you need to hit the ground running."

All the relaxation she'd basked in that morning evaporated. "We're going to work on that," she said.

"We? What's to work on?" Vinh sounded impatient. "Get a temp job. Get your résumé online. Hell, get a job at a damned Walmart if you have to. You don't have to include it in your work history." He huffed out a breath. "Damn it. If you'd focused more on your career, you wouldn't be stuck in this position!"

"Don't even start with me, anh em sinh đôi," she snapped back. "We're not all crazy workaholics like you, you know!"

"Josh focused. You *encouraged* Josh to focus, as I recall, to put everything into his dream and make it big," Vinh pointed out. "So don't make this about me being money hungry, okay? I just want to see you succeed."

"Yeah, well, I want to find someplace I feel like I belong."

"Are there unicorns there, or just leprechauns?" Vinh said.

She growled at him. "Okay, *Ba*."

It was the lowest blow she could think of, and she immediately felt bad as soon as the word dropped out of her mouth.

"Sorry. Sorry." He apologized before she could, and she felt like shit. To his credit, he really did sound it. "I just . . . okay. Tell me if you need help."

She sighed. "I'm sorry too."

"Speaking of, you heard from Ba?" She could hear the tightness in his voice. Their father wasn't a favorite topic for either of them.

"I hit him on WhatsApp for his birthday," she said. "He seems happy. That company he started sounds like it's still in business."

"Think he's got a new wife yet?"

She sighed. "Probably a couple by now. I mean, not technically—but you know how he is."

Vinh growled in frustration, then sighed. "You planning on telling our mother that you're moving back? You'll be, what, an hour away."

"I'll text her," Tam said. "Her practice is always crazy busy, and I don't know what Scott's coparenting schedule is, so she's probably busy."

Scott was her mother's new husband, who shared two kids with his ex-wife, a teen and a tween. Tam and Vinh's mother seemed to have a decent relationship with the kids—possibly because she was more open to parenting than she had been when she'd been saddled with twins at twenty years old.

It wasn't that she wasn't *interested* in what her own children were doing, per se. She was cordial and polite. But there was too much baggage in their joint history—and they reminded her of all the struggling and all the fights with her ex-husband. Tam didn't feel all that close to her.

"I gotta try to get some sleep." Vinh sighed. "Listen, I know how close you and Josh are and all, but you don't want to be in a position where you feel like you're helping but you yourself are stuck. You focus too much on other people, Tam. You need to think about yourself, okay?"

She nodded, then realized he couldn't see. "Okay, Vinh," she said.

He paused, and she heard some faint noises. "Okay, my calendar says I'm headed out to LA in a few weeks. I'm going to stop by Ponto and check on you, make sure you're doing all right."

"I'm not four," she protested, even as she felt her eyes water a little.

"You're still my little sister. Besides, sometimes you need a nudge."

She bared her teeth at that, even though he couldn't witness it.

"See you soon." With that, he hung up.

She sighed. Then she turned off the TV. He was right on one count, at least. She couldn't just take advantage of Josh's generosity. She'd gotten jobs quickly enough. She went to the guest bedroom and retrieved her laptop, then set it up on the kitchen table. She typed in a job website and then started working on a résumé.

It might not be a dream job, but she needed to get on her own feet. And fast.

CHAPTER 12

Josh came home early—early for him, at least, around five o'clock. He tended to go in to his office at the Tombs between ten and noon and then work till closing or midnight, whatever was later. But with Tam here, he wanted to make sure that he was giving her time to address her problems. He also needed to carve out some time to work on the presentation for Darius's investment group.

Amber had been assuring him for years that he wasn't needed, but the ghost kitchens were his baby, and he tended to . . . well, baby them. He was a control freak, just as she'd accused him of being. He liked checking on the line, seeing how things were going, troubleshooting where need be. The conveyor belt and ordering system had been particularly tricky when they'd started. Now, after many iterations and a lot of elbow grease, the whole system was frictionless as freshly Zambonied ice.

In a fit of pride (and boredom), he'd had Asad do up graphic design for the user interface of the computerized systems—not the customer-facing one but the restaurant-facing one. It had a cartoon ghost on it and the Ghost Kitchens Unlimited logo, just like his van, and had options for the food supply status, history, and profitability, ordering history and waste, projections, and even prep times and delivery results.

He might be a food guy, but deep down? Still a geek to the core.

He pulled into his driveway, eager to see Tam. He hoped that she'd taken his advice and just chilled out. If anyone was a candidate for it, it was his best friend. She'd looked so stomped on, so adrift, after she'd quit her job. In some ways, it was worse even than the bullshit with her ex. She needed to just rest. Relax. Have fun for a change, rather than stress.

He wondered absently if he should take her to Disneyland. They used to do that in high school. He couldn't convince her to play hooky from school that often, but they had gone during the summers when they had cash. It'd be worth it to watch her have fun and be like a kid for a while.

He opened the door, calling out, "Honey, I'm home!" and knew, immediately, that she was far from relaxing.

He'd left her on the couch, cozy in a weighted throw blanket that Amber had gotten him (admittedly as a joke, telling him to stop freaking out about his new deal with French Bistro a few years ago). Now, the TV was off. She sat at the kitchen table with her laptop open, scowling at it and typing.

"Whatcha doin'?" he asked, his tone suspicious. He put down the food he'd brought for dinner on the kitchen table opposite her.

A blush bloomed high on her cheeks. "Hi," she said slowly. "How was your day?"

"Better than yours, from the looks of it," he said, playing along. "I talked with my investment guy, Darius. He wants to know if I'm up for another round of funding. I just need to come up with a solid pitch for his group."

Her eyes widened, and her scowl turned into a bright smile. "Josh, that's fantastic!" She got up and gave him a hug.

"I was planning on approaching him in a year, to expand, but I guess he thinks I'm ready now," Josh said, smiling back. "I've got data, but I need to come up with a new concept for one of our underperformers.

Still, that shouldn't be a problem." He grinned. "Hey! Maybe you could help me brainstorm."

"Really?" She blinked. "I mean, I don't know much about restaurants, obviously, but I do love food."

"I was thinking a Vietnamese restaurant would be awesome, especially in this area," he said. He'd come up with the idea later in the afternoon . . . honestly, as he was trying to think of what Tam might want for dinner. He wanted comfort food for her. "I went to school with a Viet guy who wanted to open his own restaurant—Phillip Nguyen. Last I heard he was working downtown at some snazzy brasserie in the Gaslamp Quarter, so he might not be interested in a take-out concept. But it might be worth approaching him."

"There's totally a market here," she said. "With this surprisingly large Vietnamese community . . . I mean, it's no Westminster, but it's sizeable. And Vietnamese food has gotten so much more mainstream anyway. Oh, hey! Bánh mì. You know, the sandwiches? That's perfect take-out food." She paused, then made a yummy noise. "Mmmm. Bánh mì."

He grinned. "So, I repeat. What are you doing, sweetie?"

She sighed. "I was just, um, looking up some stuff."

He saw that she had a spiral notebook open, with some things scrawled on it. Her last two places of work. What looked like a list of skills. "You're updating your résumé?" he asked, keeping his tone neutral.

"Well . . . yeah." She sounded sheepish. "I'm going to need to eventually."

"But you'll probably want to figure out what you're going to apply for first, right? Then tailor it from there? I thought we talked about this," he said. Part of him was a little hurt. Did she not have faith in him?

Dude. This is not about you.

He clamped down on a sigh. "What are you looking for?" he asked instead.

"You know. The usual. Temp stuff. Admin positions. That's what I have experience in, anyway," she said. "And without a good recommendation, and after job jumping . . . I don't know. I'm sure I can find something." She bit her lip. "I, um, looked at some rental stuff too. Might need to do a house share to start, get a roommate."

With a stranger? He hoped he kept the appalled feeling off his face, but judging by her reaction, he wasn't very successful.

"Josh, I can't just mooch off of you," she said sadly. "And just because I keep jumping into these situations doesn't mean that I need to . . . to just give up and whine about it. I need to fix it."

His eyes narrowed. "Did you, by any chance, talk to Vinh?" He loved the guy, but his head was firmly up his ass and had been for years. "Or anybody else in your family?"

"Vinh," she admitted. Then she blinked. "How'd you know?"

"Because that's them talking. The whole 'pull your weight' and 'don't be a nuisance' bit." Josh clenched his jaw for a second, then gently rubbed his hands over her arms. "I have every confidence that you could do whatever you want, Tam. If you decided to find a place to live tomorrow, and a job, I know that you could."

She smiled softly. "Thanks," she said, her tone quiet.

"But the problem isn't whether or not you *can*," he added, with as much care as he could. "The problem is: Is that the kind of life you want? Just . . . surviving?"

She winced. "I need to be realistic," she said, her voice firm. "I mean, yeah, it'd be great to do what you love—"

"That's what you told *me* I could do," Josh pointed out. He knew her. She was firmly in the "do as I say, not as I do" school of thought. Like dreams worked for other people, but not her.

She shot him a dubious look. "I thought you should've applied to MIT or CalTech, remember?" she said. "You didn't go to culinary school because it was your lasting passion. You did it because you'd been working at the diner since you were fourteen and you thought it was all you could do."

He squirmed a little. "I didn't hate it, though." It sounded sketchy, even to his own ears. "And you know what? I don't regret it. I found out I loved it a lot more than I thought I would, and it beats the hell out of a mountain of student loans. My point is, you deserve to find something you enjoy too."

She shrugged. "And *my* point is, not everybody is going to follow their bliss. There are practicalities to making a living, and sometimes you just have to get a day job and pay the bills. I don't hate being an executive assistant," she added before he could protest. "I like helping people. I like seeing results. I like problem solving." She smirked ruefully. "I just need to not work for assholes, that's all."

He sighed. "I just don't want you to feel like you've got to grab the first thing that kind of works," he said. "And I really think that there's a perfect-fit job out there for you. One that'll pay for a nicer place to live than just some shitty house share with a roomie you don't know who might drive you nuts. Or be like that woman you roomed with after Collin," he added. "The one that liked to vacuum at two in the morning and accused you of eating her eight-year-old spray cheese."

She stretched, rubbing at her neck.

"How long have you been at this?" He gestured to her laptop.

"Since about noon," she admitted.

"C'mere," he said, turning her and rubbing her shoulders. She let out a low moan, and his fingertips paused for the slightest second as his body responded with a curious *hey, what's this?*

Knock it off, body, he scolded himself.

"Did you eat?" he asked, pressing his thumbs against the concrete-hard knots between her shoulder blades.

As if to answer, her stomach yowled. She gave an embarrassed laugh.

"I might have forgotten to eat lunch," she said. "In my defense, though, I had breakfast late?"

Shit. When she ignored food, he knew she was upset, too fixated. "Okay. Break time," he said with the slightest stern edge. He pulled out the street tacos and tortas he'd brought home. "Then let's brainstorm. You said you'd give me a chance to help you figure this out."

"I don't want to be crashing in your guest room six months from now, just watching anime and K-dramas until you get home and feed me," she protested, pulling out a box. She took a deep breath, and her stomach growled again.

He put the food on the clear end of the kitchen table, then gestured for her to sit as he got her a glass of water. "How about a quarter?" he said. "That's the traditional amount of time to see at least preliminary changes in a business. Three months. That'll go by in a blink."

"Three months as a houseguest?" she protested. "You'll want to kill me."

But you're not a houseguest! He wanted to yell it. Besides, he couldn't think of anybody he had a better chance of living with than Tam. They finished each other's sentences, liked the same entertainment, had the same passion for food. They were probably a perfect fit.

"I didn't kill you before, and we were in each other's pockets for at least four years," he pointed out.

"We haven't lived together before," she said.

He liked the sound of it, he realized. Them living together. Maybe he'd just been alone too long. He'd been on his own since he'd gotten funding and moved out of the room share with Hayden.

"Three months, then?" he said, clearing his throat.

She sighed. "One month," she said.

"Two months," he countered. "You'll barely see any results in a month."

She thought about it. "Month and a half," she finally replied. "That's the best I can do. And honestly, figuring out my work situation will probably be the best way to get a new place and all."

He nodded. Month and a half. He'd figured she'd negotiate to that, even if he'd started with six months, which was his original instinct. It wasn't ideal, but he could work with it.

"Starting after dinner, then," he said with more confidence than he felt, "here's what we're going to do. You are going to *rest*," he said, then shot her a serious look when she started to protest. "We can pick up brainstorming tomorrow. I can even loop some of the Herd in. But for tonight, we're going to eat dinner, and then I'm going to make some kettle corn—on the stove—and then you can make me watch anything."

He could tell she was still in fighting mode until he got to that last part. Then her eyes sparkled. "Anything?"

He nodded.

"Even romantic stuff?"

He sighed. "Even romantic stuff." Not that it was that much of a hardship.

"Even *Bridgerton*?"

He quirked an eyebrow. "I hear there's nudity," he answered. "Sign me up."

She laughed, then shut her laptop. "Then by all means, let's have dinner and see some hot Regency sex."

He sighed. He really ought to be working on his proposal—but this was for Tam. Work could wait.

CHAPTER 13

On Tuesday night, after a day of restless, enforced "lounging" that had her sending guilty looks toward her laptop, Tam found herself at Juanita's café in downtown Ponto Beach, a place called Uncommon Grounds. It was gorgeous, funky without being too hipster, eclectic without being precious about it. Juanita let them commandeer a long table off in the back of the café, and Josh had gone above and beyond by bringing in an easel and a giant pad of paper. Despite the short notice, Josh had managed to round up Freddie, Asad, and Hayden, and Juanita planned on sitting in when it was slow. Emily had to work—at a second job, apparently—Melanie had to watch her sister's kids, and Keith had a date.

"So. To start, we're gonna look at what it is you like."

Tam squirmed in the hard wooden chair—not because the chair was particularly uncomfortable, but because the subject matter was. "You mean, in general? Or as it pertains to work?"

"Anything. I want you to keep an open mind. We're going to brainstorm anything that makes you happy."

"Like cheese?" Tam only half joked.

To her surprise, he drew a piece of cheese, making her giggle, and then wrote CHEESE next to it.

"Actually, we could probably expand that to food, period," Tam added, a bit more seriously. "Good food, anyway. Tummy-yummy food." If she was going to be honest, she was going to be *honest.*

Josh grinned, adding TUMMY YUMMY to the paper. Hayden chuckled.

"Good one," he said.

"Have you considered working in food service?" Freddie asked. She was touched that the large man was participating. He hadn't met Asad till well after their high school years, but he seemed to snap into the Herd like a perfect puzzle piece. "From what I understand, Josh wasn't expected to go the culinary route, but did. Maybe you'd enjoy it too?"

Tam bit the corner of her lips, contemplative. "I do love food. But I am not a particularly talented cook," she admitted. "I mean, I like baking, and I'm not bad at, like, cookies and stuff, but I don't know that I'm up to any particular standard—"

"Hey! None of that," Josh said, his blue eyes alight. "We're just brainstorming at this stage. We don't need to dive into details. No bad ideas, no stupid ideas."

"Porn?" Hayden suggested. Josh smacked him on the head. "What? I have a few friends that make a killing on OnlyFans." He looked over at Tam.

Tam shuddered. "Um . . . no. I mean, not to shame or anything, I'm sure they're great at what they do. But the idea of me being all sexy?" She laughed, shaking her head. "Yeah, right."

Josh frowned at her statement, looking like he was going to take umbrage with it, and the last thing she wanted to do was get sucked into a conversation about how she hadn't felt sexy, or even *like having sex*, in ages. Especially not when it could be opened up for public debate in front of her high school friends, a guy who looked to be making his dating profile, and an older woman who was reading an Amish romance and sipping tea.

Josh apparently decided the same, because he shook his head a little at Hayden. "Again, we're not looking at, um, aptitude, just interest," he said. He looked contemplative. "The trick is to define the problem."

She felt a pang of discomfort. "Well, I don't have a lot of savings, I don't have a job, and I don't have a place to live."

"Those aren't problems."

She scowled back at him. "They are if I'm living down in a van by the river, bud."

Hayden let out a howl of laughter, and Josh sighed heavily.

"No. I mean, those are temporary states, and besides, you can live with me forever if you want."

He said it like he would genuinely be glad if she stayed in his guest room for eternity. She shook her head.

"The *problem*," he said, "is you think that the only way to pay for a place to live is getting a job you hate, because it's 'all you're qualified for' based on your previous experience. Which isn't true at all. Not that there's anything wrong with being an admin, but you keep getting stuck in these places where you're not paid what you're worth and you're crushed as they keep piling duties on you, knowing that you're not going to say anything because you couldn't draw a boundary if you had a gun to your head."

They all fell silent for a moment, staring at him.

"Judgy much?" Hayden finally said.

She saw Josh's cheeks flush. "I mean, that's what *I'm* seeing as the problem," he muttered.

"She's got recovering-honors-student syndrome," Asad said, before drinking from an Italian soda and nodding sagely. "I can't tell you how often I got a rush by pulling off the impossible when I was in school, or working for that design firm in LA. People-pleasing runs in our blood. And it feels weird to say no or that we're not capable of doing something that a superior asks for, because *of course* we can figure it out."

Tam's mouth dropped open a little. "That's it exactly," she said, feeling stupid. "They'd be, like, 'Can you help edit this creative brief,' and I'd agree. Or design an Excel spreadsheet to help monitor a subdepartment's budget. Or take on social media for the department, then the agency . . . then a client."

"See?" Josh looked triumphant. "You can do a lot. We just need to sift out what you actually *like* doing, versus what you felt *compelled* to do. What brings you joy?"

What brought her *joy*? She felt a little ping of despair. She literally couldn't think of anything that brought her joy in the "finding your bliss, pursuing your passion, waking up greeting the day with a smile" kind of way.

"I don't know, Josh. I like the usual stuff. Watching TV or movies, or online. Um . . . reading." She winced at how lame that sounded.

"Okay, reading," Josh said, adding a little cute sketch of a book and writing BOOKS, then a little doodle of a television with the word WATCHING next to it. "What kind of stuff?"

"Geeky stuff. You know," she said. "And, um, romance."

"What else?"

After half an hour, the rest of the townies were chatting with each other while Josh and Tam were at loggerheads. "I'm not trying to be difficult here," Tam protested when Josh kept pushing. "I just don't know what you're after."

"I'm not after anything," he answered. "I just . . . all right. Let's attack this from another front. What did you like best about your job?"

She frowned, ignoring the pang of guilt that "your job" brought up. She couldn't believe she'd just quit a few days ago. She liked *having* a job, period. And she sure as hell liked getting a paycheck. But she hadn't thought in terms of *enjoying* said job for . . . well, ever.

"I liked being competent," she admitted. "Is that a thing?"

"Recovering honors student!" Asad sang out before turning back to his conversation with Freddie and Juanita.

"You're competent in lots of stuff, babe," Josh said offhandedly.

"Yeah. I seem to have a talent for choosing spectacularly bad boyfriends?" Tam said.

"You *do* have a tendency to date douchebags," Hayden agreed, this time earning him a smack on the head from Asad.

"Not helpful," Asad chided. Then he turned to her. "Based on what you mentioned earlier, you built spreadsheets. For a budget or something?"

She frowned as her mind played over her duties . . . the ones that had been increasing the longer she'd stayed at the agency. "I did sort of balance the budget for a few of their bigger accounts when the account execs were shuffled around," she said slowly. "They found out that I had a degree in accounting, and it just seemed like a quick and easy solution to the problem."

She'd volunteered the information. They hadn't paid her more. She wrinkled her nose. And the new account exec had found it easier to simply let her keep going with it, given her "aptitude with spreadsheets."

"So you could do accounting," Hayden said. "Problem solved."

She grimaced. The thing was—she'd gotten the accounting degree because her parents had refused to help pay for school unless she studied something practical. The idea of *being* an accountant was hardly appealing. Also, she wasn't an MBA, and she didn't really have an accounting background . . . and it had been years since she'd graduated college. Without the experience, she couldn't get hired as an accountant, even if she wanted to.

"And social media, right?" Josh prompted, as if he'd read her mind. "What did that involve?"

"That was just putting up stuff on Insta and Twitter and stuff," she said dismissively, then paused contemplatively. "And, um, researching new platforms. And creating memes. But that was just, you know, pulling stuff together, playing with images. It was kind of fun, though."

"I do graphic design," Asad pointed out. "Do you think I just pull stuff together?"

"It was nothing like what you do," she quickly protested. "I mean, you're a professional!"

"And you could be one too," Asad said with a smile. "I think that's the point Josh is trying to make. Josh? Put graphic design on the list."

"Got it." Josh flipped the large page over, putting GRAPHIC DESIGN in one corner, and FOOD in the other. Then he frowned and wrote WRITING in the middle.

"I didn't say writing!" Tam yelped.

"I know," Josh said with a grin. "But I know you wanted to get your degree in creative writing, but your parents wouldn't let you."

Dammit. This is what she got for having a friend who knew her so well, for so long.

"And all that content? The TV and movies, the books?" He looked smug. "You know you love that stuff. Writing's a natural extension. Maybe you could . . . I don't know, write screenplays. Or books. Or even just reviews. Nothing here's written in stone."

Tam grumbled, looking at the three headers. "Now what?"

In the next half hour, they had a list of possible "careers" to try: from chef to food blogger (inspired by Lily's career as an influencer), novelist to screenplay writer, graphic designer to painter. She felt overwhelmed, her head swimming.

"How do you feel?" Josh said, sidling up to her as the rest laughed over something Hayden had said.

"Like a complete and utter fraud," Tam admitted. "I can't do any of this stuff. I wouldn't even know how to start."

"If only you knew someone who did graphic design," Asad deadpanned. "Or owned, I don't know, a restaurant, or *several* restaurants. Or a catering service."

Tam felt like an idiot. "But I couldn't—"

"You promised you'd give me a chance," Josh said. "Based on the life design book I read, the best way to figure out what you want to do is by *doing* it . . . trying different things. You need to prototype, see what works for you and what doesn't, in a real, hands-on environment."

"But . . ."

He gave her a serious look. "You gave me a month and a half," he reminded her.

She sighed. She was a woman of her word. "I'd need to get a food-handling license before I could work in your kitchens, Josh," she pointed out. "And you need to work on your proposal thing, for that meeting."

"You can still help me with the new restaurant concepts if you want," Josh said. "And we can get you a license as soon as possible. Seriously. You could have it in an afternoon."

"You can also work with me," Freddie said, his deep voice quiet and gentle, subdued compared to Hayden's off-the-cuff humor, or even Asad's hyperactive cheer. "As it happens, I'm catering a gourmet picnic for a couple that's getting engaged. It would be a bit different than Josh's kitchens . . . more assembly than actual cooking. That'd be in a few weeks."

"Thanks," she said.

"And you can help me with some concept work with whatever Josh wants for his upcoming restaurant stuff," Asad added.

That was two out of three. She swallowed. "Thank you so much, all of you," she said.

"Well, we can't help with the writing stuff, but I'll reach out, see who I know," Hayden said. And of course, Hayden knew someone who knew somebody, always, so Tam felt sure that he'd probably dig up an opportunity.

"Thanks," she repeated. "It means a lot."

Hayden shrugged. "You're one of the Herd. Of course we're gonna help."

It had been a long time since she'd felt so supported, she realized. She hadn't noticed how isolated she'd let herself get in New York until it was too late, and she didn't know how to open up to new people or make friends as an adult, especially one who worked the hours that she did. She'd relied on having a relationship, problematic as it was, for all her social needs. Now she saw her mistake. She wasn't going to do that again.

"All right, game plan," Josh said. "Freddie, when do you want to work with her?"

Freddie looked at his phone. "The picnic's the sixteenth."

She flipped through the calendar on her phone. She was going to need to take all her reminders for work off, she realized with a pang. "Sure. Although at some point, I need to go back to New York."

"What?" Josh stiffened, staring at her. "Why?"

"Because I have, like, no clothes, and I don't want to buy a whole wardrobe?" she said, shaking her head. "I have some other stuff at the apartment that I need to send here. Paperwork, some books, some keepsakes."

"Oh." He frowned. "That means dealing with Brent, huh?"

"Unfortunately," she said. "But yes, I should be able to do the catering thing. And Josh, I can help you in the meantime with the restaurant ideas." At least it was a small way she could help.

"And when Josh settles on some ideas, you can help me with the graphic design," Asad added. "Maybe next week? The eighth?"

She nodded, putting it in her calendar as well.

They finally had everything pinned down, and they celebrated with drinks—mostly teas or decaf. Juanita had a gift, she realized with a sigh, and took a picture of her chai, replete with a decorative milk-foam leaf.

They had faith in her. If only she had the same.

CHAPTER 14

Tam spent the next few days decompressing, or at least trying to. She spent time at Juanita's coffee shop a lot, using an old bike that Josh owned, her messenger bag with her laptop strapped across her back. She also went to Josh's office at the Tombs, appreciating him working, trying to help where she could with his presentation while assuring him that she was thinking about her "joy." But by Thursday, she knew that she had to tie off the loose ends of her life in New York.

As she'd predicted, Lydia had texted her, demanding forgotten passwords and what would have amounted to training manuals for her replacement, before backhandedly offering her the job back. Tam blocked her number too.

Now, she needed to deal with Brent.

Once she got her clothes and belongings out of Brent's place and down to Ponto Beach, she could figure out how to move forward in her new life—whatever that wound up looking like. If Josh had his way, she'd be some kind of weird poet who wrote sestinas about a cheesemonger, complete with accompanying illustrations. She loved Josh like whoa, but still . . . she had a feeling that the next five weeks were going to go by in a blink, and she was going to be no closer to a job or a place to live than she was now. The very least she could do was have her wardrobe and important documents with her when she finally buckled down and got to work.

She sat out in the backyard, the bright Ponto sunshine warming her cheeks and making her chest feel expansive, despite the grimness of her task. Taking a deep breath, she dialed up Brent's number.

"Tam? Jesus, where are you?" Brent said without preamble. "Are you back in New York? Let me know where you are—I'll meet you. Or come home to the apartment, and I'll meet you there. That's probably a better idea . . ."

She frowned. It was only three o'clock in New York, meaning he was still at work. He'd never been so eager to drop everything for her in the past. "I'm still in Ponto," she said. "But I'm going to be back in New York. Monday, I'm thinking?"

"Thank God," Brent said. "This never should've happened. I need to see you and apologize."

"That is for fucking sure," Tam heard herself say, then snapped her mouth shut.

Where had *that* come from?

"We can get through this. I mean it," he said, his words all but oozing with sincerity. "I will do whatever it takes to get us over this and back to where we were."

"Yeah . . . no. That's not happening," Tam said quickly. "I'm just coming back to get my stuff and drop off my key. We're not reconciling, and I'm not moving back. There's nothing to discuss."

"How can you say that?" His voice was plaintive. "We had six years. Six years, Tam!" He paused. "I was going to ask you to marry me!"

She was so surprised, she jolted to her feet. "You were going to *what*?"

"I was going to propose."

"When?" she asked, gobsmacked. "I mean, when exactly were you planning to do this?"

"I didn't have anything specific planned yet," he said. "I was still working on the timing, the location. I wanted it to be perfect."

Just like that, she knew he was lying. Telling her what he figured she wanted to hear, just to keep her on the line. To make her feel guilty, and invested, and tempted.

No wonder he was able to convince rich old dudes to throw money at investments. He was one hell of a salesman. She grimaced.

How many times had she bought what he was selling?

"You'll be at work," she said, her voice firm. "I'll get my stuff, leave my key, and then we're set. I don't need to give you any other reasons, and we certainly have nothing to discuss."

"You don't sound like yourself, Tam," he tried. "I know, I fucked this up, but you've got to give me a chance to make it right. You can't just throw away everything we've had."

She wanted to scream. "It's like you don't hear a word I say," she said sharply. "We. Are. Done. That's it. Nothing left to say!"

"I can't accept that."

"You don't have a choice!" she growled.

"I'll be here at the apartment, waiting," he said, and it had just the slightest edge to it. Challenge. Maybe even . . . a teeny threat? "We're going to talk about this, Tam. You're pissed now, and nobody would blame you. But I'm not letting you go without a fight."

Part of her really, really wanted to fight. But more like "bean him with a tire iron" fight, she realized. Lucky for him, that wasn't who she was, and they both knew it. "I'm moving to Ponto, Brent. And there's nothing you can say or do to stop me."

"To be with *him*," Brent said sourly. "Guess I wasn't the only one lying, huh? Wasn't the only one cheating."

"Are you shitting me?" she spat out. "He's my friend!"

"Sure. Tell me . . . where did he suggest you stay while you're out there?"

Brent's words were poisonous, and despite knowing that she had nothing to feel guilty about, she suddenly did feel a sharp stab of it.

"Well, I'm not staying in his bed," she said, her voice firm. "And it's never been an option."

"Matter of time," Brent said, his tone sad. "I never had a chance. Tell me you're not attracted to him."

"I'm . . ."

She tripped on the words *not attracted to him*. Because it was a lie. She'd always had a sense of him . . . a physical connection. She'd have to be blind to not look at the face she'd studied for hours, those sky-blue eyes, that smile, and *not* feel the stirrings of attraction. But whether or not she was attracted wasn't the point. He was off limits, and their connection superseded any physical liaison. Not that she could explain that.

" . . . not going to discuss this with you," she finally said.

Brent pounced. "You said that you loved me, but if he'd snapped his fingers, you would've gone running to him in a second!"

She was going to say something cutting but realized that what he said was right. And that there was a reason for it. "Josh has always been there when I needed him," she said.

"Are you saying I wasn't?" Brent had ramped himself up to fine form, outraged and hurt. She usually fell prey to it, feeling guilty and outmaneuvered.

She closed her eyes, taking a deep breath. *Don't let him do this. Don't fall for it again.*

"Brent, you couldn't take time out of your busy schedule—which included *fucking your ex*—to pay attention to me." Her voice was calm as a lake's mirror surface, but inside, she felt bitterness, like chewing an aspirin, giving her a sour taste in her mouth.

"You were the one that was too busy for me," Brent tried. "I wouldn't have—"

She cut him off. "Remember when I took an Uber to the ER, that time I got stomach flu?"

Another pause. "That was . . . I apologized. How was I supposed to know how serious it was? I'm not a fucking doctor, Tam!"

"I needed you, and you said you were going to go out with your friends. Which, for all I know, was a euphemism," she said.

Brent's voice pitched harsh, all salesmanship temporarily suspended. "And I suppose Saint fucking Josh would've driven you and slept by your bedside!"

"Josh would walk over fire and glass to get me a sandwich," she said. "You couldn't show up to take me to the hospital. And when we were teens, when my life *sucked*, he was the one thing I could count on. Even more than my actual family. If you'd ever actually listened to me, or cared about me, you'd *know* that. So yeah. If he calls me and says he needs my help, I'm going to be on an airplane before he hangs up the phone. He is one of the most important people in my life, and I can't believe I let myself get cut off from him, and from the rest of my friends here, because you have a fucking inferiority complex."

That seemed to shut Brent up for a second.

"So if you want to be there when I get my stuff, fine. You want to keep talking, whatever. I'm going to have earphones in, and I'm going to pack my bags and get my shit, and that is the last you're going to see of me."

It felt liberating. It was like mainlining . . . something. At least, she imagined so, since it wasn't like she'd ever done drugs before. She felt like she could fly on sheer righteous rage alone.

"You're going to need to call me," he said. "I had the locks changed."

She gritted her teeth. Because of course he had. He wanted to control her access to her own belongings.

"Fine. Whatever." She paused. "And if you're thinking of doing anything cute like trashing my stuff, or tossing it, think very carefully. Just because I'm not vindictive like Vinh doesn't mean I'm not capable of it. I'm not kidding."

He scoffed. "We're going to talk, Tam," he said, ignoring her warning.

She hung up and then let out a low, frustrated screech, tugging at her hair close to the scalp.

How had she let it get that bad?

Josh stepped out onto the patio, and she spun. "I . . . sorry," she said reflexively. "Wait. Why aren't you at work?"

He smiled a little sheepishly. "Thought I'd come by and bring lunch," he said. "I also bought some groceries. Don't want you to get sick of takeout."

This. This was the thoughtfulness she was talking about. "I'm going to head back to New York," she said. "Shouldn't take me longer than a day to get my stuff shipped out here. I used to be irritated that all of our furniture was Brent's, but now I'm seeing that it was a blessing. And the kitchen stuff . . . well, I'm not gonna want to ship a KitchenAid mixer, because they're heavier than hell. I hate losing it, and my cookware, but it's worth it to just get clear of him."

Josh gave her a hug. "You okay?"

She sighed. "I just feel like such an idiot. Can't believe I let this crap go on this long."

"It's okay," he said against the crown of her hair. "Or it'll be okay. Promise."

She felt herself crumple a little, leaning against him.

"So you're going when?"

"I was going to go Monday," she said. "I figured he'd be at work. But it turns out he changed the locks, so at this point, it doesn't matter. Better to just get it out of the way," she mused.

He nodded. "Tell you what. Let's go Friday. That way you can still ship stuff on Saturday if it takes a while, then we can fly back on Sunday. Sound good?"

"We? What are you talking about?" She blinked. "I don't . . . you've got all your stuff with the investor proposal . . ."

"I want to help," he said. "You might not have all that much stuff, but it'll still be bulky, and you're gonna need manual labor at the very least, right?"

She bit her lip. He did have a point.

"Besides," he said with a soft laugh, "I'd walk over fire and glass to get you a sandwich, after all."

She groaned. Because of course he'd heard that bit. "I . . . that probably came out weird."

"Nah. It's true. You're my best friend." He laughed. "And you'd bail me out of jail or break me out if need be. It kind of balances between us, you know?"

She felt her chest heat. "All right. I'll get tickets," she said slowly. "Actually, it'll be good for you to be there. He tends to wear me down, and while I'd like to think that I wouldn't buckle, I think he won't act up as much if you're there." She gritted her teeth. "And I *hate* that I'm ducking behind a man to try and get another man to leave me alone."

"I get it," he said, and to her surprise, his cheeks were flushed with color. "I mean, I used you as a shield for Heidi the Pierogi Princess. It's the least I can do."

Tam burst into laughter. "God, we are a pair."

"Yeah. Yeah, we are," he said with a broad grin. "C'mon. I brought you a bánh mì from a little place across town. It's not as good as what we'll make, I don't think, although I might steal the cook if it is."

"You're kidding." She laughed. "You actually got me a sandwich."

"Glass, fire, and all," he said with a wink. "Anything for you."

She snickered, following him into the house. "Why don't the men I date treat me like you do?" she teased.

She expected him to laugh, but instead he looked at her over his shoulder.

"I genuinely don't know," he said, his tone serious. Then went back to the food as if he hadn't said anything at all.

CHAPTER 15

They caught a red-eye on Friday, which was hardly Josh's favorite thing, but it got them into New York on Saturday morning. All things considered, the sooner they got in, the sooner they could get out, and Josh knew how much of a toll this was taking on Tam. The easier and quicker he could make it, the better. As it was, he'd had to basically arm wrestle her to get the hotel room for the night, even though he was planning on not letting her pay for anything. She barely had any savings—her time in New York had been expensive—and he hated the thought of money freaking her out any more than it already had.

It occurred to him that it might be considered weird for them to be sharing a room, rather than getting separate ones. Still, he'd shared rooms with people from the Herd plenty of times. Hell, he'd shared a hotel room with Tam before. Granted, once they'd also shoehorned Tobin, Lily, Keith, and Melanie in there as well, so it wasn't like he was *just* rooming with Tam, but the principle was the same. Also, he figured if he made the argument that he would've paid for his own room anyway, then there was no reason for her to kick in any cash.

Besides, it would have two beds. There . . . weirdness abated.

They dropped off their luggage with the concierge at the hotel since they were too early for check-in. Then they went and rented a wheeled dolly and bought some cardboard boxes and a tape dispenser so she could ship her stuff. As they got closer to the towering building where she'd lived with her boyfriend, she started nervously fidgeting, tucking her hair behind her right ear.

"It's going to be okay," he reassured her, dragging the dolly with the flattened boxes balanced on it. "Don't worry, okay? You've got this."

"You remember what you promised, right?"

"I won't kick his ass," Josh said solemnly, and she snickered.

"I said don't start a fight."

"That's basically the same thing," he said, gratified by the slight relaxation of her tension and her tiny smile.

When they walked into the lobby, a livery-wearing, overweight man with graying hair surveyed them. "Hello, Ms. Doan," he intoned, sounding regal. "We haven't seen you in a few days. Everything all right?"

Tam didn't seem put off by his somewhat snooty attitude. "I'm moving out, Harvey," she told the doorman, and while he still looked concerned, he nodded, waving them through, calling Brent to announce them. Before they went to the elevator, she stopped. "Harvey—who's on Brent's approved visitor list?"

Harvey reddened. "Ah . . . you, obviously."

"I lived here," she pointed out. "Who else?"

"His parents . . . sister, I believe . . ." He cleared his throat. "And a Ms. Long?"

Josh saw a muscle by the corner of Tam's eye twitch. "Thanks," she said quietly. "Good to know."

Josh wanted so badly to hug her, but he got the feeling she was hanging on by a thread. Instead, he followed her to the elevator. They took it to the twelfth floor, then headed down the hallway. It was a nice building, at least. Brent was some kind of finance guy, he seemed to remember. She rapped on the door quickly, a few sharp raps.

Josh had never met Brent, so he wasn't sure what to expect when the door opened. The guy had brown hair that reminded Josh of weak coffee, even if it was stylishly cut. He was wearing brown slacks, a white button-down, and a pair of loafers. He seemed kind of dressed up for a Saturday, but then, Josh tended to stick to casual unless he was meeting with financial professionals or going to the local business meetup. Of course, Josh was predisposed to hate the man for how he'd treated Tam, so the jerk could've been wearing jeans and a T-shirt and still seemed like a total douche canoe.

"Tam, sweetheart," Brent said, reaching for her as if to hug her, and she let out a strangled yelp, taking a step back. He blinked, his expression one of reproach and longing. "I've been worried. Why didn't you—"

His reproof broke off when he took in Josh and the dolly in the hallway.

"You brought him? Here?" His voice cracked, and he looked at her like she'd kicked his puppy. "In . . . in *our* apartment?" His eyes were wide and solemn as he shook his head, projecting a profound sense of loss.

The guy should've gotten a fucking Oscar for his little self-pitying performance. Josh could see his tactic: make Tam feel guilty, knock her off balance.

"In the apartment you *fucked your ex-girlfriend* in? In *our bed*?" Tam snapped back. "Want to think that through again, and stable your high horse?"

Brent made a sour face, glaring at Josh. Josh just grinned back, proud of Tam's composure.

"We really need to talk," Brent tried again as she grabbed the boxes off the dolly. "I can't make this right if you don't talk to me."

Josh was about to step in and say she didn't need to do anything, but Tam's expression was growing more and more lethal, and it wasn't his place, so he bit his tongue.

"I told you before: this isn't up for discussion," Tam said. "I'm packing up and leaving. Period."

"But we haven't . . . you can't just . . ." Brent let out an exasperated huff. "Damn it, Tam. This isn't fair."

"Isn't *fair*?" She stared at him, briefly stopping in her tracks. "And you cheating on me *is*?"

Another tactic, Josh realized. The guy was manipulative as hell, but skillful at it. He was trying to get her to engage. And apparently after six years, she was used to falling into it.

Josh reached out and touched her shoulder, and she stopped, taking a deep breath as she looked at him instead of the jackass who was still trying to play mind games. When he was sure she was focused, he nodded, stroking her shoulder ever so slightly. He watched as her breathing evened out, and she nodded back.

"Whatever, Brent," she finally muttered. "It's not fair. Poor you. I don't give a shit."

Brent looked like he was going to physically stand in her way, which Josh would've loved—it would've given him an excuse to ditch Tam's "don't start a fight" warning—but finally, the guy clenched his jaw hard enough that Josh could hear audible teeth grinding. Then he stepped out of the way.

Tam took her armful of collapsed boxes and the tape dispenser and headed for a room off to the side, what Josh had to assume was the bedroom. "Just wait here, I'll be right out," she said to Josh. He wanted to help, but he got the sense that she needed to do it alone—both to make her decisions, but also to regain her composure. When Brent went to follow her, she glared at him. "You too. I don't need your help."

"How do I know you won't take anything of mine?" Brent said like a total dickhead. Which he obviously was.

From the way she rolled her eyes, Josh could tell she felt the same way. "I don't want a damned thing of yours, and you know it. Knock it off."

"It's *my* apartment, Tam," he said with enough of a threat that Josh's hackles went up. He gripped the handle of the dolly a little harder, imagining it was Brent's throat.

"Yup. With Daphne on the approved visitor list," Tam replied, and Brent flushed. "So now it'll be *all* your apartment. Don't worry. This shouldn't take long." She stalked away, muttering to herself.

Which left the two men standing in the living room, awkward and belligerent, with tension thick as nitroglycerin.

Josh looked around, afraid that if he struck up a conversation with the asshole, it wouldn't be the only thing he wound up striking. The apartment didn't look like someplace Tam would live at all. Tam loved gentle nature colors: rich earthy browns, different gradients of blue, sage greens. Calm, inviting colors.

Kind of like the colors in his own house, he realized with a jolt.

He turned his attention back to his surroundings, trying to distract himself as Tam packed this chapter of her life away. The place was painfully boring, all black and white, with glossy chrome accents. There was a Peloton bike in the corner, and . . . jeez. A cigar humidor and a small beer fridge? When Tam didn't even drink beer, and her seasonal asthma made even secondhand smoke a problem? He was gritting his teeth as he stared at the "artwork": framed black-and-white posters, all noir films.

Tam hated noir films.

Beyond that, the apartment looked like one of the least comfortable places he'd ever seen. No knickknacks or photos of the couple. No pillows on the hard-looking couch. He knew that she loved lap blankets and thought napping on a couch was one of the greatest indulgences known to man.

This place looked like a bachelor pad, Josh realized. And wondered if Tam had ever put that together.

"So, since Tam isn't introducing us," Brent said as Josh heard the shrill squeak of packing tape as Tam put together the boxes, "I'm Brent. Her boyfriend."

"*Ex-boyfriend*," Tam shouted from the bedroom.

Brent kept glaring at Josh. "And I have to assume you're her little high school friend. Josh, was it?"

Josh thought about ignoring him, but it didn't seem worth it. At least hopefully it'd shut the guy up for a second. "That's right."

He took a step back, sizing Josh up. Josh hadn't been in a fistfight in years, but God, if he hadn't promised Tam he wouldn't, he would be beating this guy senseless, right in his bougie living room. Even if he got arrested, it'd be worth it.

After what felt like forever, during which time Josh checked on their flight and got a message that they could check into their hotel room, he sensed Brent was gearing up for something. Some new way to screw with Tam's head. He cleared his throat.

"Soooo," Brent said slowly. "You're fucking her, then?"

Josh heard Tam's strangled sound of protest. He knew that he shouldn't. He'd promised he wouldn't start a fight with the guy.

That said—she hadn't said not to *mess* with him. Specifically.

"I am now," Josh announced, throwing in a wide, cocky smile for good measure. "And I've got you to thank for it. If you hadn't been such a dick, screwing around on her and treating her like crap, we never would've reconnected. I owe you a solid."

Brent's mouth dropped open. Then his expression turned irritated.

"You honestly expect me to believe you two never hooked up?"

"I know, right?" Josh agreed easily, loving the way that it made the guy turn an ugly purple red. "Talk about wasted time! I mean, I had a feeling that it'd be incredible, but I think if we'd *known* what we were missing . . . holy shit."

Brent's eyes bugged out, and a vein pulsed in his temple.

"I don't blame you for not wanting to let her go," Josh continued blithely. "She is the best I've ever been with. Hands down."

Tam came out with a box, awkwardly put it on the dolly, then retreated to the bedroom and came back, putting another on top of it. Then she nodded at her haul. "That's it. All my stuff."

"Really? That's it?" Josh knew that the stuff in the apartment—the furniture and whatever—wasn't hers, but Christ. She'd lived with the guy for nearly six years, and this was all she'd accumulated? Stuff she was able to pack away in less than twenty minutes?

"I know," she said, and she sounded embarrassed and let out a little laugh. "Thank God for Marie Kondo, huh?"

Josh nodded, knowing that she was playing it off, trying desperately to keep it together. "All right. Let's get out of here."

"No way," Brent interjected, and it took Josh a second to figure out what Brent was protesting. He thought the idiot was going to try to stop them. Instead, he crossed his arms. "No way you two are fucking."

"Oh, sure, now you believe me," Tam muttered darkly.

But he kept going. "Want to know how I know? Because she's a goddamned puritan. She made me wait for months before we had sex." He tried a grin, his expression turning smarmy. "You blew it as soon as you said she's the best you've ever been with. Trust me, she's not that good. Next time, don't oversell it."

Josh looked at her.

Please. Please let me knock him the fuck out. I can make it quick. We'll be gone before the cops get here.

She must've understood what he was trying to communicate, because she shook her head, ever so slightly. Then, before Josh knew what was going on, she stepped up to him, putting her hands on either side of his face and tugging until he was at her eye level.

Then she kissed him.

He wasn't quite sure what was going on at first, simply because it so wasn't *them*. But then he registered her lips, so unbelievably soft. The fucking *heat* of that mobile mouth of hers. The sexy, needy little sounds she made.

He really wasn't anticipating tongue, but when she teased his lips, he opened his mouth because hey, he wasn't rude.

That may have turned into a strategic error, because then he closed his eyes, and . . . *holy hell.*

It was like getting dragged under by a whirlpool, only a really sexy, overwhelming one. He tilted his head for better access, his tongue tangling with hers as she made a small, deliciously needy noise of surprise and desire. His hands clenched reflexively at her hips, pulling her tighter to him, a low growl building in his own throat.

Mine.

"The fuck, Tam?" Brent squeaked. His voice seemed really far away.

Josh couldn't give less of a fuck, audience or not. He was getting hard, with her body pressed against his, her hands moving from his face to his shoulders, almost clawing at him like she wanted to climb him like a tree. He didn't care if it was obvious that he was responding to what had to be the most unexpected, hottest moment of his life. All he cared about was the woman currently shocking him with her passion and her heat.

Finally, Tam pulled away, looking dazed. Then she cleared her throat.

"Yeah. Okay," she said, as if she was answering a question no one had asked. She blinked, her pupils dilated so wide it was like her eyes were black. She looked stunned.

Josh stared back. He knew how she felt.

"Is this your way of getting back at me?" Brent squawked. "Because if you wanted to hurt me, then you succeeded."

"Hmm?" Tam turned, as if she'd suddenly become aware of Brent's presence. "Oh. Right. So . . . yeah. Bye." It was like she couldn't even hear him anymore. She gestured to the dolly, put a key on a ring on the counter, and then walked out the door.

Josh nodded at Brent, who looked shocked.

"Thanks for that 'overselling' tip," Josh said with a wink and just enough smart-ass to make Brent livid. And the guy was, definitely. Which probably shouldn't have made Josh as happy as it did.

But hey, no one was perfect. He jogged down the hallway with the dolly and boxes, catching up with Tam, who still seemed in a fugue state.

They waited for the elevator. "Sorry about that," she finally said, sounding breathless.

"Don't be," Josh said. "Was worth it to see that asshole's face."

She giggled. It sounded a little hysterical, but at least she wasn't sad.

The problem was, his body had woken up and was now throbbing painfully. He was a little breathless himself.

And we're about to spend the night together in a hotel room, he thought, as he tried valiantly to calm his unruly body down.

Her kiss was totally unexpected—and it was like they'd let a genie out of a bottle. One he'd certainly never anticipated.

This, he realized, could be bad.

CHAPTER 16

A few hours later, Josh was convinced he was right.

This was *bad*.

It was like they'd opened Pandora's sex toy box or something. His body was vibrating like a tuning fork—and it was attuned specifically to *her*. When she took his hand, the softness of her palm against his was a revelation. She tugged him through the crowd. She stayed by his side, chattering about their plans for the day, seemingly unaffected . . . even as he fought against getting hard from smelling her jasmine shampoo.

It hadn't gotten any better by the time they'd hit the small shipping store where they'd returned the rented dolly and shipped her boxes of clothes to his house in Ponto. Then they'd stopped by the hotel, dropping their bags off in their room after checking in.

"Wanna sightsee?" she then said with a bright smile. "I know you've never been to New York, and I don't know when I'll be back. Maybe you won't make that scrunchy face when I say it's an awesome city."

He was more fixated on her smile than the topic, so he found himself saying yes. She hugged him with an excited squeal.

He went rock hard in an instant. Which was both unexpected and unsettling.

While she'd searched for tourist attractions and pieced together a plan of attack, he'd surreptitiously looked for earlier flights home, just in case. Unfortunately, all the nonstop flights were booked, and all the flights with stops were these hideous multicity affairs that would take all day and into the night. As much as he didn't want to face his body's new heightened awareness of Tam's tight little figure . . .

Knock it off with that shit! He visualized hitting himself on the nose with a rolled-up newspaper.

. . . that was, his new awareness of *his friend*, he didn't want to subject her to a flight that sprawled around the country and was three times as long as their original flight, just because he was unnerved by his physical reaction to her.

He sighed.

"C'mon," she said, tugging at him until thcy hit a subway.

Unfortunately, there was some kind of festival or event, and the trains were teeming with people. Their compartment was standing room only. Ordinarily, he would've found the experience fun—he rarely took the train from Ponto Beach to San Diego or LA—but in their sardine-like position, she was yet again pressed against him. He'd adjusted himself and was forcing himself to try to think of the least sexual things possible. Honestly, just the smells and the heat of the train should've done the trick. But then the train gave a lurch, throwing her against him. He held her tight, and she *clung*.

He sent up a silent prayer for perseverance and held her tighter.

By the time they'd gone through Central Park, seen the waterfront, and hit up a snazzy seafood restaurant off Times Square after some people watching, he was both exhausted and wired. They headed back to their hotel, where a convention of some sort was in full swing. He was starting to get burnout from all the "energy" of New York, and all he wanted to do was go back to the room and crash.

The elevator banks were, of course, packed.

"Wanna take the stairs?" he asked, his voice rasping slightly.

She looked at him like he'd lost his mind. "To the twenty-third floor?"

"Um . . . right. No." He swallowed hard.

Just get through this.

They crammed their way into an elevator with a bunch of drunken dentists. When one leered at Tam, Josh glowered at him until he backed down, repentant. Then Josh turned, and . . .

Yup. Yet again, he was crushed against Tam's body, to the point where he could see her heartbeat fluttering in her throat, watch her swallow, feel her breathing grow uneven. Every time someone moved, it seemed like the two of them brushed against each other, sliding over each other like bunched-up silk. She gasped softly, and he thought he was going to explode.

"You okay?" he asked. It came out hoarse.

She simply nodded.

Thankfully, by the time they reached the higher floors, there were fewer people and more space. He flanked her instead of pressing against her, but the damage was already done. He prayed that she didn't look down where his bulge was pretty much unmistakable.

They retreated down the hallway to the hotel room. It was basic, nothing to write home about: a simple small room with a TV, a dresser, a nightstand between two queen-size beds. He let them in with his card key and turned on the lights.

"So. Wanna, um, watch a movie or something?" she asked. She seemed off. Not quite upset. There was a hyperactive forced cheer to her expression, and he realized he'd been too distracted by his own body to realize that she'd probably been dealing with the emotional fallout of Dickhead Brent all day.

"Hey, hey. You all right?" Without thinking, he reached for her, tugging her in for a hug.

Which meant she felt exactly what he'd developed in the elevator.

They both froze. Then, carefully, he tried to play it off by . . . *patting her head*.

He winced at his own stupidity. What was he *doing*?

He pulled away. "I think a movie sounds, um, great," he said, realizing he sounded like an idiot, but not sure how to say *oops, sorry about my hard-on!* "I want to, ah, take a shower, though? First, I mean?"

She was staring at him. Then she nodded, quickly, just once.

He grimaced. "Unless you wanted to take a shower?"

Instantly, his brain provided a visual of Tam in the shower, water sluicing down her naked body as she arched her back . . .

Maybe even the two of them, together . . .

Whoa! No! Stop being helpful!

"Not with me!" he spluttered out, then realized she hadn't commented and probably hadn't thought that at all. "I mean, you know. If you want to use the bathroom first? To take a shower?"

"I'll take one in the morning, I think?" she squeaked.

"Cool, cool." Oh my God. He was devolving into a gibbering dipshit. He needed to get out, now. "Then, um, I'll take a quick shower and then we can watch a movie. Anything you want!"

Which reminded him of sitting on the couch with her, watching the damned Bridgertons bone buck naked. He'd gotten kind of . . . *bothered* at that point too. Then, he had felt awkward because he'd essentially been snuggled up with Tam as they watched all the sexy shenanigans.

"Right!" With that, he marched into the bathroom and shut the door, breathing hard.

Man, I need to jerk off.

That was obviously the solution.

He just needed to release the pressure, as it were. He hadn't had sex in a good few months. Last time was a quick hookup that he could barely remember, some woman he'd picked up at a bar. She'd been looking for a good time and then had told him to leave before the sweat had cooled because her roommate was due home. Of course, he was slowly starting to figure out that *roommate* probably meant *boyfriend*, and he cursed himself, which is why he hadn't gotten with anyone since. He had no time or interest in dating apps, and he was very wary of setups by the Herd or Amber because if things went south, it could create blowback to the whole friend-network dynamic.

So the one-two punch of celibacy, combined with being plastered to Tam for most of the day after sharing a toe-curling kiss, was making his body go haywire. He'd just take a shower, take himself in hand . . . and come out with Tam none the wiser, a relaxed, sane, comfortable man.

He stripped out of his clothes, then grimaced.

Is this skeevy, though?

This was brand-new territory. It wasn't like they were in the same room, after all, which helped, but still. Was he crossing a line here? Just because she wouldn't know didn't mean *he* wouldn't know. And probably feel guilty about it. It was . . . weird.

Besides, it wasn't like he was going to *think* about her while he was . . .

He stopped short. *You sure about that, sport?*

He looked at himself in the mirror. His dick stuck out like a missile, and he was glaring like he wanted to kill somebody.

God damn it. He respected Tam, and he cared about her. He probably shouldn't do a damn thing but get his ass in the shower, turn it all the way to "C," and freeze his balls off until he got his shit together.

He then glanced around and noticed that he'd forgotten his toiletry bag. Because *of course he had.* In his haste to dive into the shower and get himself off, he'd left his toothbrush and shaving kit and whatever-the-hell-else behind.

Sighing, he threw a towel around his waist, keeping his dick tucked in the band but hidden from sight. Then he stepped out. "Sorry, just forgot . . ."

His words dried up in his throat.

Tam was lying in one of the beds, with only a sheet pulled over her. She was wearing her nightgown. One of her arms was draped over her head. The other had disappeared beneath the covers . . . and from the outline of the thin fabric, he could tell that her hand was still caught between her legs, working furiously.

Her eyes flew open, meeting his. He tried to speak, and sheerly, utterly *couldn't*. The vision of Tam, arching like a cat, panting softly, her eyes closed, was probably going to haunt him for the rest of his life.

That said, the vision wasn't really helping his whole *situation*, either.

They stared at each other for a long moment.

"Um . . . ," she said, as she yanked her hand up from between her thighs and pulled the sheet to her chin. Her face went red as a raspberry with a blush that could've set fire to her hair. "Sorry?"

"I forgot my toothbrush," he said inanely.

She grimaced. "I thought you were going to take a longer shower."

CHAPTER 17

Fuck. My. Life.

Tam wanted a time machine. Something that would take her back five minutes or so, to the moment when she'd brilliantly decided to address the sexual tension that had been frying her system since the moment she'd kissed Josh in Brent's apartment. So she could smack some sense into herself.

Or better yet, she'd go back to the moment just before kissing Josh, and smack herself then.

What were you thinking?

The thing was, she *hadn't* been thinking. At least not with her brain. Her body was apparently like a sex-starved desert, parched and sun-baked, until Josh had kissed the crap out of her and made her wet.

No pun intended. Although let's face it, there was a whole lotta truth there.

She groaned, flipping over and burying her head in her pillow. "You didn't see anything," she mumbled, going for her best Jedi mind trick. "I was just lying here. Sleeping."

"What was that?" She heard Josh's amusement, felt the mattress dip as he sat down next to her. "You okay?"

She turned to face him, and he was grinning softly. "I said, let's just forget all this happened."

"I can try," he said slowly, then huffed out a breath. "I can *pretend* I forgot, anyway."

She sat up. She could still feel the damp slide between her thighs, and her nipples were like diamonds, and *oh God*, why couldn't she just *stop*?

The problem was, she hadn't had sex with Brent in a while, way before they'd broken up. Hadn't been interested in sex in even longer than that. Honestly, sex tended to be a stressful occurrence for her. She was always so in her head about it—intent on making sure her partner was happy. She frowned. It was recovering-honors-student syndrome all over again. She'd people-pleased to the point where she rarely experienced pleasure herself, unless it was the pleasure of a "job well done."

Sex was a chore. And she'd rather have the orgasm than the accolade at this point, but she couldn't seem to get her mind and body on the same page.

Which is why just *kissing* Josh had been such a revelation—and today had been such an intoxicating, painful, teasing *mess*. It was like her long-dormant hormones had suddenly decided to crash in on her, all at once. She was a time bomb of sexual tension, and she just needed to explode. She figured it would have taken less than five minutes for her to silently get herself off while Josh was in the bathroom. Then she'd get ready for bed, and they'd watch a movie, with Josh none the wiser.

And I would have gotten away with it, too, if it weren't for his meddling toothbrush!

"Not to make this weird, though," Josh said softly, "but I think that's going to be imprinted on my retinas? For, like, ever?"

She growled, forcing herself not to hide in the pillow again. "Well, can we try to unweird this?" she begged. "Because right now, I kind of want to throw myself off a tall bridge. I can't even imagine how I could be more humiliated."

He chuffed out a breath of laughter. "It's only weird," he said mischievously, "if we make it weird."

"God, please, don't quote Hayden to me right now," she said, but at least she laughed too. And thoughts of Hayden did kill her libido quite a bit.

Josh got up and went back to the bathroom. She watched the play of muscles in his back as he strode shirtless across the small hotel room. And that ass. How had she never noticed and admired the perfection of that bubble butt? For a skinny guy, he . . .

What are you *doing?*

She shook her head, hard, clutching the pillow to her front. She needed to get a grip, ASAP.

"Man, am I tired," she lied, forcing a yawn. "We should just go to sleep. Yes! Sleep. That's a good idea."

He was quiet, staring at her from the bathroom doorway, and she frowned at him.

"You said you'd *pretend*, at least," she muttered.

"Okay." With that, he disappeared into the bathroom, this time with his toiletry bag. She heard him brushing his teeth.

For a brief, frenetic second, she thought about picking up where she left off. Then she gritted her teeth and counted her breathing until the thought passed.

"All yours," he said, after a short period of time. He was still draped in the towel that left little to the imagination, and she forced herself not to look.

Although he had good legs, she realized. Despite his wiry frame, he had solid calves and thighs. "You're still running?" she blurted out.

He looked at her with surprise. "Yeah. I mean, not lately, but it's usually a part of my daily routine."

"Oh. You seem . . . fit." She felt her cheeks burn.

Stop digging the hole deeper, you twit. She hurried to the bathroom, where she brushed her teeth, washed her face, and got ready for bed.

When she emerged, he was lying on top of his covers, still shirtless, but now wearing a pair of pajama pants instead of a towel, which she supposed she ought to be grateful for. She shut the lights off and clambered into her bed.

"Um . . . good night?" she said.

"Good night."

She felt more than heard the buzz of city noises far below. She swore she could almost feel the building swaying, even though there was hardly any wind. There was a thin ribbon of light from the slight gap in the blackout curtains, and the soft red glow from the alarm clock.

"It's because of the kiss, isn't it?" Josh broke the silence, surprising her.

"What is?"

"How turned on we are."

It was like holding a match to flash paper. Her body just went *fwoomp!* as heat exploded through her.

"We?"

"Because I have to admit, I didn't think kissing you was going to be like that, at all."

She turned to face his shadowy form, both irritated and relieved that she couldn't make out his expression. "What did you think it was going to be like?"

"I don't know. Just not like *that*."

"Huh."

She heard him rustle on the bed, his voice sounding closer, suggesting he'd turned toward her. "Haven't you thought about it?"

"About what?"

"Us. Together." He cleared his throat. "Kissing and . . . I don't know. Whatever."

"Well, sure." She sensed his surprise, and she rolled her eyes, even though she doubted he could see her. "Hey, you're hot, and I'm human. Don't act shocked."

"When you thought about it, did you think it was going to be that hot?" he said, his voice tinged with frustration and amusement in equal parts.

"I didn't think *anything* could be that hot," she admitted, then closed her eyes and wished, yet again, for a time machine.

He was quiet for a long moment. "Fair point," he said, and his voice sounded strained.

Another long moment, and she heard him snicker in the darkness.

"Why aren't you more surprised that I thought about it?" he asked.

"Not to stereotype, but . . . I've known you since you were a pubescent, cis het male," she pointed out. "Of course you thought about it."

"That feels a little reductive."

"You probably thought about what sex was like with Galadriel, every single one of the Golden Girls, and our sixth-grade teacher, Mrs. Russo, who smelled like overcooked cabbage and sad."

"Hey, Betty White's on my top ten list," he said, and she burst out laughing. Slowly, it felt like they were relaxing back into their old groove. The weirdness was slowly dissipating. *Nature is healing.*

"Wanna watch a movie?" he asked. "I know our flight is early, but I'm still kinda keyed up."

She knew exactly what he meant. "A movie sounds great," she said. She fumbled in the darkness for the remote, then turned the TV on. She scrolled through the on-demand selections. "Have a preference?"

"Something funny, I think," he said. She saw him, outlined in the light from the television. He'd gotten under the covers at some point. His hair was a tousled mess, and his eyes shone. He smiled at her. "Or maybe something action—with lots of explosions, and no real story to follow?"

It took absolutely everything in her not to get up and crawl into his bed. For the first time in their history, she knew that if they started snuggling, it wouldn't just be snuggling . . . and she was nervous about what it would turn into.

She cleared her throat, looking absently at the list she was hastily dashing through. "Indiana Jones! Classic."

She didn't even know which one it was, just haphazardly clicked until the thing cued up. She looked over to see him studying her, rather than the screen. She found it hard to look away.

"Well, well, well, Dr. Jones," she heard. "You're looking hotter than ever."

Wait. What?

She snapped her head back to look at the screen, to see a woman dressed as the iconic character—fedora, leather jacket, even the bullwhip. She had huge breasts that were practically falling out of her shirt, tiny booty shorts, and serious thigh-high boots.

"Call me Indiana Jane," the woman said, and within moments, as Tam watched in horrified fascination, "Jane" was suddenly bent over a nearby desk, stripped of her clothing (except for the hat) and . . .

And . . .

"Oh, shit!" Tam shouted, as her brain finally put together what was happening. She hastily pounded buttons on the remote—which initially resulted in fast-forwarding, then rewinding, then pausing (on a particularly lascivious scene of Jane enjoying the attentions of several other adventurers?) before finally shutting the movie down. "What the hell was *that*?"

Josh started laughing—deep, uncontrollable belly laughs that had tears running down his cheeks. "Oh my God," he said, when it seemed like he could finally catch his breath. "It's internet rule number thirty-four. If it exists, there is porn of it."

"No exceptions," Tam muttered. "For pity's sake. Why . . . is . . . *today*? I swear, this is the Universe's way of saying the hell with it, just have sex with Josh!"

Josh's laughter abruptly cut off. "Wait. Seriously?"

"Oh my *God*, Josh, not seriously."

Although . . . kind of seriously? Her body tingled. She hadn't quite meant to say it, but all things considered, it really did seem . . . fated?

"It'd be a bad idea," she murmured. "I mean, wouldn't it?"

He was quiet. "Probably," he finally agreed.

Strangely, she didn't feel comforted by his agreement. "Because we're good friends, and we don't want to screw that up."

"Exactly." This time, his agreement was more pronounced. "Sex comes and goes . . ."

"Ha ha," she said dryly.

"Wha . . . oh, ha. No pun intended," he said with a grin. "But having a best friend like you? That doesn't happen every day, and it's not worth screwing up. I wouldn't lose you for anything."

She smiled back at him, feeling warmth in her chest, even as she felt the weirdest knot of disappointment in her stomach. Strangely, it reminded her of high school.

Back when you had a crush and you knew it would be disaster.

God. She hadn't thought about that in years. Had buried it so far into her psyche that she'd (almost) forgotten she used to feel that way.

He started chuckling. "Man. Can you imagine what would've happened if we'd gotten together in high school?"

As usual, he was reading her mind. Albeit not completely. "Yeah," she said with a weak half-laugh. "That would've been awful."

"Train wreck," he said. "We would've broken up, and it would be like when Vinh and Emily split. Remember?"

She bit her lip. "I mean, I was in Vassar when that whole thing happened, but I know it was a mess. Vinh's still screwed up about it."

"Emily's still bitter too," Josh said. "The Herd didn't want to take sides, but it was pretty bleak . . . and Vinh just sort of vanished. Emily's still a townie, so we just support her, you know? If Vinh had been back in Ponto, I don't know what would've happened."

She grimaced. She didn't want to think about it either. Vinh had not had a single serious relationship since he'd broken up with Emily. He seemed to wall himself up in ice, and she still didn't have the whole story on *why* they'd broken up. But Josh was right. It was a disaster.

She didn't want that to happen between them.

"All right." She scrolled way more carefully, this time settling on *Deadpool*. "This ought to do it."

"Hey, Tam?"

"Mmm?" She glanced over to find him staring at her.

"You know I love you, right?" He looked so earnest. So sincere. "You're the most important person in my life. And I don't take that lightly."

She sighed. Then she crawled out of bed, went over to his bed, and gave him a huge, almost bruising hug, breathing in the scent of his neck. She felt tears prick at the corners of her eyes.

"I love you too, Josh," she whispered.

And that's *why we're not sleeping together.*

CHAPTER 18

Tam groaned early the next morning in the hotel room as she looked at the text update from the airline. "What the heck? Do planes hate me now?"

"At least it's just a flight delay," Josh said sympathetically, "and not a complete grid shutdown like last time."

"Oh God, don't even joke," Tam said, knocking on the nearby table. Superstitious? Yes. But the way her luck had been running this trip, she wouldn't be surprised if all flights were grounded and they'd be forced to stay here. And the hotel would move them to a honeymoon suite with just one bed, for some reason.

She rubbed at her sandy eyes. She'd gotten barely any sleep, and the snippets of sleep she had been able to get were frustrating, to say the least. She'd kept replaying the kiss with Josh, until she was panting and sweaty and ready for more . . . but when she tried to take them back to the hotel room, all the doors were locked and the key card wouldn't work. And people kept interrupting. She was starting to get desperate enough to consider simply boinking him in plain view of anyone and everyone, because she was pretty sure she'd be capable of bending steel rebar out of sheer frustration if she didn't get an orgasm, like, *now*.

She woke up grumpy. Josh telling her that their flight had been pushed off until late that evening did not help matters at all.

"You could try to get more sleep," Josh suggested.

He looked all rumpled and sexy as hell. His honey-blond hair was tousled, and he had stubble that she wanted to rub herself all over, like a cat. And that was not going to help her with her oath not to sleep with the guy. "Harrumph," she said instead, rolling over and gripping the pillow like she was wrestling it. "Don't know if I'll be able to. Once I'm awake, I'm just . . . up. You know?"

"Um, yeah." He got up and hurriedly used the bathroom, but not before she got a glimpse of what had to be morning wood. It made her body tense and tingle, and she squirmed uncomfortably.

This is intolerable!

When he was done showering and brushing and whatever, he came out wrapped in a towel again, yawning and rubbing the back of his head.

"Did you sleep like shit too?" she asked.

Why did that sleepy-eyed grin of his have to be so damned sexy? He nodded slowly. "Barely slept at all," he admitted.

She almost asked why, then caught herself. Because . . . well. The why was obvious. She could be oblivious, but she sincerely doubted he was up all night worrying about, say, the tax code or the grandfather time-travel paradox.

She forced herself to get ready for the day, showering quickly. She briefly considered taking care of herself in the shower, but she was too self-conscious at this point. And, again, with her luck, a fire alarm would go off or something.

She came out wrapped in a terry towel, having forgotten her clothes in her haste to get cleaned up. Her eyebrows jumped up as she saw that there was a wheeled cart with an assortment of breakfast items on it. Josh smiled at her, wearing a pair of jeans and a Neon Genesis Evangelion shirt.

"Thought you might be hungry," he said, nodding at the selection, "but wasn't sure what you wanted."

She smiled. "You spoil me," she said, sitting next to him at the little desk.

"I called down and saw if we could do late checkout, too," he said. "The convention ended, so everybody's leaving. They said we could stay until this afternoon, no problem."

"That's good. I don't think I'm up for any more sightseeing," she admitted. "And hanging out at the airport sounds exhausting."

They ate in companionable silence, and she found herself watching Josh. The way his strong hands broke apart a bear claw. The way his Adam's apple bobbed as he took a long sip of orange juice.

"I think we should try it."

She blinked, shocked out of her reverie. "Sorry, what?"

He finished the pastry, then wiped his hands with the linen napkin, his eyes blazing as he stared at her. "I said," he repeated, slowly, intensely, "we should try it."

She swallowed as best she could against the sudden lump in her throat. "You mean . . . *it*?" She shot a nervous glance at the bed.

"Listen, I don't understand it either," he said, his voice gravelly in the best possible way. "We've been friends forever, and to my knowledge, we've never come close to being this . . ." He gestured futilely between them.

"This horny for each other?" she clarified, then wrinkled her nose. "Ick. Hate that term."

He chuckled, even as his blue eyes kept burning into her like a welder's arc. "I haven't been this turned on with anyone. And I don't want to screw anything up between us, but I'm starting to wonder if we'll screw things up if we *don't* have sex with each other. If we just let this tension keep building up."

She blinked. "You're saying . . . we have to have sex," she said, enunciating each syllable, sure that she was misunderstanding something. "To save the friendship."

He shook his head, rubbing his eyes with the heels of his hands. "When you put it that way, it sounds—"

"No, you may be on to something here," she found herself saying.

What are you doing?

"If we do this," she said, not sure what words were going to come out of her mouth since apparently her body had decided to take over this portion of the group project, "we would just be . . . satisfying an urge and addressing a curiosity. I mean, maybe it's just the taboo, right? Like, we've always looked at each other as off limits, and now it's kind of hit a tipping point?"

Josh moved his hands away, arching an eyebrow at her. "Okay . . ."

"And we've been under a lot of stress," she reasoned. "I mean, I know I have."

He leaned forward. She could smell him: the familiar scent of some beach-inspired deodorant, and the underlying, comforting male scent that was just *him*. "Then if we have sex, we'd be scratching an itch?"

"That's right up there with *horny* on the ick scale," she said, "but . . . I was thinking more . . . getting it out of our systems?"

She winced. She was grasping at straws now, but her body couldn't seem to stop making excuses.

He took her hands. Then he tugged her onto his lap, nuzzling her neck. Unlike with their usual affection, she could feel the heat of his breath tickle across her skin, and she shivered.

"It'd be like an experiment," he said, nipping at her jawline.

"Okay. Sure." At this point, she would've agreed that it was going to save the world if he'd just keep making her body react like that. "Whatever."

"And it's not going to be weird?"

"Only weird if we make it weird," she said, and they both snickered.

"Um. Maybe . . ." He frowned. "I just don't want to screw anything up."

"Tell you what," Tam said. "This is a onetime exclusive deal. We do the deed. Then we go home to Ponto Beach, and we never speak of it again. Take it to our graves."

"What happens in New York," he intoned, even as an amused grin teased his lips, "stays in New York."

"Exactly."

"All right." He kissed her, slowly, and she felt like her skin was on fire. "Then . . . let's have sex."

She sighed happily against his mouth. She would think about consequences later. Right now, this was all her body wanted, and it felt so incredibly *right* she couldn't imagine there being a price she wouldn't theoretically pay, in the future, just to have this now.

He leaned back, pulling his T-shirt over his head and tossing it to the floor. Then she tugged him to his feet, undoing his fly and pulling at his waistband. He was chuckling as he pulled down his pants, removing them and his socks, leaving him in a pair of boxer briefs that outlined a not-insubstantial erection that seemed to be getting harder by the minute. She felt her mouth go dry.

"Wow," she whispered.

"Second thoughts?"

She shook her head. "Are you kidding?"

He was still laughing when she took a deep breath, braced herself for possible humiliation, and took off the robe she was wearing.

She didn't make a habit of being naked in front of other people. Her sexual history was pretty scarce, and she didn't really flaunt herself at the showers in the gym or anything. She might be a bit self-conscious, especially when Brent had poked at her "cheese tummy" or remarked that her cup size was a bit small.

She bit her lip, looking at Josh, praying that he wouldn't judge.

But it was Josh. No one made her feel more comfortable being herself. No one accepted her the way he did.

And judging from the way his expression burned with pure, unadulterated lust, no one wanted her, just as she was, the way he did.

She nodded at his underwear. "Your turn," she said, her voice hoarse.

He grinned, winked . . . then pulled down his briefs in a smooth motion, kicking them aside. His cock bobbed, slapping his stomach.

"Wow," she repeated.

He barked out a surprised laugh. "C'mere," he said, and before she could follow the instruction, he grabbed her and tossed her lightly onto the bed. It was her turn to laugh as he playfully tussled with her. His skin was hot against hers, and the sprinkling of hair on his chest and thicker hair on his legs rubbed against her smooth skin. She ran her calf against his, enjoying the difference in texture. He rubbed his stubble across her chest, no doubt leaving beard rash. She didn't care. Nor did she care when he sucked hard against her neck. She arched her back, wanting more.

He was breathing hard, but still smiling. She smiled back. It should be weird, she supposed, but it wasn't. His palms stroked over her breasts, over her stomach, over the slight flare of her hips. He kissed her everywhere, it seemed. And she just gasped her way through it. When she finally got too self-conscious, she returned the favor, kissing whatever she could get her mouth onto—his neck, his chest, the happy trail that led down to his cock. Then she kissed the bead of precum that had formed, and he jolted. She looked up, grinning at his astonished face, before sucking lightly on the head.

"Whoa, none of that," he said quickly, tugging her off him. "Not unless you want me going off like a bottle rocket in, like, two seconds."

"Challenge accepted," she said, starting to go for him again, but he rumbled with laughter, holding her tighter.

"When I go off," he said, nibbling at her lips, "it's going to be inside you. And you're going to be there every step of the way."

She was about to say, *Of course, where else would I be?* like a smart-ass, when he reached down between her legs. After stroking around her entrance, he delved between her curls, finding her clit, which was already hard and eager to be found. He stroked it like a master, and had her seeing stars.

"Inside me," she said quickly. "No. Wait! Damn it. Do you have a condom? Please say you have one. Don't make me call down to the desk."

He let out a ragged laugh. "Should have a few in my luggage," he said. "I think. I was optimistic the last time I was on vacation."

"Thank God for preparation," she breathed.

He moved away, and she felt immediately cold and frenzied, eager to regain what she'd lost. He scrambled to grab a foil packet, opening it with hands that shook, which she registered as sweet. Then he rolled the condom onto himself, then moved toward her with purpose.

"How do you want to do this?" he rasped. "Have a favorite position? On top, on the side, missionary?"

"Dealer's choice," she said.

He teased her with his hardness, and she wanted to just explode. "No," he said firmly. "I want to make sure we do what makes you feel good. There are enough selfish assholes out there—I'm not going to be one of them."

Not with you, she could almost hear him say.

She sighed. "Whatever you do," she said, "I promise I'll enjoy."

He smiled in response, and she knew he *got* it. She wasn't just saying it to please him, like she would have with someone else. He knew her better than anyone . . . and what he didn't know about her body, he'd learn, because he was careful and observant, and because he wanted to make her happy. He didn't need her taking over the experience, even of her own pleasure.

Which was a relief, because right now, she was quickly losing her mind.

He stretched out over her, blanketing her with his body, notching himself between her thighs. "It's a classic for a reason," he murmured, and she giggled . . . right up to the point where he started to breach her. She was wetter than she'd ever been in her life, but he was still sizeable, and they carefully fit themselves together, breathing unevenly. She gasped as he finally slid all the way in, bottoming out against her.

"Wow," she breathed. It was becoming her default word with him.

He kissed her, and she kissed him back, hard, her hands gripping his shoulders like they were keeping her tethered to the earth. Then, with slow, deliberate strokes, he started moving.

Within minutes, she was gibbering like she was speaking in tongues, shaking and grasping like she was possessed.

Good grief, is this *what sex is supposed to feel like?*

A little part of her wanted to sue all her previous boyfriends. Or at least leave bad Yelp reviews.

She felt deliciously, deliriously filled, her body trembling, every nerve ending lit up like a bonfire.

"Tam," Josh muttered in a harsh voice, his hips swiveling slightly as he angled up a bit higher, supporting himself on his arms over her . . . just enough so that the base of him rubbed against her clit on the upstroke. Then he angled again, and . . .

"Oh, *ngh*, there, right there," she stammered, barely coherent.

Apparently, the G-spot was real, and he'd found it.

He started pounding it like a man possessed, and in all of a few seconds, she lost her mind. Yelling his name, biting his shoulder, her hips juddering like she'd hit a live wire, she came with the force of a lightning bolt. She almost passed out.

In the onslaught, she barely registered him slamming against her, calling her name on a deep, sensual groan as his hips jerked and he came shortly after her. Then he rolled to his side, cradling her to him so he didn't crush her.

Because of course he did.

"Wow," he finally said, and she chuckled quietly as she tried desperately to catch her breath. He got up, took care of the condom, then climbed back into bed, snuggling her.

He was a snuggler. Which she knew. Just not in this context.

She yawned as sleepy, sated pleasure rolled through her. "I couldn't have even begun to imagine it would be like that." She smiled at him.

"You feel so damned good," he rumbled, and she kissed his chest without thinking about it. She felt his breathing go even, and she smoothed her cheek against his chest.

As she started falling asleep, she heard him ask, tentatively, "Tam?"

"Mmmph?"

"You know . . . how you said this is it? One time only, get it out of our systems? What happens in New York, stays in New York?"

She tensed slightly, but her body was too tired to truly throw up defenses.

"How are you defining *once*?"

She let out a peal of laughter, even as her body started to try to rally. "One . . . day?" she said slowly.

She glanced up under her lashes to catch his heated smile.

"And we are, technically, still in New York," he mused.

She leaned up and kissed him. "Power nap," she said. "Then . . . well. Flight's not till tonight, and we've got late checkout."

"We'll take it to our graves," he said. Then he kissed her back.

Things escalated from there.

They did make their flight . . .

. . . but they never napped.

CHAPTER 19

They hadn't talked about it since they left New York. They'd barely talked at all, something that made Tam feel a little ill. They'd come home Sunday night, and Josh had spent long days at the Tombs on Monday and Tuesday . . . and she'd gone to bed early, after hanging out with Juanita at Uncommon Grounds, taking quick peeks at admin job postings on indeed.com, and looking at nearby temp agencies. Not that she wasn't giving Josh time to help her out—she was still open to finding her bliss, or pursuing her passion, or whatever he wanted to call it. But since they *weren't talking*, it was hard to really pin down what her next steps were going to be.

He was right. This was a huge mistake.

But they'd get past it. It was just sex, after all. Great sex, admittedly, but at the end of the day, it wasn't a relationship. Their commitment as friends outranked anything physical, and soon enough, they were going to say, "Hey, remember that time in New York?" with a fond laugh and shake of the head. It'd be seen as a poor decision that they'd walked away from, unscathed.

She just needed to keep repeating that to herself, and she'd get there.

"You okay?" Asad said.

"Huh?" She jolted out of her own thoughts.

"I said, we've got a potential client coming in to talk about a new brand identity and some marketing ideas," Asad said. "You were a million miles away."

"I'm so sorry." She felt guilty and forced herself to be more present. She was sitting at a large tilted design table with Asad, in the little office he rented for his graphic design business. Even though he was the only person who used the office, he was adamant that it helped him focus and also helped give him a better work/home balance because he could "leave work at work." The fact that he was doing well enough to rent the little storefront was fantastic, and he was obviously happy with it. It was stylish and neat as a pin, with high-end computers as well as places where he sketched and did mock-ups. It was really quite cool.

"Things going okay with Josh?"

"Hmm? Sure. Why wouldn't they be?" What, was he psychic now?

Asad sent her a strange look. "It's different when you're actually living with a friend as opposed to just, you know, *being friends*. I love Tobin like a brother, but I stayed at his place for a week while my place was being fumigated—this was before I moved in with Freddie—and *ugh*. It is a miracle I did not kill that man."

She snickered. "No, I don't want to kill Josh. We are actually surprisingly compatible." She frowned as she said that. "From a roomie standpoint, I mean."

Not that Asad needed clarification.

"So, what do you want me to do?" she said, forcing herself to focus on the business at hand.

"You're just going to take notes, see what I do. If you want to suggest something, I'm open to it," Asad said with the confidence and ease of someone completely at home in his life, doing something he loved. "This guy's a referral, not a big business or anything. He runs a contracting service for a bunch of handymen or something. I'm working with him as a favor to an interior designer I work with often."

"Okay."

"Oop. There he is." Asad got up, then walked over to the door and opened it. "Are you Clint?"

"Yes, sir." Clint nodded. He looked slick, somewhere in his thirties, maybe early forties at the oldest. He was wearing a suit that looked like it had pretentions of being expensive but probably wasn't, and his dark hair was shellacked with a lot of product. "Hey there," he said, shaking Asad's hand. He seemed to size up the small office, then looked at Tam, offering his hand again. "Clint. Clint Halliday. Nice to meetcha."

She smiled. "Tam Doan."

"She's shadowing my job," Asad said, and Clint frowned momentarily. "Don't worry, I'll be doing the work on your account—this is just an opportunity for her to see the details of graphic design and branding and judge if it's a path she wants to pursue. I hope that isn't a problem?"

Tam immediately felt her stomach knot. "I don't want to intrude," she said quickly. "I can just—"

"Nah, that's fine." Clint looked as nervous as she felt, although she could tell he was valiantly trying to hide it. "So. Peter tells me that you're the man when it comes to, like, logos and business names and stuff."

"Peter's too kind," Asad said smoothly. "And you're looking for a business name, I understand? For a new company?"

"Yeah." Clint fidgeted until Asad gestured to a small conference table in the corner, by the window. The three of them took a seat. "My uncle died, and I inherited some money, and I used to do all kinds of odd jobs, you know? Not bonded or anything. And I knew a lot of people who did a lot of different things."

"All right," Asad said encouragingly. "So you're becoming a contractor?"

"Hell, no," Clint said. "I just want to be . . . what's it. A clearinghouse. For handyguys," he clarified. "You know. Like, if you need a leak fixed in your toilet, or you want some light landscaping or a fence fixed or new doors hung or whatever. I'd have different, whatchacallum, specialties. But people wouldn't have to go through and pay an arm and a leg for small jobs."

"That makes sense to me," Asad said, writing some notes on graph paper in his leather portfolio. Clint looked proud, pleased, and relaxed. Asad was really, really good at this, she noticed—the graphic work she'd seen was good, but just putting this nervous man at ease was a talent in and of itself. "So. Did you have any name ideas in mind?"

Clint nodded, leaning back in his chair. "I was thinking: *HandyJobs*."

Tam choked. Asad glared at her.

"Sorry," she said, pointing to her throat. "Allergies."

"Yeah, I get 'em too," Clint commiserated. "Early spring? I sneeze like crazy."

She stood up and got herself a mug of water, forcing herself to calm down. What was she? Twelve?

"All right," Asad said casually, as if his new client hadn't just suggested calling his "private service" business after hand jobs. "Any other candidates?"

"I really like HandyJobs," Clint said, and thankfully she wasn't drinking, or else she'd have choked again. She bit her lip, hard.

"It works best if we have a wider selection," Asad said, putting a little more sternness in his tone. "Just so we have options. How about something more descriptive? Like . . . Small Jobs? Or Simple Solutions?"

"Nah," Clint said, pouting slightly. She hadn't seen a grown man pout like that, perhaps ever. "*HandyJobs* just feels right. I'm comfortable with HandyJobs."

Okay, now he's just messing with us.

Asad's poker face was legendary, and he steepled his fingers, tapping them against his mouth. "If you could humor me," he said, as if asking Clint for a favor. Clint reluctantly nodded. "Maybe we could come up with something besides the 'Handy' appellation. What do you think?"

Clint drew his brows together, thinking hard. Then he looked up.

"Jacks," he said. "You know. My grandfather used to call 'em jack-of-all-trades."

"Now we're getting somewhere," Asad said, writing that down. "I think—"

"We could call it Jack-for-You!" Clint crowed.

Don't laugh. Don't laugh. Do not *laugh.*

Asad jotted it down, then nodded. "I'm thinking . . . tradesman. Trades. Tradeworks?"

Clint frowned, then nodded. "That actually sounds kinda classy," he said.

Asad got up, retrieving a sketchpad and a thick black pencil. "I was thinking . . ."

Within minutes, he'd sketched a rudimentary drawing of tools around the word *tradeworks*. He held it up.

Clint stared in awe. "You did that in no time flat," he marveled. "And it looks amazing! How did you *do* that?"

"It's what I do," Asad said with a humble smile. "But I'm going to come up with a few more ideas. You don't want to just jump on the first one, necessarily. This is your business: you want it to be a good fit, and those things take time and a lot of thought."

For the next hour, they talked, and Asad sketched and took notes. Despite the disastrous opening salvo (and her own adolescent reaction to Clint's proposed names), it turned out beautifully. Clint had, indeed, gone with TradeWorks, and Asad promised to send him mock-ups of the logo design and brand identity within a few weeks.

When Clint left, Asad sighed and locked the door behind him. Then he looked at Tam, and dissolved into giggles.

"Oh my God," he said. "*HandyJobs.* He loves HandyJobs. Good HandyJobs are *comfortable*." He hooted. "I can't wait to tell Freddie about this!"

"I don't know how you kept it together," Tam admitted. "Actually, I don't know how you did *any* of this. You sketched, like, eight concepts in under an hour."

"Doodles, not concepts," he corrected. "Just rough ideas so he could get an inkling of where he was going. And I've been doing this for a while."

"I can't just pick up a pencil and start drawing things." She slumped in her chair, feeling defeated. Josh meant well, encouraging her, but this seemed impossible.

Asad sat next to her, looking at her with curiosity. "Why don't you tell me what you used to do at your old job?" he asked. "Come at it a different way."

She sighed. "I just did social media stuff. Occasional memes, banners, Insta graphics, stuff like that," she said, feeling totally outclassed. "Things you could do on Canva, for God's sake . . . plug-and-play templates, simple pictures building on existing material. Nothing like this."

She pointed to a gorgeous brand identity set he'd been working on for a company that made sailboats. Brochures, logo, even merchandise. It looked like a million dollars, luxe and yet still almost whimsical.

"Don't worry about that," Asad said, looking into her eyes. "What did you *like* about what you were doing? How did you even get into it? Did they say that was going to be part of your job when you got hired?"

She let out a snicker. "Yeah, right," she joked, then realized he was serious. "No. They just said it was 'administrative duties' and . . . well. Let's just say that it covered pretty much anything they could think of."

"We graphic designers call that scope creep," Asad said, looking irritated. "When the client says they just want one thing—like a logo—then starts adding shit, because they don't think it's a big deal. They say stuff like: 'You're already doing the logo, why would you charge more for letterhead?' And, 'How long would it take to do some simple GIFs advertising a special?'"

"Exactly!" Tam shook her head. "They needed somebody to take over the social media accounts for the agency, but nobody was able to take it on. Or wanted to, or something. My boss just said, 'We need to post something from the newsletter on Twitter,' and next thing I know, I was running to Creative to get some graphics and running their Instagram and Facebook."

"You must've been doing a good job, then."

She shrugged, feeling sheepish. "They seemed happy with it. Happy enough for me to do the social media for a small flashlight account and a small candy brand."

"You would've hated it if they were unhappy, huh?"

She raised an eyebrow. "Wouldn't you?"

He laughed, nodding. "Remember that recovering-honors-student thing I mentioned? I think all of us in the Herd have some amount of overachieving hardwired into us," he agreed. "I'm just trying to figure out if graphic design is something you got kind of good at because it was expected of you, or if it's something you could really love."

She tilted her head. "Is this a follow-your-bliss thing?" She hated how dubious she sounded. "Because I have to say, I haven't really tried, but I feel like I couldn't find my bliss with two search dogs, a floodlight, and a bloodhound."

He grinned. "You're just a little lost, sweetie. And it's not easy, especially when you've been listening to pretty much everyone *but* yourself when you were trying to figure out what you wanted," he pointed out. "Josh may be overenthusiastic, and a little fixated on the process, but he's not wrong: you need to find out what you love. And then have the courage to actually go for it."

"I've just been a secretary . . . ," she started, and his eyes widened.

"Gonna stop you right there. I have known *way* too many secretaries for there to be a *just* in that sentence," he chided. "And I have to imagine that other assistants feel the same way, so I know you don't mean that!"

She reluctantly smiled. "That's true, actually," she said.

"That's your family's deal, isn't it?" he said. "Your dad's a business guy, your mom's a doctor. And Vinh's—whatever the hell he is. Corporate hitman."

She snickered. For all she knew, that was probably true.

"They're the ones that think what you're doing isn't enough, right?"

"Oh, not you too," she muttered. "I swear, if one more person tells me I have to figure out my true passion . . ."

"Variation on a theme," Asad said easily. "I was just trying to say, you don't have to do anything, no matter what anyone tells you. If we're pressuring you, tell us to shove it." He waited a beat. "And if your family has opinions on what you should be doing—technically, you can tell them to shove it too. Though you'll probably be a bit more polite."

She bit her lip. "They'll be disappointed," she said. "They are *already* disappointed. My father thought I should've gone into business somewhere. My mother doesn't understand why I didn't pursue a hard science. Vinh always tells me I should've pushed for a promotion. And they've all hated my boyfriends."

"Well, you have seemed to make your choices based on what your boyfriends suggest, and that's a whole 'nother conversation," Asad said. "But when it comes to the actual job, from what I've gathered, it sounds like those people were . . ." He frowned, trailing off.

"Challenging?" she suggested.

"I was going to say heinous abusive shit stains, but okay," he said, and she let out a surprised giggle. "There is nothing at all wrong with being an assistant, if it's something you enjoy doing. But doing something you hate—and doing it *really well*—isn't good for you. And if you don't like graphic design, if you feel like it's too much pressure, then don't do it."

They sat quietly for a moment. Then Asad reached out and squeezed her hand.

"I don't want to be one more person telling you what you ought to be doing with your life," he said, his voice gentle. "I just love you, sweetie. You're one of my oldest friends, and I hate to see you so unhappy."

She took a deep breath. "I can't just binge-watch streaming channels and play around on social media and take pictures of food while camping out and hiding away in Josh's guest bedroom," she said softly. "I have to get my shit together."

Asad's eyes gleamed. "First of all: Are you really just in Josh's guest room?"

It took her a second to catch his question. "Um . . . yes? Why?"

"The way he looks at you, I was surprised you hadn't moved into his actual bedroom by now," Asad said with a smirk.

"You *know* it's not like that with us!" *What happens in New York stays in New York . . .*

He arched a perfect eyebrow at her. "Are you two really still playing that game? Because really. You're worse than Tobin and Lily." He huffed out an impatient breath. "If you two were any more perfect for each other, the universe would break or something."

"We're friends," she said.

"So?" Asad replied. "Freddie and I are friends. He's my best friend. And I love him more than anything."

"It's . . ." She sighed. "Different?"

He sent her a withering glare. "Because we're gay?"

She shot back an irritated look of her own. "Obviously not." She took a deep breath. "Because if I lost him, I don't know what I'd do."

"Oh, hon." Asad got up and gave her a quick hug. "You know you couldn't possibly lose that guy. He's . . . he's Rory from *Doctor Who*. He would wait two thousand years for you. He's waited this long, hasn't he?"

"This is *not* a conversation I'm ready to have," she said, pulling away from him and clearing her throat. "Anyway, I think I like graphic design, but not to this extent. Social media level, not design logos and advertising and brand identities level."

"Your social media is funny," he agreed. "Hey! You should talk to Lily. Maybe you could be an influencer?"

She felt herself shrink, her chest caving in on itself. The thought of being "on" twenty-four hours a day, without some kind of buffer, felt just as intimidating.

"God. I'm sorry. I know you're just trying to help," Tam said helplessly. "I feel like I'm whining, but I just can't seem to figure out what I want."

"It'll get easier," Asad reassured her. "I know it seems like you're just throwing stuff at the wall and seeing what sticks, but sooner or later, you're going to find something you love, I swear."

She smiled weakly. "I don't think love and business really go together."

"Sure they do. Love improves everything you add it to. It's like salt." He paused contemplatively. "Or Giancarlo Esposito."

It got her nowhere closer to her desire for employment, but she knew Asad had a point. Everyone was telling her to find more than just a job—to find what she loved. It seemed scary, and maybe a bit naive, and sort of impossible. But damn it, if all these people who cared about her were willing to drill it into her head . . . the least she could do was actually *try*.

CHAPTER 20

Josh met Darius that evening at Uncommon Grounds. Darius walked in, dressed in business casual—a deep-purple polo shirt and a pair of charcoal slacks. He had very dark skin, and his hair was cut short in a simple fade. He smiled at Juanita as he gave her his coffee order, winking when she told him it'd be ready in a second. "Josh," he called out in greeting, making his way to the table Josh had managed to snag. "How're you doing?"

Other than being utterly confused by having sex with my best friend a few days ago? Peachy.

"Can't complain," he said instead, shaking Darius's hand. "I've got an idea for pivoting the underperformer that I wanted to run by you, actually."

"Oh?" Darius sat down. Juanita brought him a large ceramic mug of coffee, and Darius thanked her with a broad smile that had Josh's normally confident friend blushing.

"I was thinking Vietnamese food. Especially if we can separate the components, which people who eat Vietnamese food are used to, so the bread doesn't get soggy with the fresh ingredients. And we've got the packaging ready to go, since we pack up the street tacos for Oaxaca that way already. The assembly process is part of the whole deal . . ." Josh started to go into his spiel, but he was distracted, and he knew it. Even as he shifted to other possibilities—Italian sandwiches, picnic foods, whatever—he realized that he was babbling. "Anyway, I'll narrow it down to three and then crunch more numbers and come up with a few packaging concepts and design ideas."

Darius made a hum of assent as he took a long swig of his coffee. "Ah, caffeine," he said, his eyes low lidded. "You okay there, Josh?"

Josh shifted nervously. "Sure. Why? Does something sound wrong?"

"Other than the fact that you just went through all those options like a hyperactive six-year-old who just discovered Pixy Stix?" Darius studied him intently, his dark eyes probing. "You nervous?"

"No!" Josh realized that his voice actually sounded nervous. Which he was.

Just not about the presentation.

He knew exactly what was going on with him. It had been three days since he'd landed with Tam, after having mind-blowing sex that they were absolutely never going to talk about again. Except part of him wanted to shout it from his backyard.

I HAD SEX WITH TAM DOAN, AND IT ROCKED MY WORLD!

They'd agreed to pretend it never happened. They had known that it wasn't a good idea, so the best, most logical approach was to pretend it had never happened. But the problem was, no matter how hard he tried, he couldn't ignore the electricity that ran between them every time they were in the same damned room. He'd always been aware of her. Now, it was like he could *see* the lines of attraction that seemed to arc between them like a Jacob's ladder.

He cleared his throat. "Just a lot on my mind," he tried to dissemble, and Darius sent him a quizzical look before continuing to talk.

"You don't need to have that much detail on a new restaurant by the twentieth—you just need to show how easy it is to retool. Although the more I thought about it, the more I realized it might be better to hook up with another established restaurant, one with a track record of sales, and provide delivery service for them on a streamlined menu. Kind of like your deal with French Bistro, you know, where you picked the most popular items that were best for delivery? That way, we can prove that there's already success, and you're just contributing to it. I know that probably means ditching the Vietnamese food idea, but it might be an easier sell."

Josh frowned. "That's a great idea," he agreed quickly. "It would take less time to show your investors that it's viable. We could ride on their sales numbers, which would be easy to provide." He grimaced. "I . . . sorry. I should've thought of that. Don't know why I didn't."

"You can't come up with everything," Darius said with a deep chuckle. "Like I said, though, you seem distracted. What's going on?"

Josh sighed. "I had a friend come into town," he tried explaining. "Looking for a new start, new job, new place. Kind of in a bad situation."

"Man, that sucks," Darius commiserated. "What job did he used to have?"

"She used to be an assistant, for an ad agency in Manhattan," Josh clarified. "But she hated it. I'm trying to help her figure out her next steps."

"Okay. Any sense of what she wants to do?" Darius asked, opening the black Moleskine notebook he always carried and pulling out a pen.

"We've narrowed it down to things related to food, graphic design, or writing," Josh said. "Sorry, I know that's broad. But I'd hate for her to rush. I want her to find something she loves, like I did."

"Sounds like you're pretty invested in her outcome, there," Darius observed, his expression wry. "Just a friend, huh?"

"You wouldn't believe how often we get that," Josh said around a groan, even as his mind helpfully supplied images—graphic images—of just how *close* their friendship was.

Damn it, not now.

He forced himself to focus. "She was really instrumental in helping me start Ghost Kitchens Unlimited, actually, and I'd like to return the favor."

"Just curious," Darius asked as he jotted down a few notes on a blank piece of paper. "What'd she do to help you?"

Josh took a sip of his own chai latte, remembering. "I was in a bad place myself," he admitted. "You know how I mentioned, when you first invested, about losing the job at Sergio's?"

"I remember thinking it was ballsy of you to reveal that kind of weakness right from the jump," Darius said. "You were fearlessly transparent. Just this side of foolish, actually, but really brave. And then when you told me why he fired you—because you wanted to update his systems and improve his ordering and stuff—I did some digging. You were right. That Sergio guy's an asshole."

"I don't think I used those words."

Darius made a small *pfft* sound. "Dude. This is between you and me, no bullshit. So where does the girl fit in?"

"And around that same time, I . . ." He grimaced. "I broke up with a girlfriend who was running me ragged and who dumped me when I lost the job. She thought I was on track to be executive chef or something, or at least some kind of restaurant manager for a fancy four-star place, although how she thought I was going to swing that *and* give her all the attention she felt she needed was kind of baffling. Anyway, I was living with my mom at the time." And this was the hard part. "My mom then sold the house out from under me, which I didn't find out about until she closed the damned paperwork and gave me a few weeks' notice, so I was kind of screwed."

"Oh, shit," Darius breathed.

"Yeah. She figured I'd land on my feet, and that it was high time I should, which . . . yeah, okay, I guess she wasn't wrong?" The fact that he'd been paying all the utilities and half the mortgage hadn't stopped her—she'd taken the money and run, leaving him surprised as hell with a text message before blocking his number. "At least I found out before I was evicted. It was messed up. So there I was, getting hit with everything at once, and Tam—that's my friend—she flies in from New

York. And she tells me about this study from these guys in Stanford, about designing a life you want."

"Oh, yeah. I've read those guys."

"I was feeling beyond hopeless," Josh admitted. "But she was just cheerful as a damned anime character, and she had this adorable little stern face, and she said, 'We are *going* to figure this out.' And we camped out in the desert for a weekend, and talked and talked, and sketched all this stuff out on Post-its. And drank Jäger." He grinned. "And she took everything I was good at, and the stuff I liked, and she just *believed* in me. And before I knew it, I took the little idea that I'd had after reading an article on the potential of the delivery driving services, and the commercial kitchen stuff, and my systems for improving Sergio's place, and . . . I don't know. It just all *clicked*."

"You bet your ass it did," Darius agreed. "I don't generally invest in restaurants or anything food related. Too much chance for failure. But your concept? Was ironclad. I don't regret it for a minute."

"It changed my life," Josh said with no hyperbole. "*She* changed my life. You both did."

"Huh." Darius nodded. "So you're going to help her, huh?"

"I'm going to do everything I can to try."

"I respect that," Darius said, nodding. He took another long swig of coffee, then his expression turned serious. "But I have to tell you: Meeting with my investment group is a big deal. I don't want to freak you out, but I think it's going to be bigger than you realize. I need your head in the game, Josh."

Josh nodded immediately. "Trust me. I can handle this."

"If you need to help your friend, I get that. But just make sure that you're clear, all right?"

Panic washed over him in a wave, and Josh forced himself to settle. "I'm clear. I've got this."

"Good man." Darius nodded with approval, then stood, reaching to shake Josh's hand. "Get me a prelim draft of that presentation, with some possible established restaurants you could partner with, or new concepts. We can present both as options for the partners. Then we'll get it all polished before we meet with my group."

"Thanks," Josh said, standing as well and returning Darius's strong grip. Then he pulled himself together as Darius walked out the door and finished the rest of his chai.

"Who's the hottie?" Juanita said, waggling her eyebrows as she grabbed Darius's empty cup.

"My investor," Josh said, shaking his head at her.

"Think he might like to talk to me about investing in the coffee shop?"

"He generally doesn't do restaurants, or coffee shops," Josh said, feeling uncomfortable. "I was an exception."

Juanita rolled her eyes like he was dense. "I don't really want the money," she said with a broad smile. "I just want to watch him talk, preferably in private. Those *lips*."

"I'll pass that right along," he said with a chuckle.

"How was the trip to New York? Tam said it went okay, but she seemed . . . weird."

"Weird?" Josh stiffened, walking behind Juanita and bussing his own mug. "Weird how?"

"Just distracted. Sort of off."

"She's got a lot on her mind," Josh tried to justify.

"That ex of hers wasn't too much of a jerk?" Juanita said protectively.

Josh's chest warmed. "He tried to be," Josh admitted. "But she stood up to him. He seemed pretty pissed about that."

"He didn't deserve her," Juanita spat. "He's just lucky he wasn't around here. The Herd would've been on the ground and ready to pound some sense into him if he had been."

Josh thought about his own murderous thoughts. "Damned right," he growled. Then he sighed. "Do you think she'll be okay?"

"Tam?" Juanita smiled. "Of course. She's got us—and most of all, she's got you. How could she not be okay?"

Josh hung on to that thought. She did have him. She trusted him. He was going to make it up to her.

Which meant they had to get things back to normal.

Which meant he had to talk to her—tonight.

CHAPTER 21

Josh got home at around seven that night, intent on talking to Tam. "What happens in New York" be damned.

In the few days since they'd returned from New York, they'd kept up a front of almost stylized pleasantry, but it was forced. The tension that had started since she'd kissed him in Brent's apartment was by now thicker than Jell-O and permeated every single interaction they had. They hadn't shared many meals since. They didn't snuggle on the couch anymore. They didn't hug each other good night. And when they did make physical contact, there was this awkward cha-cha of "oops, I didn't mean" and other incoherent muttered apologies. He also found himself looking at her more—noticing the curve of her lips, or the way she nudged her glasses up, or tucked her hair behind her ear. Or he'd find *her* looking at him and then quickly looking away. But in the split second their eyes met, he could've been scorched to the earth by the sheer *need* she communicated with those brief looks.

And yeah, he'd jacked off pretty much every day. He wasn't even sorry.

This morning, he'd given her a lift to a coffee shop by Asad's office in awkward silence and then headed to the Tombs to bury himself in work. Now that he'd had his meeting with Darius, he found himself wanting to talk to her about it. And he wanted to see how she'd done with Asad—if the graphic design life path might be something she wanted to pursue. So even though there was still sexual tension thick enough to cut with a knife, he still couldn't stop himself from wanting to see her. They needed to get back to normal. He wanted his friend back.

Something you should've considered before you slept together.

"Hey honey, I'm home," he tried joking, which would've worked better if he hadn't croaked it out. The first thing he registered was the scent of food cooking. He blinked as he saw her in the kitchen. She grinned.

"How was your day, dear?" she sent back, grinning and making a *mwah mwah mwah* sound as she blew him kisses.

He grinned broadly back, taking the first deep breath in days, it seemed. Maybe she'd just gotten over the weirdness, somehow processed through the confusing feelings or the guilt or the worry. Whatever it was, he'd take it. This was how they always joked. Surely he could keep his act together enough to show her he was equally unaffected. He walked up and wrapped his arms around her, nuzzling her shoulder, and he got a deep whiff of her: something citrusy and clean, with a hint of floral. He took another deep breath before he could stop himself. It just felt like such a *relief.*

"Smells good," he said. He wasn't sure if he meant the food or her.

He felt her stiffen in his arms; then, with just a teeny motion, she leaned back against him, molding her back to his front for just a second.

His body tensed. Especially one particular part of his body.

He took a careful step back, trying not to jolt or startle her, and willed his unruly body to calm the fuck down.

We just got this back! Don't screw it up!

"I hope you don't mind," she said, giving him a sideways glance. "There was a farmer's market by Asad's office, and I stopped by before I Ubered home. I thought you might be hungry. Unless you already ate?"

"No, actually." He investigated the counters and the stovetop. She had sliced up peppers, cauliflower, broccoli, onion, summer squash. She also had what looked like tri tip, marinated in something. He thought he smelled lemongrass and lime. "This looks fantastic. I never eat like this."

"I try to incorporate veggies, and there's so much stuff in season," she said, sounding embarrassed. "I mean, it's not restaurant quality . . ."

"Shut up, it looks delicious," he countered. "It's not that I don't eat veggies—I just usually eat from one of the restaurants, when I remember. And when I get home, it's usually midnight. If I'm not hyperfocused, or if Amber rags on me, then I'll eat something at work, but I forget and have cereal a lot too."

She shook her head, tutting, which made him smile. "Much as I loved the restaurants in New York, it wasn't cheap to eat out all the time, and left to my own devices, I never order enough veggies when I get takeout," she said. "Hope you like stir-fry. Oh, and I'm gratified to see you've got fish sauce."

He grinned. "Of course. Fish sauce kicks ass," he said. "I've got sambal oelek too, if you want it."

"Dinner'll be ready in about five?" she said. "Might want to set the table."

"It's a nice night," he noted. "Want to eat out on the patio?"

She nodded eagerly, her warm smile making his stomach swoop. He cleared his throat, taking cutlery, napkins, and place mats out to the outdoor table. The sky shifted from deep salmon to a rich indigo. It was going to be dark soon, so unless they wanted to eat blind, he should probably do something to add illumination. Still, the patio light seemed too harsh. Without thinking, he pulled out some candles of different heights, grouping them in the center of the table. Then he got them both glasses of water and popped lemon slices in.

By the time he was done, she had rice in rice bowls, covered in sauce, and she'd plated up a perfectly cooked veggie-and-beef stir-fry. He helped her carry it out to the table. "Oh," she said, sounding surprised. "This looks pretty."

He immediately realized: it did look pretty. More noticeably, it looked *romantic.*

"The candles made sense because it's getting dark," he said inanely, not sure why his voice was sounding so scratchy. She looked at him curiously, eyebrow arched.

Get it together! Don't mess this up!

"So how was your day with Asad?" he said finally, as they sat down.

She grinned, using chopsticks and holding the bowl up. "I have a whole new appreciation for what he has to go through," she said. "And I have one word for you: handjobs."

He choked on some rice. His brain immediately provided him with a picture of her, naked, wrapping her soft, delicate fingers around his . . .

Nope! Abort! Abort!

"I beg your pardon?" he said, when he could breathe.

"Or rather, HandyJobs," she said and proceeded to regale him with the story of Asad's clueless client. He burst out laughing, feeling the tension from the day ease out of his muscles. Maybe it would be easier than he thought. "So how was your day?" she said, once she'd wrapped up her story.

He smiled. "It was good," he said, hmming around a bite of food. "This is really delicious, Tam. Thanks for cooking."

"It's stupid simple. Really no big deal," she said. "What good things happened at work?"

He blinked. He wasn't used to talking to anybody about his day, he realized.

He hadn't had a girlfriend since he'd started Ghost Kitchens Unlimited. If he was honest, he was used to picking out women who were self-absorbed and narcissistic, his own stupid pattern, so they had hardly had the comfortable domesticity of *how was your day?* It had taken him years to finally realize that he was replicating the dynamic he'd had with his mother; if, by some miracle, he could find a self-centered drama queen and finally get her to love him, he would prove he was actually "worth it."

Beyond that, in the past years that he'd been running the business, he didn't talk to Amber about his day, because . . . well, because she was working at the same place, she knew everything that was going on, and she was busy.

Finally, he didn't hang out with the Herd half as much as he could. He was usually too fixated on making GKU the most successful thing possible.

He frowned. He hadn't considered himself a workaholic, like Vinh, or even Lily. He'd just been busy.

Now, he realized he might've overshot the mark a little.

"All right, spit it out," Tam pressed. "What's going on?"

"No, it really is good," he said. "It just occurred to me that I don't usually have someone ask about my day."

Her smile was small and gentle.

"I, um, had a talk with my investor, Darius."

"Everything okay with the presentation?" she asked before picking up a slice of pepper and eating it delicately.

"It's on track." Josh sighed. "He just hammered home how big a deal this is, bringing it to his partners. I can't lose focus. If anything, I need to push harder."

"Does that mean more hours?" she asked. "I know that you could be a huge success—I mean, you're already a huge success—but I would hate to see you go down the Vinh route and just bury yourself in business. It does catch up with you, health-wise."

It was like she was reading his mind, unsurprisingly. "You know me too well."

"Yeah, well, I've got history to back it up." She frowned a little.

He knew that her father's health was compromised by work stress, the man having had two heart attacks before he turned forty-five. "I think I didn't realize how far down that road I was going until you got here," Josh admitted. "I've been careful about exercise and sleep and stuff. Maybe not as careful as I could be, but it's taken me this long to get here, and I haven't wanted to jeopardize it. I think having you here is good for me."

"Good," she said with a solemn little nod. "I worry about you. I want you to be all right."

He felt his heart warm. She had always been like this, even when they were teens. Just tiny throwaway comments that were so obvious to her—and meant so fucking much to him. He didn't think she'd ever understand that.

They were silent for a second, watching the sun disappear into the water. She sighed.

"It really is beautiful here," she murmured, tucking her hair behind her ear. "I can't believe I stayed away so long."

Even though he hadn't really paid attention to a sunset in years, he focused on her face, looking a beautiful rosy gold in the waning light. "I missed you," he blurted out, then frowned at himself. "When you were gone, I mean."

She smiled, reaching over with her free hand and taking his, giving it a squeeze. "Missed you too," she said, sounding raspy. "I promise I won't stay away so long again."

He squeezed back. "Better not," he said. "Or I'll come looking for you."

She smirked, releasing his hand, only to hold out her pinky. "Pinky promise," she said.

He grinned, hooking his pinky in hers, holding her gaze. "You're my girl," he said. He took a deep breath, releasing her pinky only to tangle the rest of his fingers with hers. "Listen, about New York . . ."

"We promised not to talk about it," she said quickly.

He nodded, feeling disappointment in his chest. "I just wanted to say it was really important to me." He saw her eyes widen. "I mean, it's not . . . gah. I'm not saying it was anything other than what it was, or that it's going to happen again, or any of that. What I'm saying is, it was weird afterward. It's *been* weird." He grimaced. "I missed you this week too. We avoided each other. We *never* do that."

She bit her lip. "I know. And I'm sorry."

"We should've expected it. *I* should've," he clarified. "But . . . it's more important to me that we're friends. So we're not going to let it get weird again. Right?"

She smiled at him. "I'm glad."

He saw her pulse beat heavily in her throat, and she swallowed hard even though she hadn't taken another bite. Then she cleared her throat. "So. I'm, um, working at Freddie's this week," she said, quickly switching the topic.

He released her. He'd said the important bit, and they weren't weird anymore. They were friends. That was the crucial element.

But what if he wanted to be more than friends? Was that something he really wanted to entertain?

And if not—why couldn't he stop thinking about it?

CHAPTER 22

Tam was a little nervous as Freddie ushered her into his commercial kitchen. It wasn't quite as shiny as the Tombs, but it was still obviously a nicely maintained kitchen, with ovens and stovetops along one wall, a large kitchen island with a stainless top, and plenty of counters. It was early, around six o'clock in the morning, which was rough considering that yet again, she'd had a hard time sleeping.

She blamed it on Josh. They'd had a great dinner, but there was still that lingering *awareness* between them, and as hard as she tried, it was impossible to tamp down.

For pity's sake! It was just sex!

Amazing sex.

Really mind-blowing, panty-melting, can't-stop-thinking-about-it sex.

Just not the relationship kind.

Not that she had a whole lot of personal experience with casual sex, but it was literally a thing people did, every day, out in the world. She needed to stop being so damned precious about it, and focus on more important things . . . like what she was supposed to do with the rest of her life.

"Welcome to Graham Catering," Freddie said, his deep voice rumbling pleasantly and yanking her out of her distracting thoughts. "These two are my sous chefs, Divina and Timothy. They are the hardest-working people I've ever met."

"Nice to meet you," Tam said, feeling a little self-conscious.

"Tam's just shadowing today," he said. "She wants to see if she wants to make a living doing what we do."

Divina, a short, squat Filipina woman with a bright smile and sparkling eyes, laughed. "Oh, no! Save yourself!"

The other chef, Timothy, was a tall, lanky Black man who smiled at her shyly, giving her a nod of greeting.

"I'm just here to help where I can," Tam said immediately. She was wearing a T-shirt, a pair of jeans, and sneakers, since Freddie had said to dress comfortably. She'd braided her hair and put on a Ghost Kitchens Unlimited baseball cap. She'd taken her food handler's course, which was startlingly like taking traffic school online—a couple of hours, and she was now qualified to prepare food for other humans. That was actually a bit more daunting. She just hoped she didn't screw anything up too badly.

Freddie and his chefs, on the other hand, were wearing checked chef's pants and their chef's whites, looking every inch like total professionals. Divina's dark hair was tucked up in a short white toque, while Timothy had a nicely shaved head. Freddie put his own black toque on.

"What are we working on?" Tam asked. "And what can I help you with?"

"You're in luck," Freddie said. "Today's an easy day. We're catering a corporate lunch. I suggested you work with me today because they're just charcuterie boxes, very straightforward."

"Charcuterie boxes?" Tam squealed with joy before she stopped herself. "Those are my favorite thing ever."

"I'm well acquainted with your love of cheese," Freddie said with a small smile, surprising her. She didn't really know Freddie that well, other than on social media—he'd been with Asad for a while, but it wasn't like she'd been around the Herd that often in the past five years—but she guessed that her love of cheese preceded her. "Actually, I started following your Instagram because I appreciated your food pictures," he revealed.

She bit her lip. "Well, I do love food," she said. "That's why I'm here today, after all."

"In fact, the cheese we're using today is one of your favorites," Freddie continued, surprising her. "Once you described that truffle-and-fig triple-cream brie, I couldn't stop myself. And you're right, Cloud City Creamery is amazing. We order from them often now."

She was grinning so hard she thought her face would split. "I love them! I broke up with my boyfriend over them!"

She hadn't meant to blurt that out. Freddie, Divina, and Timothy all stared at her.

"There were other mitigating circumstances," she muttered.

"All right, we're going to make three different boxes that showcase that cheese," Freddie said after an uncomfortable moment. He looked over at his crew, briskly shifting back to business. "How'd prep go?"

"We got the fresh fruit in this morning," Timothy answered. "That's cut and portioned. Cheese has been sliced too. Still need the crackers and cookies bagged, the boxes prepped, and then everything assembled."

"All right. Let's walk through the assembly."

Tam watched as Freddie set up the example boxes: one with salami and prosciutto, one with fancy jerky that he'd locally sourced, and finally a vegetarian version. She knew the basics of setting up a charcuterie board, but their attention to detail—balancing meat and cheese, fresh and dried fruit and nuts, little lidded containers of pickles, and even the tiny glass jars of preserves or honeycomb, all in a gorgeous cardboard box with a clear window on top—was inspiring. It was like magic. Her fingers itched to take a picture with her phone, but she felt that probably wasn't professional, and she was trying to get the experience of actually working, not just playing tourist.

She'd see if she could convince Freddie to let her take one when they were done, though.

"Ready?" Freddie asked, as Timothy and Divina started moving quickly through their tasks.

Tam nodded. She was assigned the duty of individually wrapping the small tuiles that Timothy had baked that morning—almond dipped in chocolate. They looked amazing, but they were delicate, as she quickly learned when one broke in her hand. To be careful, she had to move slowly, which made her self-conscious as Timothy, Divina, and Freddie flew through the rest of prep. They were like machines, moving quickly and efficiently, their smooth actions almost like a dance. It helped that they had music. Freddie allowed everyone to have an hour block where they got to choose their own music. Timothy liked electronic dance music. Divina liked local bands that Tam hadn't heard of, most with an indie/folk flair to them. And Freddie was a fan of '90s R & B, which apparently the others teased him about constantly. She was too shy to share her Spotify playlist, so she just enjoyed what they listened to.

Of course, by hour three, her legs were aching, as were her shoulders. She was tense because she didn't want to break the cookies, and the repetitive motion of bagging the cookies and then wrapping them in the shiny silver twist ties grew exhausting. They were waiting on her, and that made her feel worse.

"I'm so sorry," she said, as Timothy moved next to her, helping her bag faster.

He shrugged, his smile lopsided. "It takes a little while to get used to," he said with kindness. "Don't worry about it."

"So you want to be a caterer?" Divina asked, as her hands flew across the counter, making salami look like roses, placing cheese and figs and grapes in the boxes, and matching the drawing Freddie had posted.

"I'm not sure," Tam admitted, wincing as another cookie snapped. "I know I like food. I'm still kind of looking at my options."

She looked at both of them. They didn't seem to have any problem holding a conversation while working, even if they'd largely been quiet.

This might be the best way to find out more about whether or not this would be a good fit for her.

"What do you two like about catering?"

"My parents owned a restaurant in Los Angeles," Divina said. "Sold it when I got to high school. I like catering because I don't have to wait on customers if I don't want to . . . that's Sherry's job."

"Who's Sherry?"

"Sherry is the woman who's responsible for setup," Freddie said. "We're responsible for menu planning, cooking, packaging. I used to do the staging and the service side of it, too, but after a few years on high-profile events in Los Angeles, I got tired of it."

Timothy snickered. "He was a terror," he stage-whispered.

"Freddie was?" Tam stared at Freddie, who looked like a big ginger teddy bear. "Really?"

Freddie smiled, shaking his head. "I really was a total bastard," he said, shocking her. "On my way to becoming one of *those* celebrity chefs."

Tam was fascinated. She simply couldn't picture it. "What happened?" she asked.

"Asad, actually." Freddie's smile was beatific, his gaze soft, like he was remembering the whole thing. His hands still worked tirelessly, assembling the boxes. "He was still in LA at the time, working with one of the best design firms in Brentwood. I had been unhappy with their designs for my packaging and branding, although in retrospect, I wouldn't have been happy with anything. Because I was just unhappy in general." He cleared his throat. "I'm embarrassed about this, but I sort of stormed into their office and threw a fit, demanding I be reassigned to someone 'competent.' They then put Asad in charge of my account. I think they gave me to Asad to punish him. He was new, and they just dumped me onto his desk and ran."

"And instead," Divina said with an amused smile, "Asad not only came up with beautiful work, he teased Freddie and then made him dinner."

"Really?" She'd known Asad was gay in high school, obviously. But it was funny to hear about him cooking. Usually he was the one who was pursued—he was quite handsome, and charming, and flirty.

Freddie's cheeks pinkened a little, and he shut the box he was working on with a tiny satisfied pat. "People usually feel self-conscious cooking for a chef," Freddie rumbled. "But Asad made me b'steeya, of all things. He wasn't scared of me. And he kind of pointed out that I was miserable and asked why I kept doing what I was doing when I wasn't happy. And I realized that he had a point."

She grinned. Now that was the Asad she knew.

"When he quit the design firm and said he was moving back to Ponto Beach—someplace I'd never heard of, mind you—it occurred to me that I didn't want to lose him. Not as a designer, but also not as more than that."

Tam's chest warmed. "I love everything about that story."

"He thought I was insane when I moved down here," Freddie said with a laugh. "Hell, *I* thought I was insane. But it was like I was able to breathe for the first time, you know? It was totally worth it."

Tam smiled. That's what she wanted. She wanted to feel at home someplace. And, if she was being honest . . . she wanted to feel that *with* someone.

They got the boxes done, and it felt like she'd packaged thousands of cookies, although it had only been maybe a few hundred. They handed the boxes off to Sherry, who had a van and her partner to deliver the goods to the event site.

"All right," Freddie said. "Lunch break, then we'll get the food ready for tonight's gala."

Tam tried not to quail at the thought. She took a picture of the boxes they'd made for themselves—"factory irregular," essentially. She sighed with pleasure as she took a bite of cheese with a piece of dried apricot.

"What do you love best about your work?" she asked Freddie.

"I like the variety. I love food, just like Divina, just like Timothy," Freddie said. "That said, I'm glad I don't have an actual restaurant. I like being able to do different things. I like making events special, but not having the pressure I felt in LA to impress for the sake of one-upping someone else or proving that I had what it took. I like the pace I have here."

"What don't you like?" If Tam was going to do this, then she ought to know.

He frowned. "Well, the lease is going to be up on this kitchen soon," he said, "and I'm thinking of maybe a different place. The landlord's slow on fixing appliances, and it's not an ideal setup for deliveries, which isn't great for catering," he said. "And there's the usual stuff you're going to get in the restaurant world. Ordering from suppliers, food waste . . . they're a constant pressure."

She thought about Josh—how Darius had said that maybe Josh ought to look at getting an established successful business to replace the current restaurant that was in trouble, rather than trying the original but risky bánh mì idea.

"So you tell me," Freddie said, interrupting her thoughts. "What do you think? How do you feel about food as a career?"

She smiled. "Um . . ." Her body was aching, and she didn't want to look at another cookie for a while. Which was disturbing. "It's not my Giancarlo."

He looked startled until she explained Asad's comparison to him, then he laughed. "He really does make everything better," he said ruefully. "And I get what you're saying."

She took a picture of the box in front of her, posting it on Instagram. "What's your handle? I'll tag you in," she said.

"I barely go on Instagram," Freddie admitted. "I like seeing other people's, but it's intimidating."

"But your food is gorgeous!" she protested. "Here."

Within a few minutes, she'd updated his page with a picture of an open completed box and added a caption, as well as a bunch of hashtags. He looked startled, but grateful.

"You're good at that."

She shrugged. "It's just social media," she said.

"If you say so." His eyes narrowed. "But maybe you should think about it."

CHAPTER 23

On Friday, Josh was in his office at the Tombs. Having Tam in the house was great in a lot of ways. She helped him with his presentation. He knew she was stumped about the job thing, so he'd suggested she brainstorm some little writing projects. Not to mention they took turns cooking dinner and doing laundry and cleaning the kitchen. It was like having a roommate again.

One that smelled nice when he cuddled with her on the couch, watching some of their favorite shows and movies.

One that danced on the lawn when she didn't realize he was watching as she listened to her music.

One that made him wish, quite desperately, that he wasn't friends with her so he could ask her out.

Despite turning the corner on their "New York weirdness," he was still so hyperaware of her he could barely think straight. He went to bed every night aching, and he felt stretched thin by his efforts to maintain the facade that their friendship hadn't altered at all . . . when the truth was, it had changed, subtly and, he was afraid, irrevocably.

So he went into the office on Friday, knocked out a bunch of invoicing and orders, had a stern talk with a supplier who had botched one of their deliveries, and had lunch after helping Amber in Monster Sandwich. They really needed to hire another cook for that one. He made a note on his to-do list.

Now, it was the afternoon, and he'd barricaded himself in his windowless office, typing away at a list of restaurant chains that might want to expand their market to the North San Diego County area and that could be a good fit for a ghost kitchen partnership. He thought there were several promising candidates, but they would take convincing. He'd need to know who to talk to, and then he'd need to set up meetings—it would take research, and data, and persuasion. He didn't need to have a partnership in hand prior to the presentation—that was probably unreasonable. Still, he'd like to show the legwork when he did the pitch.

By three, his eyes were crossing, but he kept at it doggedly. If nothing else, it helped him keep his mind off Tam. The only problem was, he wasn't sure if he was actually accomplishing anything, or if he was spinning his wheels at this point. Maybe he'd take a break, get a soda.

There was a knock at his door, which opened before he could answer. He'd forgotten to lock it, and cursed himself. Heidi wandered in, wearing one of her usual outfits that was designed to draw attention to her award-winning breasts.

He sighed. He liked boobs as much as the next guy, but he really, really wasn't in the mood to deal with Heidi today.

"Kinda busy, Heidi," he said, his tone cool.

"Oh, sugar, no gentleman's too busy for a lady," she said with a smile and a wink. To his consternation, she closed the door behind her. He bolted up. "Got a second?"

"Just a second." He clenched his jaw. "Open the door, please."

"I need to talk to you in private, though," she said, waving her hand.

"I can't imagine why. Is it business related?"

He figured she'd come up with some kind of fabricated, tissue-thin excuse, but to his surprise, her expression actually turned serious. "I have to break my lease."

"Wait, what?" he blurted out. "But . . . your lease isn't up until February."

"That's why it's called *breaking* the lease," she said, rolling her eyes. "Peter, my damned ex-husband, is getting remarried. And he's decided that my little 'unprofitable hobby' isn't worth investing in, so he's cutting me off."

Josh frowned. He wasn't actually surprised. The restaurant *was* essentially just a hobby for Heidi. She hired cooks, and they did their best, but they often had no one to ask questions of when things went wrong since she only spent time at the restaurant erratically, and the recipes that Heidi used were cribbed from things she'd found on the internet—not things she'd tested or developed, and certainly not things that took ingredient spoilage or food waste into account. She'd mix stuff she liked from Texas with things she thought sounded Southern Californian or fancy. (He shuddered at the memory of her ill-fated ahi pierogi offering.) Beyond that, she didn't really market beyond going to business mixers and having a Facebook page.

Honestly, it was kind of amazing that it had stayed in business this long.

Josh took a deep breath. "I'm sorry to hear that," he said politely, even as his mind raced.

God, I don't need this.

He was supposed to give this presentation in less than a week, and it was going to look like shit if he had an underperformer *and* a vacant kitchen. Darius had made it clear: he needed this pitch to hit it out of the park. For all he knew, his second location depended on it.

So . . . now he had to find yet *another* existing restaurant to fill the gap?

Add it to the list. He felt his shoulder blades pinch together with tension.

He was so in his head trying to come up with some solutions that he didn't initially notice Heidi taking a step closer to him. "You know . . . I could stay," she purred, her hips wiggling a little as she sauntered in front of his chest, reaching to stroke a palm over one of his pecs.

"Whoa." He dodged, quickly moving away from her, toward the door. "I thought you said you were cut off."

"Yes, but . . . ," she said, her bottle-green eyes bright—and shrewd. "You could make an exception and let me stay, couldn't you? You're a super-successful restauranteur. You made this place out of nothing, and now you're, like, a multimillionaire or something. Aren't you? If you invested and helped me out, we could turn it around and show everybody that Pierogi Princess is a brilliant idea. We could even make it a chain!"

Oh, for fuck's sake. "No, Heidi."

She pouted, arching her back. It was as if she was putting herself on a platter, like her pierogies. "But it'd mean *a lot* to me."

Was she kidding? Did this actually *work* on anyone? "Heidi," he said firmly, "I am not interested."

She toyed with her neckline. Seriously—*toyed with her neckline*. Next thing she'd be doing was unfastening a button. He found himself growing more and more irritated. "You won't know you like something," she said, her voice husky, "until you try it."

He rubbed a hand over his face, then opened the door. "I'm really sorry."

She narrowed her eyes as it slowly sank in. "Are you serious? You're . . . just . . . no?"

Finally! "*Absolutely* no." He shook his head, all but standing in the hallway. "Amber?" he called out.

Heidi was fuming by the time Amber made it to the office. "Yes?" Amber said, looking at Heidi curiously.

"Heidi will no longer be renting the kitchen," he said. "She needs to break the lease. Would you see what it'll take to help her get whatever equipment or ingredients she might own out to her car?"

Heidi goggled. "What?" she screeched.

Amber nodded. "Sure thing, no problem. I'll have one of the guys help me."

"You can't just kick me out!" Heidi shouted.

Josh sighed. "You said you were breaking your lease. Were you planning on paying for next month? No?" He steamrolled over her stuttered protests. "Then there really isn't any reason for you to stay. You will need to let your staff know, but otherwise, it's not a problem. I'm not even going to charge you a penalty. Good luck on your future endeavors."

Heidi's face flushed unpleasantly, and her glare was murderous. "Maybe I'll sue you," she murmured. "I want to make my restaurant a success, and I want you to help me. Is it to get back at my husband? Sure. But if you're going to be this way, maybe I'll call a lawyer and say that you made me uncomfortable, and *that's* why I had to break my lease. See where that goes."

She let that threat hang in the air, and he stared back at her.

"I am *standing right here*," Amber pointed out. "While you're threatening him."

"Yes, but you weren't when we were in his office. With the door closed." Heidi crossed her arms, smiling smugly. "Besides, you work for him—he could pressure you to lie for him, to keep your job. You're hardly credible."

Josh took in a deep breath, then let it out slowly as he counted to ten. As he'd hoped, it prevented his head from exploding.

Then, silently, he pointed to a corner of the office.

"Security camera," he said. "With mic."

Now the flush drained from Heidi's face, and she went white as sour cream. For once in his life, he was grateful for having worked at Sergio's and learning to put a camera where you keep your cash after they'd had that incident of embezzlement *and* when they'd been robbed. The fact that he had a mic on this camera had been a fortuitous extra, something he'd been hesitant about, but had accepted when the electrician offered it as a bonus.

"You . . . but . . ." Heidi tried to rally. "That's not legal! You can't just record me without my knowledge!"

For once, Heidi's haphazard approach to business was saving his ass. "You expressly agreed to permission when you signed the lease and our business agreement, remember? It even said explicitly where the cameras were," he growled. "Now get out."

Heidi stormed out, Amber on her heels. Josh felt like every muscle in his body was a tight, hard knot.

This is the last thing I needed.

Not long after, Amber came up to his office. "I escorted Miss Thang out to her Lexus," Amber said with an undertone of glee. "She was *pissed.* It never occurred to her that she couldn't get exactly what she felt entitled to."

"The timing sucks," Josh admitted, "but I gotta say, it's probably for the best that she's gone. Her numbers didn't play into any of our work, but having an unprofitable restaurant attached to Ghost Kitchens Unlimited was not going to help our image. Of course, now I need to add not just one, but two restaurants, one way or another." He rubbed small circles on his temples with his fingertips.

"You look like shit," Amber pointed out. "You've been working at this all afternoon. Maybe knock off early?"

"That's like a half day," Josh said. "I used to work fourteen-hour shifts, remember?"

"Yeah, because I told you that shit wasn't sustainable, remember?" Amber shot back. "Go home to that girl of yours, relax a little."

He was ready to protest. *Tam's not my girl.* And the fact that he was starting to suspect he wanted her to be was just one more layer of *fuck my life* that he didn't need.

But even as he was ready to protest, his brain shot up a flare. Even with the sexual frustration—even with the *pining*, as Amber would call it—he knew that nobody made him feel better than Tam did, no matter what.

"You may have a point," he finally agreed. "All right. I'm headed home. I'll be back in tomorrow."

"I've got the fort," Amber said with a sly smile. "Don't worry about me, boss. Just go have some fun for a change."

He rolled his eyes, but he dutifully went back to his house. When he got there, Tam was on her laptop at the dining room table, frowning and typing.

"You're not applying for temp jobs again, are you?" he said suspiciously.

"You're home early," she said, and for a second, he thought of the last time she'd said something similar. *And I thought you were going to take a longer shower.*

He frowned at himself.

"Had kind of a crap day," he said. "Heidi broke her lease. Which means I have two restaurants to replace and loss of rental income until I do." He leaned over her shoulder. She was on some kind of photo-editing software, with a picture of a charcuterie board. "What are you doing?"

"Just coming up with some memes for Freddie," she said. "I had fun over there yesterday. I mean, I think it's obvious that I'm never going to be a culinary artist like him, or you. But it was still a good time."

Josh smiled, resting his chin on her shoulder. She absently nuzzled his face with hers, and he took a breath of her scent: lemon, white clover, and an almost candy sweetness that was pure Tam.

He felt the tension from work leave his body, even as a new tension crept in.

He glanced at the memes. There were a lot of cheese puns, he noticed, and a SHARK CUTIE joke. He grinned.

"You're good at that."

"Can you believe that Freddie's catering hasn't posted on Insta for eight months?" she said, sounding scandalized. "I'm going to talk with Asad about it. I can't believe he's letting his boyfriend slack like that."

Josh grinned as she finished and shut her laptop. She studied him intently as he stepped away to get himself a glass of water.

"So. Are you going to be working?" she asked, nodding her head toward his home office.

He groaned. "I should," he admitted. "But Amber says I'm getting burned out and that maybe I should take a break."

Tam stood up, looking into his eyes. "She's right," she pronounced. "You do look kind of crispy. And a break sounds good."

"But I have so much that I need to do," he countered.

"It'll still be there, and if you're refreshed, you'll be able to tackle it better," she said. "At least, that's what this pushy best friend of mine told me when I first got back to Ponto."

He grinned. "Really? He sounds like an asshole."

"Yeah, but a smart one," she answered, and he barked out a laugh. "You know what I could go for?"

He shook his head.

"Trip to the beach," she said. "I haven't been in years. It could be nice."

"It's September," he pointed out.

"Yeah, but it's not that cold," she answered. "It's Southern Cal, dude, and it's sunny as hell today. I'll be fine."

He thought about it. It had been years since he'd been to the beach, other than occasionally running along it. When was the last time he'd just had a trip for fun?

Besides—if Tam wanted to go, then of course he'd go. It really wasn't even a question.

Still, he had to put up at least a token resistance. "I guess," he drawled, trying to sound as reluctant as possible. "But only because you want to go."

She kissed his cheek. “You’re a sweetheart,” she said with a hint of sarcasm, then grinned. “Let me get my suit on, and I’ll meet you back here.” Then she scooted back to the guest bedroom.

He looked at the closed door, then adjusted himself.

Swimsuits.

He hadn’t thought about that aspect of this.

Maybe it was a bad idea, after all. And he was still recovering from their last good bad idea.

CHAPTER 24

Ponto Beach had a long stretch of sand that wasn't particularly tourist friendly. While most people thought of million-dollar houses right on the beach, new hotels going up every day, and a decent crab-shack-style restaurant out on the pier, Tam always thought of Ponto as the craggy, isolated bits of beachfront where you parked along Highway 101 and then hoofed it across scraggly brush until you got to the sand. It was less crowded, for one thing, and it was where the Nerd Herd had tended to go when they'd decided to go to the beach. She remembered hours of playing Frisbee and splashing around in the water, coming home with sand stuck to her sunscreen, smelling like coconut and salt and sea air.

She hadn't realized how happy those days had been. Now, stepping out of Josh's van in a pair of sandals, shorts pulled over her swimsuit, and a hoodie zipped up, it all came crashing back down on her. The afternoon sun was high and hot, so the cool air off the Pacific felt like a benediction, gently blowing her hair off her face.

"Careful," Josh said, taking her hand as she stepped down the bank. Then he went to the back of the van. It had taken him what felt like forever to get ready, and she saw him pull out one of the coolers, a beach bag, and two large plastic buckets, stacked up. She looked at the latter curiously.

"Help me with these?" he asked, handing her the buckets. They were empty, more awkward than heavy. She then watched as he slung the bag over his shoulder and hefted the cooler. "C'mon. You pick a spot."

She finally chose a nice bit of sand that wasn't too rocky and wasn't too strewn with washed-up ropes of kelp. "Here," she pointed. "Should I put the buckets down?"

"Not quite yet." He put the cooler down, then opened the bag, pulling out a king-size fitted sheet, complete with elastic. "Help me stretch this out?"

She did, puzzled. Then he put the cooler in one corner of the sheet, the bag in the opposite corner, and then the buckets in the remaining two. When he was done, it was like having the world's lowest, weakest playpen. She started laughing.

He shrugged. "I may have learned this from Martha Stewart or something," he grumbled. "The important bit is, I hate it when my towel gets covered with a ton of sand, and I really hate getting sand in my food. Hop in."

She carefully shook off her feet—he'd done all this work, after all—and clambered into the sheet, eventually landing ungracefully on her butt. "So. Wow. This is a thing."

He grinned, following her lead and climbing onto the sheet, making sure he didn't get any sand in. He was wearing a pair of orange board shorts and a zip-up navy sweatshirt. His blond hair was tousled by the wind, and his eyes were lighter than they were when he'd gotten home from the Tombs. He looked more relaxed.

She stretched out, feeling the sun heating her like a lizard on a rock, and she moaned slightly. The sound of the waves crashing against the sand was incredibly soothing. "I can't believe I let this much time pass," she said. "I remember loving coming down here."

He stretched out next to her, and she could feel the heat coming off him . . . which, given the strength of the afternoon sun, was saying something. "Me too," he agreed, letting out a deep breath.

"Times like these, I don't even care that I can't figure out my life," Tam added, arching her back a little and wiggling to settle herself more comfortably in the sand under the sheet.

Josh rolled to one side, propping his head up on his hand. "You've barely scratched the surface," he pointed out. "It's not like you're running out of time. You set an arbitrary deadline—you can give yourself some slack."

"I've shadowed two jobs," she said.

"And just because you don't like working with unconsciously pervy design clients or stuffing hundreds of cookies into cellophane bags doesn't mean that you aren't still going to fit in graphic design or some kind of culinary career. Look at me. I never would've guessed I'd be in the restaurant business, especially not ghost kitchens."

"That's because there weren't really ghost kitchens when we were in school," Tam said with a rueful smile.

He tugged a lock of her hair, and she gave him her attention. "My point is, you never know what life's going to throw at you," he said. "And you definitely don't know what you're going to be great at. Don't shut off your avenues before you give yourself a chance, okay?"

She felt those words, like a hot-rock massage—soothing and warm, comforting and relaxing. She smiled at him. "You are my best friend in the entire world," she said.

He grinned back. "Back atcha. So, what are you going to try for writing?"

She bit her lip. "I don't know," she admitted. "I have no idea how to write a book, and honestly, I don't think I'd want to. I don't think screenplays would be any easier. So maybe articles, I guess?" She sighed. "Or . . . maybe a podcast? That's not writing, per se, but . . . maybe?"

The wind kicked up, blowing her hair in her face, and she spluttered. Chuckling, he used his fingertip to brush her hair out of her face and tuck it behind her hair.

Her heart started thumping erratically.

Stop it. We talked about this.

They were friends, and that was more important than any kind of sexual relationship that might crash and burn. It wasn't worth the risk.

Then he smiled at her . . . that slow, sugary, downright incendiary smile of his that had made stronger women than herself drop their panties on command.

It was getting hot, wasn't it?

She peeled off her hoodie, leaving her in her tankini top in good-luck red. She needed to get back on track, and quickly. She flipped onto her stomach, resting her face on her interlaced fingers, and changed the subject. "So. Today really sucked, huh?"

He scowled. She felt a little bad, but at the same time, it felt familiar to try to solve someone else's problems—even if they were her best friend's. "I'll work it out," he said but sounded frustrated. "I mean, the timing could be better, but the more I think about it, the more I'm glad that Heidi's gone. She seemed nice enough when she and her husband signed the lease, but the divorce made her really jump the rails. I think that she misses Texas. And she wanted to have her own success . . . her ex has a lot of money, and he's a lot older. She wanted the money and the status, and it was a train wreck. When he divorced her, I think she just started latching on to me as a kind of replacement. You know, younger guy who makes money, and who could make her restaurant a success." He pulled his lips into a thin line. "Anyway, whatever her reasons, she was manipulative and a problem. I just wish that I had another restaurant lined up to replace the slot. Now I need to find two new restaurants to fill the gaps before my presentation. I didn't think I'd be able to sign anybody prior to the presentation, but this looks like I don't have my shit together."

He huffed out an impatient breath, and she could see him stressing out. She propped herself up.

This is probably a bad idea, she told herself, but then ignored the little voice inside her. "Flip over. Onto your stomach."

His eyes widened. "Why?"

"Just shut up and flip over." She bit her lip. "And, um, take off your sweatshirt."

He did as instructed, stripping out of his sweatshirt and stretching out on his stomach. For a second, she just reveled in the look of his long, lean, but well-defined back. His muscles tensed and danced as she smoothed her fingers over the planes of his back.

"You are tense as hell," she pointed out, trying to sound clinical, which would've worked better if her voice hadn't gone as husky as a frickin' cam girl's. She coughed lightly, then dug in the beach bag. As she'd suspected, he had sunscreen. "I'm going to get you covered in sunscreen and give you a little massage, okay?"

"I could make so many jokes," he said, his voice a little muffled against the sheet. She snickered, poking him in the side and making him wince. "Hey! Ticklish!"

"I know, you baby," she said, rolling her eyes. She started smoothing the sunscreen into his skin, working on the knots between his neck and shoulder blades, which felt like blocks of granite. "Man. You are a mess."

"Thanks," he drawled sarcastically.

"So," she said, squeezing harder, putting some of her body weight into it. "Your investor, what's his name . . ."

"Darius."

"Yeah, him. He said that it might be better to hook up with an established restaurant, like French Bistro, so you've got a winning track record with brand recognition from the jump? Instead of a brand-new restaurant?"

She felt him sigh beneath her fingertips, both out of resignation at Darius's suggestion and with relaxation as slowly his muscles unknotted.

"Does it have to be a restaurant?"

She could see him try to shoot her a skeptical look from his prone position. "Well, I could try partnering with a furniture store, but I don't think it'd be as effective."

"Smart-ass." Just for that, she poked him again, and he jerked. "I mean, does it need to be an established restaurant that wants takeout? Or could you partner with a catering company?"

He flipped to look at her more intently. "What are you talking about?"

"Freddie's lease is coming up, and he's unhappy," she said. "I heard him mention it. And he's got problems with food waste and supply ordering. I know that you like ordering local, and you seem to have a lot of that handled with the software you developed. Also, you are totally set for delivery, which would work with his setup person, I think." She shrugged. "Then, you could replace the underperformer with Graham Catering, which has a proven track record that your investor would appreciate, and which would show the versatility of the space. Which still leaves you with Heidi's spot, but I figure, it'd still be good to show that you can start a new concept from scratch very quickly, so you can do the bánh mì restaurant. I mean, that's the whole appeal of ghost kitchens—or at least, that's what you told me. This way, you have the best of both worlds, and you have both your spots filled. Win-win."

He stared at her, silent, long enough for her to be embarrassed. Then, before she could react, he tackled her in a huge hug.

"You. Are. Brilliant," he said vehemently. "That is *perfect*. That is . . . how did you . . . oh my God."

She felt his praise sink into her like butter into toast, and she wriggled happily. "I was just trying to help."

"What would I do without you?" His eyes were shining and his smile was so beatifically happy that she realized she wanted to capture that forever. Just looking at him so happy made her feel like she'd swallowed the sun.

"Here's hoping you don't have to find out," she quipped, then reached into her shorts and pulled out her cell phone. "Selfie. I want to document this." She scooted closer to him, smiling and holding her fingers up in a V.

She got a shot of the two of them smiling. Then he leaned down and kissed her, right in the crook of her neck.

She couldn't help it. She gasped. It felt like every nerve ending she had lit up like the Eiffel Tower at night. She shot him a look of shock.

"Was aiming for your cheek," he said, but his pupils were blown wide, and his gaze gleamed, hot and harsh and full of . . . *nngh.*

She felt her pulse start to go haywire, and she put her phone down, staring at him the whole time.

They'd talked about it. They'd sworn they wouldn't do anything again.

Bad idea?

Hell, yes.

But she wasn't going to let that stop her. Not this time.

So she leaned over and kissed him.

CHAPTER 25

Josh knew, on some level, that there were things like public indecency laws. But in this moment, with Tam pressed against him, he gave not. One. Single. Damn.

He tilted his head to get a better angle on that full, mobile mouth of hers, weaving his fingers into her hair to hold her tightly against him. She let out a soft little moan against his lips that made his whole body—and yes, he meant his *whole* body—go hard.

He traced the line of her lips with his tongue, and she parted them without any hesitation, letting him sweep his tongue in before tangling it with hers. He felt as well as heard her gasp, and she writhed against him in a way that had him aching. Her nipples were hard little points underneath her tankini top, and he felt them against his bare chest. He tugged her slightly, until she was riding his lap. She had to feel the erection that was now steel hard and straining against his board shorts.

A tiny little voice in his subconscious warned him that this might be a bad idea, for the sake of any passersby, if not for the whole "what happens in New York stays in New York" agreement. But his body, on the other hand, wrestled that tiny voice into submission by warning it: *Don't mess this up, or I will hurt you.*

Obviously my body is very invested in this outcome, he thought . . . just before she shimmied her hips slightly, notching him closer to her heat, and shivering. His eyes rolled back in his head.

He released her hair and smoothed his palms down her back, moving his hands to her hips, tugging her flush against him. Not that it was possible for her to get any closer. She whimpered, eager and intent, wriggling and blindly repositioning to wrap her legs around his waist. Her fingers grasped his shoulders, holding him tight. She was devouring him just as much as he was devouring her, rocking against him.

If they weren't wearing clothes, he'd be inside her by now. He just knew it.

A high-pitched whistle tore the air, and they jerked apart, breathing heavily.

"Whoo!" a surfer said, grinning wolfishly. He was flanked by a few buddies, all wearing wet suits and bearing short "potato chip" boards. "Get some!"

"Don't mind us—just keep doing what you're doing," another guy said, laughing raucously, as the third guy just leered.

Sanity hit Josh like a slap. He was practically having sex. With Tam.

In public.

This would probably be the exact situation that tiny voice was yammering on about.

Tam's face was deep red, and she bit her lip. He couldn't help himself. He leaned down, soothing it with his tongue, ignoring the catcalls of the surfers. "Maybe you'll let me bite your lip next," he said, against her mouth, before pulling away.

She started to get off his lap, but her eyes bugged out as she saw his erection. Not that he could hide it at this point. "Um. What are we . . . that is . . ."

He stroked her chin, then leaned in and kissed her neck. This was stupid, he just knew it. But at the same time, even with the audience, he simply didn't care. "Maybe we should take this back home," he said, his voice rough as sandpaper.

She looked low lidded, almost sleepy, even though her gaze burned with incandescent desire. "We said that we weren't going to do this again," she pointed out.

"Weren't going to do what again?" he teased, nipping at her jawline, gratified by her breathy little sigh.

"You *know*."

"We were pretending," he said, punctuating each word with open-mouth kisses against the column of her throat, "that nothing happened. If nothing happened before, then this is a brand-new thing. Right?"

He felt her throat work as she swallowed, and her hips canted again. "Sophistry. It's still a bad idea, though," she said, but the protest was weak, especially considering she was still pressed up against him. "I mean . . . isn't it?"

He grimaced as his brain tried, yet again, to agree with her. Then he frowned. "Why does it have to be a bad idea?"

"Because . . . because if we have a relationship, and it jumps the rails, and we wind up getting weird and avoiding each other again, or being hurt and blaming each other, or—"

"Wait a second," Josh interrupted, seeing the fear in her eyes. "I'm not saying that. The friendship comes first, always." He paused. It felt like standing on the edge of a high dive. Finally, he just said *fuck it* . . . and leaped.

"What if it wasn't a relationship, though?"

She blinked at him. "You're talking friends with benefits?" She looked startled.

He wondered for a second if he'd insulted her. *Dammit, body. This is what I get for listening to you.*

But before he could take it back, her expression shifted to something contemplative.

"I suppose . . . if we knew it, going in," she said slowly. "Then it wouldn't . . . do any damage?"

She yelped as he picked her up, wrapping her legs around him like a koala. "I can get you home in about ten minutes," he said, giving her earlobe a nibble. "Just let me grab this stuff."

She laughed, but it was breathless. He carried her to the van and unlocked it. Then he sprinted back to their stuff, piling it pell-mell and throwing it in the back of the van. He drove faster than he probably should have back to his house. When they reached his driveway, he pulled in, then shut off the van. "Inside, inside," he urged, and she laughed, shaking her head.

"We had a deal in New York for a reason," she said, and her serious tone put some of his horniness on hold. "We were both turned on, but I can't lose you as a friend, Josh. I was already stupid for years, and I've missed you. If we hook up, and it gets . . . complicated, or if we have hard feelings and stop talking to each other . . . I don't think I can deal with that."

His chest warmed. Of course she'd think of that. And she was right, and, at the same time, not quite right.

"Do you know why I called you, when everything went wrong, five years ago?" he asked quietly. "There were plenty of people right here in town that I could've asked for help, or drowned my sorrows with. You were three thousand miles away, and the first person I wanted to talk to. Because I know you cared then, and you care now. You have always been my constant. You're my fucking North Star."

She smiled at him, slowly, her eyes glistening a little with tears.

"And you know why you called me at three in the morning?" he continued. "Not because you didn't have anyone. You could have called Vinh, because even if you've grown apart, and even if you joked that he might have killed Brent—"

"Was it a joke, though?" she interjected.

He rolled his eyes. "The thing is, you know Vinh would have helped. But you called me because you know that I care about you, more than just about anything. I can't think of a single person I'm closer to than you. We've counted on each other for too long."

He held out his pinky.

"I promise," he said solemnly. "Nothing's going to ruin our friendship. If you need me, I'm there. Period. If you don't want to have sex now, I'll completely respect that. If you have sex with me now, and then never want to again, I will still be your best friend. I swear, no matter what happens between us, I will always, always, *always* have your back, because you are the closest person to me in the whole world, and I'd never jeopardize that."

He meant every word.

She smiled, holding out her pinky, linking it with his.

Then she released him, hastily fumbling with her belt buckle. "Race you inside."

They rushed back into the house. He shut the door behind him with his foot, slamming it, then pressed her up against the nearest wall. She moaned.

He hadn't bothered to put his sweatshirt on—it was still in the van—and she was still in a swimsuit and shorts. They kicked off sandy sandals. He was tempted to just take her on the couch, but no—she deserved a bed.

Laughing, stumbling, they made it down the hallway to his room. He pulled back the covers, shucking his board shorts off as she tugged and struggled with her suit. Finally, she was gloriously, deliciously nude in front of him. For all of a second, she looked self-conscious.

He wanted to eat her alive.

"C'mere," he said, reaching for her. Her smile was slow and warm, heating him from the inside. She kissed him eagerly, and it was maybe the most tender kiss he'd ever experienced, turning their frenzy into something more tempered. Something stronger.

"Now, where were we?" she murmured, just before she clambered on top of him on the bed, mimicking the position they'd been in before being so rudely interrupted on the beach.

He groaned against her, enveloping her in his arms, stroking her petal-soft skin. How in the hell had he thought that he could give this up? That they could have one time in New York, and then somehow—he laughed internally—pretend that it had never happened?

She was molten in his arms. He'd always seen her as his goofy, sweet, completely reliable bestie. Now, he wondered how he'd missed that this girl was a sex goddess all along.

He tilted, off balance, and she pinned him to the mattress. Her body, soft and supple, contoured itself to fit him. His cock was going absolutely crazy, desperate to get inside her sweet heat.

"Tam," he rasped. Her only response was a mischievous smile . . . then she moved lower.

He wasn't expecting to feel her mouth circle the head of his erection, and for a second, he almost blacked out.

Holy. Shit.

He'd had blow jobs before, of course. But not one with the warm wet heat, the snug fit, that playful tickle of her tongue as she searched out his most sensitive spots. He let out a yell of pleasure as she sank down a bit. He was too big for her to take, but she still licked him like an ice cream cone, making little yummy noises of happiness, as her soft palm circled the rest of him and tugged with just the right amount of pressure.

How had Brent, or anyone, actually thought she wasn't good in bed? The woman was a goddamned prodigy.

He felt his heart hammering like an overrevved engine in his chest, his breath coming out in gulping pants as she continued to work her magic. He was sorely tempted to just let her go to completion, maybe return the favor. But he remembered how it felt to be that physically close to her, and he knew that, if they only had one more shot at this, that was what he wanted. He tapped her, getting her attention.

"God, you are too good at that. But I want to be inside you," he said. His voice sounded broken and rusty.

She released him with a wet pop, nodding. She stretched out next to him as he got out a condom from his nightstand. She looked perfect—like a present, like everything he'd ever wanted. Putting the condom down on the bed, he leaned down, pressing hot kisses on whatever flesh he could reach. He cupped her breasts, which were perfectly sized to fit his palm, like peaches. He licked around the nipples, first one and then the other, as she arched her back, pushing herself deeper into his mouth. As he kept licking and laving, he reached down, smoothing his palm down her stomach before carefully stroking between her legs.

She gasped, jolting. "Josh," she panted, her breathing uneven.

He pressed, stroking until he felt the wetness. He slicked her growing response between her folds, searching out and finding the hard bump of her clit. Smiling against her breast, he sucked as he gently but firmly worked her over.

"*Holy shit*," she said, echoing his earlier thoughts, and he couldn't help it. He laughed, delighted.

"You like that?"

"*Love* that," she answered, still sounding shocked. "Keep doing that."

"Oh, I will," he said. "But maybe . . . well. See if you like this."

He rolled on the condom, barely realizing that his hands were shaking. He'd never had sex affect him like this. Normally, with a hookup, he obviously made sure that his partner had a good time. But there wasn't this sense of connection, of closeness. This woman knew him, inside and out. He couldn't love her more if he were two people.

The fact that Tam had obviously been with guys who didn't put her pleasure first made him both angry on her behalf and a little proud that he was finally doing the job properly. He wanted her to feel every ounce of pleasure that she could.

And then he wanted to do it all over again.

He pressed himself at her opening, the hard tip nudging her open, and she moaned. He knew that he wanted better access, and after their interval in New York, he had a better sense of where her pleasure points were. He propped her leg up on his chest, spreading her, slowly working his way deeper. Then he used the broad pad of his thumb to keep working her clit as he moved in and out, slow and steady.

"Oh my God," she breathed, staring at him with rapt attention. "Oh my *God*!"

He knew what she meant. Her body was clamped around him like a vise, and he wanted to come so badly. They started moving together, in unison, getting a rhythm that made him want to howl. She lifted her hips to meet his every thrust, and he tugged her. She shook her head from side to side, almost speaking in tongues.

"Harder, Josh," she said. "Fuck me *hard*."

It was the tipping point. He lost his rhythm, starting to buck against her as his body lost control. She let out a low cry, and he felt her muscles ripple around him, milking him. And he just snapped. His orgasm roared through him, his vision all but going white, and he groaned, his hips jerking against her.

It took a while for him to get it together enough to get rid of the condom. When he was done, he came back to bed, collapsing at her side. She rolled against him, both their bodies slick with sweat, and she kissed him.

"That was . . . wow." She blinked. "I can't believe I'm saying this, but . . . were you holding out on me in New York?"

He stared at her, then started chuckling, then flat-out laughing until they were both laughing and couldn't stop. He felt happiness bubble up in him like champagne.

He'd never felt like this about anyone else. Ever. The sex was incredible.

The aftermath? Even more so.

Why, exactly, shouldn't we be in a relationship, again?

He frowned. Dammit. That was a really good question.

CHAPTER 26

Tam locked Josh's bike in front of Uncommon Grounds, feeling just the slightest ache from muscles she'd used recently that had nothing to do with cycling.

Honestly, I should get a car.

Tam frowned as she entered Juanita's café. *I need to get a job before I can afford a car,* she thought absently. That said, she'd need a car to get a job, more than likely. It had never been an issue in New York. She probably should've included that in the pros/cons list that she and Josh had worked out, but for now, she was sort of stuck.

She hadn't thought a lot of things through. Especially where Josh was concerned.

The sex this past weekend was . . . she didn't even have words for it. She'd thought the New York interlude was a fluke, or at least, she'd desperately tried to write it off that way. She'd been in an emotionally intense state after packing up her stuff and having her quasi-showdown with Brent, and they'd both been stirred up after a period of celibacy, and . . . things had . . . *happened.*

But Friday?

That was simply an afternoon with my friend, she tried desperately to argue to herself. He'd had a rough day. They'd just hung out at the beach.

Then a kiss.

Then . . .

Fireworks. Mind-blowing, paradigm-shifting, world-shaking sex.

She groaned softly to herself. She probably should say she hadn't been expecting it, but on some level, it made perfect sense. Josh had always paid more attention to her than anyone else in her world. He simply *got* her on a level that nobody matched, ever.

Of course he could read her like a damned book.

Of course he'd give her more pleasure than she thought her body was capable of.

Now, she was still trying to figure out her life. As sweet as Josh was about her "finding her bliss," she knew, ultimately, that at some point she was going to have to face facts. Not everybody got their dream job. Not everybody hit that perfect work-life balance.

Not everybody got their perceived soul mate. And the sooner she stopped fantasizing about Josh in that role, the better for both of them, because *that* was what was ultimately going to screw over their friendship.

He'd been so awesome about assuring her that he'd never stop being her friend, no matter what happened. But he kept couching it in ways that made it seem like he wouldn't get too attached. If *she* left, if *she* changed her mind, if *she* pulled away.

Apparently it had never occurred to him that she might fall in love with him. What would he do then? God, what would *she* do then?

"Hey, you!" Juanita came out from behind the counter and gave her a hug. "Glad you could come have breakfast. Emily's running a few minutes late—some family trouble, you know how that is. Can I get you something?"

"I'll pay like a regular customer," Tam said with a smile, going to the counter, where a girl with red hair pulled back in a ponytail and a septum piercing was smiling congenially. "Then maybe we can grab a table?"

Juanita grudgingly accepted, and Tam ordered a promising egg-brioche soufflé-type thing and a vanilla latte. Red Ponytail—whose name turned out to be Mabel, per her name tag—promised to deliver her food and drink, so she met Juanita at a tiled-top table by the window.

Juanita looked at her shrewdly. "You okay? You look different."

Tam forced herself not to look guilty. "Didn't sleep that well, that's all," she demurred. Which wasn't a lie. On Friday, she'd wound up showering with Josh, then eating a haphazard dinner of Tater Tots, carnitas, avocado, and cheddar cheese that should've been disgusting but worked, well enough that Josh joked about opening a Tater Tot restaurant. Then they'd had sex again before collapsing into sleep in Josh's bed (after changing the dirty, somewhat sandy sheets, of course). She'd been surprised to wake up there.

To avoid the weirdness of "morning after," they'd then had sex *again.*

This pattern had continued all weekend, stopping only when Josh had gone off to the Tombs to work. She'd catnapped, cooked, and cleaned the house while he was gone. She'd also made time to watch a few K-dramas and sun herself lazily in his backyard.

Long story short: she was the best kind of exhausted, despite her recent bouts of rest and recuperation.

She shook her head, trying to clear the cobwebs, and thanked Mabel profusely when she delivered the latte in front of her. It had a smiley face in the broad cup face, painted in foam. Tam let out a little happy hum as she took a sip.

"How's the job hunt working?" Juanita asked, sipping what looked like a green tea. "Sorry the brainstorming turned into such a shit show. I mean, it was funny, but in retrospect, it probably wasn't that helpful."

"It's going," Tam admitted, shifting uneasily. "Josh's good at staying on track, and I did identify the stuff I liked. I still do like graphic design, just not the way Asad does it. And I like food. But I guess I like eating it more than, you know, making it." She shrugged, laughing at herself.

"What's left?"

"Writing," Tam said, feeling herself tense. "The thing is, I can't imagine what I'd write. I can't think of any ideas for a book, and even if I could, the thought of all those words? *Ugh.*"

"Maybe you could write articles?" Juanita supplied.

Before Tam could answer, Emily came in like a whirlwind. "Sorry, sorry," she said. "I overslept. Hold on, let me grab a sticky bun and some coffee."

Tam smiled. She was glad that Emily had the day off, even if it meant that she'd been working all weekend. Tam almost felt guilty at how she'd spent the weekend.

Emily settled down at the table, throwing herself into a chair. "So? What'd I miss?"

"Tam was just talking about narrowing down what she wants to do for a living," Juanita said with a grin.

Emily looked at Tam, then her eyes narrowed. "What's different about you?"

Tam stiffened. "I don't . . ."

"*Oh my God,*" Emily said, eyes rounding. "You finally slept with Josh!"

Tam choked on air.

Juanita started laughing. "Is *that* it? I thought there was something different, too, but I figured she just got some sun."

"She got some *something,*" Emily said, snickering as Mabel delivered her food. "Spill! Spill! Was it good? What was the tipping point?"

"Who's got this September in the betting pool?" Juanita said, pulling up her phone. "It's on the Slack channel, right?"

Tam glared at them, nudging Juanita with her foot. "Okay. You two have to *swear* you won't tell anybody."

They looked at each other. "Only if you give us details," Emily said.

Juanita rolled her eyes. "Emily," she chided, then looked at Tam. "If you don't want us to talk, we won't."

"But I need someone to live vicariously through." Emily faked a whine, then winked at Tam. "Juanita and I are too single!"

"She does have a point there," Juanita muttered.

Tam sighed. "We did, um, sleep together," she said. "But we said we weren't going to say anything. To anyone."

"Oh, come on," Juanita said. "I bet if you two were in the same room, it'd be obvious to absolutely everyone. Even Hayden, and that guy is the definition of oblivious."

Tam frowned.

"I actually would've guessed you'd already slept together," Emily added. "But then, I was really early in the betting pool for when you two were going to get together."

Tam sighed. "It's not going to *go* anywhere," she said. "He's still my best friend. We're just friends." She took a long sip of her latte. "Who, um, have sex occasionally."

Emily and Juanita exchanged a look of disbelief.

"Makes sense," Juanita said, rolling her eyes.

"Yeah," Emily agreed. "Totally foolproof."

"Hey," Tam protested. "Like I said: he is my best friend! I'm not going to jeopardize that, ever. If you know us at all, you know that. I would take a bullet for Josh."

"And he'd jump in front of a train for you," Juanita agreed. "But sex changes things. You honestly telling me that you're just going to be friends?"

"Yes." Tam hoped that sounded more confident than she felt.

"Why, though?" Juanita said, sounding genuinely baffled. "That guy is your soul mate. Do you have any idea how rare that is? He treats you like gold and loves you to distraction. What in the world is the point of you two just staying friends? What are you scared of?"

Tam stiffened. "I can't afford to lose him as a friend," she said, slowly and carefully. "And a relationship? What if it didn't work?"

"Yeah, but what if it *did*?" Juanita pressed.

"No, Tam's got a point," Emily agreed, and she looked surprisingly somber. "No offense, Tam, but you have a tendency of putting your entire life on hold for whatever guy you're with. You cut us off because of your last boyfriend."

"I feel like shit about that," Tam interjected as guilt nibbled at her, but Emily made a dismissive motion.

"Not the point. You moved across country for the one before that—we started losing touch with you when you graduated. You didn't even like New York, but you applied to Vassar because of Collin."

"Josh isn't like that," Juanita protested, reading Tam's mind. "He's not going to insist that she do anything just because he's selfish. If anything, he'd sacrifice everything to make sure she's happy."

"Yeah, but this isn't about Josh. This is about Tam," Emily said, then shifted to look at Tam seriously. "Nothing hurts more than seeing the person you love, one of your best friends, walk away because of whatever is going on in his life. You know Josh has a lot of stuff going on with his business. And I know you. You'd probably do whatever you could to help him out and then just sort of limp along with whatever *you* want to do with life. Or not look into what makes you complete . . . just keep devoting yourself to making *him* happy. Am I wrong?"

Tam poked at her eggs with her fork. Unfortunately, Emily had a point. And seeing the pain etched in Emily's expression, she knew the woman had every reason to have this stance . . . thanks to Vinh, Emily's first love.

"I'm not saying you shouldn't be in a relationship with Josh if you want to," Emily said, reaching over and patting Tam's forearm encouragingly. "I'm just saying, Josh may have a point about you designing your life. You need to figure out what *you* want to do. And you can do it. You just need to stay focused."

Tam nodded, feeling a little sad.

"Josh loves you," Emily added. "Maybe not as a girlfriend, but we all know that you are the closest person to him on earth, and he'll back your play no matter what you figure out."

Tam swallowed hard against the lump in her throat. Then she took a bite of the breakfast dish. "This is really good," she said to Juanita.

Juanita beamed. "I know that my parents thought I was crazy to open the café, rather than be an oncologist," she said with an impish grin. "But, weird though it seems, this was following *my* bliss. I can recommend it highly."

"Yeah, well, until I can stumble across a job that lets me screw around on social media while eating cheese, I'll just have to manage," Tam said. "I really missed you guys. I'm glad you could come out and have breakfast with me."

"Wanna take a selfie?" Emily said, pulling out her phone. Pretty soon the three of them were squeezing together, taking photos with all their phones. Mabel even helped.

Juanita went back to work, and Emily chatted away while Tam uploaded the photo onto Instagram, adding the caption, alt photo description, and hashtags:

Hanging with the Nerd Herd in Ponto. [Image description: Juanita Guitierrez, Emily MacDonald, Tam Doan at Uncommon Grounds, Ponto Beach, CA] #BFFs #BeachLife #CoffeeHouseLove

She then tagged in Juanita and Emily as well as the coffee shop.

She noticed that there were a lot of comments on her previous photo, the one with her and Josh. She didn't have a huge following, although she had online friends who shared her interests—cheese friends, K-drama friends, book friends. Normally, she got a few likes. This number seemed unusually high. Granted, Josh was cute, and she had to admit, the picture was sexy.

She opened it . . . only to stumble on the first comment.

"TAM DOAN IS A WHORE."

She choked in utter shock. "What the *hell*?"

CHAPTER 27

Josh had a kick-ass Monday. He'd spent only a little bit of time in the Tombs on the weekend, and today, he'd left Tam in bed—*his* bed—and attacked the day with a vengeance, because he knew he had something (some*one*) amazing to come home to.

Before the kitchens opened, he'd already had a conversation with a Vietnamese chef about the bánh mì delivery restaurant concept, which had been amazing. Phillip Nguyen was getting frustrated in his current restaurant situation, and he loved bánh mì in general—the versatility, its simplicity and unpretentiousness, the way it reminded him of his childhood. They talked about potential menu options and overlap with ingredient ordering with Oaxaca for things like fresh vegetables, pickled sides, even bakery items—they'd sourced a good bakery for bolillos for their tortas, but they could probably provide the small baguettes that made bánh mì so great. He and Phillip also talked names, possible branding, and packaging. They had a meeting scheduled to discuss it in more detail and hash out a partnership agreement, and how Phillip would work with Amber, tying in to the overall ghost kitchen "ecosystem" and working with the existing structures.

Then he'd called Freddie and discussed the possibility of moving Graham Catering over to the Tombs. Freddie actually drove over that day, since he'd never actually visited Josh's kitchens before. (Asad had been over several times.) Freddie was impressed with the size, the working conditions, and the possibility of consolidated ordering reducing food waste. Granted, catering meant his "menu" would be constantly changing, but Josh had made sure there was plenty of refrigeration and freezer space prior to opening, and there were a lot of ways they could consolidate costs. By the time they were done, Freddie had agreed verbally, which thrilled Josh. Having proof of a delivery partnership in writing prior to the pitch meeting, plus a chef on board for the bánh mì restaurant concept, was going to be huge.

"I can't believe Tam thought of this," Freddie said. "Or rather, I can't believe she did when it never occurred to us."

"I didn't know you were looking, honestly," Josh said.

"And I didn't know you had space available!"

It was all working out perfectly . . . and Josh had Tam to thank for it. It shouldn't surprise him. She was brilliant at connecting things: seeing a big picture and identifying what worked together.

When they were younger, she was always the creative one. He'd be tenaciously beating his head against a wall, and she'd take one look, go, "You know, this feels like," and solve the problem in, like, a second. Hell, that's how she helped him get his head out of his ass and create the Tombs in the first place. They were at her mother's house—her father had already moved back to Vietnam by then after the divorce—and they'd ordered food from some delivery service.

"You could do this," she pointed out.

"What, be a food delivery driver?" He shook his head. "They work their asses off for shit pay. Don't think that's a step in the right direction, although I guess it's good to know I can fall back on it."

"No." She opened her phone, typing something in. "What was it you were telling me about? A few months ago. Some weird, neat thing you'd heard of."

"Was it the octopus holding a knife?" he asked, amused. "Because I don't see how that's relevant."

She shot him an irritated look. "No. The group kitchen thing."

"What, a ghost kitchen?"

"Yes. That." She typed faster, then held up the screen, handing him her phone. "Could you do that?"

"You mean . . . rent some commercial space to open my own restaurant, delivery only?" He rubbed his jaw. It would be less of a financial investment, he realized. But even if it was only $10,000 to $15,000 . . . that was money he didn't have and wasn't sure he could get.

"No," she said with a confident smile. "You could *run* all the kitchens. And you could sublease them out, or come up with multiple restaurants."

His mouth had dropped open at the sheer audacity of her plan, and he'd balked. "No way. I can't even get the money for one restaurant! How the hell would I get the money for multiple restaurants in a . . ."

And just like that, the vision clobbered him. It was a *eureka* moment like he'd never had. He saw the potential . . . not just for money, but for the macrocosm of the multiple kitchens, and what he could do with them. He'd been nervous and had wanted to play small, but it only really worked if he bit the bullet and went for the bigger number. It was what had prompted him to dive deep into the research, do a trial run at a ghost kitchen with another chef . . . and finally approach venture capitalists who might be hesitant about investing in a restaurant.

It had taken six months, and a lot of luck, but he'd found Darius. From there, he'd been on a rocket ride that vaulted him and Ghost Kitchens Unlimited into the stratosphere, more successful than he'd ever dreamed. Unfortunately, he'd gotten so fixated on the day-to-day, he'd lost touch with the best friend who had made it possible, both in her creative suggestion and in the sheer belief and moral support that she'd provided.

Now, it was seven o'clock, and he was eager to get back home, to have dinner with her.

The sex was incredible. But even more incredible was the fact that she was simply *there* . . . in his house, in his life.

He knew that he had trouble taking risks, but once he committed, he went all in. The Tombs was a prime example of that. He knew that his friendship with Tam would be at risk if they tried shifting from "friends with benefits" to something more, but the more he thought about it, the more he realized—they *were* in a relationship. They just hadn't ever acknowledged it. He loved her, and she loved him, and they both knew that. But he was *in* love with her and suspected that he had been for a long time. He'd been a bit stupid about it, and he'd taken advantage of the fact that she'd just be there for him . . . until she fell in love with other people and wasn't "just there" for him anymore. He'd missed that window, and had convinced himself that it was for the best. If he was risk resistant, she was downright risk phobic.

He just needed to convince her that they wouldn't screw things up irrevocably if they started dating. He chuckled at himself. Although *dating* seemed too tepid a term for what they had.

He came in, finding her at the table, as usual. She'd taken it over as a sort of home office. He didn't mind, although he'd thought about buying her a desk for the third bedroom, where he had his computer setup, so she'd have a place of her own. He didn't want her to think "temporary" when it came to living at his house.

Which was another thing he needed to convince her of. They were living together, but he knew that she thought it was "mooching" or taking advantage. He didn't want her to think that. He wanted her to think of his house as her own.

Because I'm in love with her.

He smiled, putting the French Bistro food he'd brought on the counter. "Hey there. How are—"

He stopped abruptly. Her face was splotchy, her eyes puffy, her nose pink. There was a wad of tissues next to her elbow.

"What the hell happened?" He rushed to her side. "Are you all right?"

She shook her head. "Brent," she finally said, her voice scratchy, probably from crying.

That fucking guy. Josh felt his hands form into fists. "What did he do now?"

She turned, showing him her laptop screen, opened to an Instagram page with the picture of him kissing her neck. And then he saw the comment beside it, in all caps.

TAM DOAN IS A WHORE.

"I'm going to kill him," Josh spat out.

"I blocked his account, but I forgot to choose the 'block all new accounts from this user' option," Tam said, sniffling. "Trust me—I did that after I deleted his comment."

"So that's not still up?"

She shook her head. "Just took a screenshot, just in case. Evidence beats anger."

It was a paraphrase of one of Vinh's favorite sayings, something their grandfather used to say. Jeez, that family had baggage.

"Then I went and checked his social media," she said, her eyes welling with tears again. "You would not believe the shitposting he's doing. He paints himself as a total victim. Says that his 'ex-girlfriend' and the 'love of his life'—which, mind you, he rarely posted about, when we were dating, but now has pictures of me *everywhere*—cheated on him for years with her 'high school flame.' And that I moved out and shafted him, leaving him to shell out for his super-high rent. And that he was going to propose."

Shock jolted through him. "He was?"

She shook her head. "He said he was, but he was lying," she said. "I know that. I just . . . why is he doing this? What's the point? *He* was sleeping with *his* ex! And he treated me like crap when I lived with him, and I *let* him. What is the purpose in this? Why is he *like* this?"

Josh growled, feeling anger course through him. "The guy's an asshole," Josh said, then held up his hands when she rolled her eyes at him.

"That's facile, I know, a gross oversimplification. But I know guys like this from the restaurant business. They make stupid business decisions out of sheer spite."

"But *why*?" she repeated.

He sighed. "Why did my mother feel the need to neglect me unless she was screaming at me? Why did your parents have screaming matches that made you feel scared in your own home?"

She frowned. "Your mother . . . may have a drinking problem," she said, and her tone was as careful as her expression was compassionate. "And my parents got married way too early because they got pregnant and had twins, and neither of them were ready for what they landed in. I'm not saying any of the lot of them were *justified*. I'm just saying they had *reasons*. Bad ones, maybe, but still."

He sighed. She had a point. "Well, maybe Brent has some dark past or something. Maybe he has a sympathetic supervillain origin story, I don't know. But he made you feel like shit and acted like you didn't matter . . . until you finally had enough. Now, he can't deal with the idea that you're happy without him, that you stood up to him. He feels . . ." He thought back to Heidi. "He feels *entitled* to you. Now that he's lost you, and he's alone and doesn't have anybody to kick around anymore, he's going to make you pay for it."

She rubbed her eyes with her fingertips. "That actually sounds right," she admitted.

Despite wanting to beat the guy to a pulp for making Tam feel bad, the more important thing here was helping Tam feel better, so he took a deep breath, stroking her shoulders. "He doesn't have that big a following, does he? Will this impact you? I don't know . . . professionally? Or did you share friends or anything?" Even though he assumed anyone who could stay friends with that dickhead was probably an asshole as well.

"We had some mutual friends," she said. "I mean, nobody I was close with, although now I've gotten some sharp DMs on Twitter and

Insta, calling me out. But I feel like . . . it's not fair. He gets away with shit *constantly*. And now he's going to get all this sympathy from people because he's the supposed victim?" She shook her head. "Maybe it's stupid, but I just feel like he shouldn't get away with it. Not this time."

Josh stroked her shoulder. "What're you thinking?"

"I don't know. Posting on my social media accounts. Clearing my name, I guess?" She sighed. "At least giving my side of the story."

He nodded. "Whatever you need."

She leaned on her hands. "This is why I need to stay single," she muttered. "Obviously I can't be trusted with relationships."

Josh stiffened. That wasn't right—wasn't fair. But at the same time, he knew that she was speaking out of her current tumultuous emotions.

But what if she did believe it?

He grimaced. Now was not the time to pressure her. She was working through stuff. He needed to be there for her. That was what was most important.

"Well, why don't you have a bite to eat," he said, gesturing to dinner. "And maybe take a break. Then you can write up what you want. Sound good?"

She smiled at him, looking wan, but thankful. "See? Why do I need a boyfriend, when I have you?" she tried to joke.

He forced a laugh, knowing that her compliment wasn't really the praise she thought it was.

CHAPTER 28

The next day, Tam was back at Juanita's café. She was crawling out of her own skin, and she'd spent the night tossing and turning until Josh had essentially cuddled the hell out of her until she'd slept.

She felt . . . angry. And hurt. A little guilty, somehow. And confused that this was happening at all.

She'd known when she started dating him that Brent had his issues, insecurity and control being two of them, but she'd never thought he was capable of this level of selfishness and cruelty. Now, she was wondering what the hell was wrong with her that she'd never noticed it before.

This morning, she'd dropped Josh off at the empty ghost kitchens and taken the van to go back to Uncommon Grounds. *I* really *need a car if I'm staying in Ponto Beach,* she reminded herself. Armed with her laptop and messenger bag, she ordered herself a large latte and a cinnamon roll, which were two of her favorite indulgences, then settled at a table in the corner.

She'd had a lot of time to think about exactly what she was going to post. She was going to go through multiple drafts of this, she knew it, but unlike people like Brent, she wasn't about to just dash off something when she felt pissed. Especially after running the social media accounts for the ad agency for a few years, she knew just how dangerous writing off the cuff was. You had to be timely, but it was better to be a little slow and not screw up than to snap something off, only to have to walk it back with apologies that would be scrutinized even more than the original stupid post.

She didn't want to be foolish. She'd been that enough, dating Brent, thanks very much.

She knew that she had that picture of Brent and Daphne in bed together. Simply posting it, with the word *liar*, would probably be enough to shut him up, but . . . maybe she was too nice, but it didn't feel right. Vinh probably wouldn't have hesitated for a second. Actually, Vinh would have never let himself get into this position—he was choosier about relationships than anyone she knew, which was why he hadn't been in anything long term since Emily—and he would have crushed someone if they'd tried to slander him the way Brent was character assassinating her. But as much as she didn't like Daphne, she didn't know what Daphne's situation was, and posting a scantily clad photo of her without consent simply felt wrong. Even as much as she hated Brent right now, the same applied to him. Granted, he was outright dragging her on social media, going so far as to name her. Still, two wrongs didn't necessarily make a right.

She bit her lip. That said, she still felt like he'd gotten away with this for long enough. She'd slept on it. It was all systems go on sharing her side of the story, and, hopefully, leaching some of the poison from the situation by being a little bit funny.

She didn't want it to be a highly impassioned grudge fest or airing of grievances, either, although she got the feeling that, if she opened the pressure valve on that particular topic, she'd probably spew out a fountain of issues that had bothered her over the course of their relationship. She didn't want to make it a "he said, she said" social media war. This was just to help herself get closure, and to somehow feel like she'd taken some kind of step to prevent him from feeling like he'd simply gotten away with his lies, scot-free.

She started to type.

"This is weird to write, but my ex-boyfriend has been posting about me on his social media. He's been lying about our relationship, and why we broke up. It doesn't matter, in a lot of ways—we're over, and if people are going to believe him, then they don't know me at all. But he's been getting away with things for the six years we were together, and I feel like, for my own peace of mind, I want to set the record straight."

She paused, thinking of how to lighten it up. Then she grinned, took a bite of cinnamon roll with her fork (so she didn't get her keyboard sticky), and then started typing again.

"Strangely enough, we broke up because of Cloud City Creamery cheese . . ."

From there, the story spilled out. The shitty day. Finding him asleep with another woman. How he'd thrown out something that was so important to her, that she enjoyed so much . . . simply *because* she enjoyed it. Because it was another way of controlling her.

She snickered as it started to flow. This was the background.

Now, she just needed to figure out how to frame it in a comedic way.

She took the van to the grocery store, blowing some of her saved money on utter indulgences—a lot of cheese. By the time she'd made it back to Josh's house, she had a plan. Hunkered down at his kitchen table, she revised, grumbling, drinking tea. She decided to take the cheese idea and run with it, because it took the sting out of all Brent's actions, and because . . . well, cheese.

She set up a food shot on Josh's granite countertop, artfully displayed on one of his stark white plates. "Have the blues because your boyfriend refuses to put you on the lease without giving a good reason? Cloud City Creamery's Blue Period Artisan Blue Cheese is the perfect replacement. Especially melted on fresh potato chips." Granted, she didn't *have* freshly made chips, but the kettle chips still held up in the air fryer, the blue cheese crumbles melting like a dream. It was literally picture perfect.

She snickered as she set up the next shot, taking advantage of her experience with Freddie's catering by putting together a tiny charcuterie board. "Maybe I could've gotten over him sleeping with his ex. But throwing out my award-winning Signature Sensation? UNFORGIVEABLE!"

Then she put up a candid picture of her and Josh from the Herd brainstorming. She was eating some goat cheese on a cracker—because, again, cheese—and he had an arm looped around her, grinning and moving in as if he were a breaching shark going after her cracker. This was the tricky bit, since he was the one she was supposedly cheating with.

"Josh has been my best friend, through all of this . . . and for years before. I would take a bullet for my bestie. He's the GOAT. And so is CCC's herbed goat cheese."

She was essentially writing an infomercial for Cloud City Creamery, she realized, but by the end of it, not only did she feel vindicated, she felt silly and relieved. She wound up making a long Twitter thread and posted a bunch of cheese pictures on Instagram and Facebook as well. She doubted that Brent would see any of them at this point, especially since she had him blocked, but it didn't matter. She'd gotten her point across, and had some fun doing it.

It didn't take long for the responses to start rolling in. Some were from Brent's friends, which didn't quite surprise her.

"Are you saying that he cheated on you? Why should I believe you?"

She sighed. She'd expected this, and answered.

"You don't have to believe me. I don't care either way. I do have proof, but I don't owe it to you, and if you know who I am, you know I don't need it. You can think I'm lying or making this up so I don't have to show it, but Brent knows the truth. I don't know why he decided to start all this crap, but I'm tired of just being quiet and taking it and letting him play the victim. Maybe the next girl he tries to date won't be so gullible. He didn't think I'd stand up, and I am. So you ask him."

She took a deep breath, then forced herself to stay off social media for a few hours. Instead, she went back to the beach, bringing a chair and letting the cool air and the waves soothe her. She even read, which calmed her mind more than anything.

When seven o'clock rolled around, she went and picked Josh up. "How'd it go?" he asked, climbing into the van on the passenger's side.

She shrugged. "It was probably a bad idea," she admitted. "But, I don't know. I felt better."

"What'd you say?"

"See for yourself."

He pulled out his phone, and she knew he was opening it to her pages. He started chuckling. "This . . . is a lot of cheese," he remarked.

"Um, yeah. I might've run the cheese idea right into the ground, but I was having too much fun," she said, squirming a little as she drove them back to his house. "But hey, if I can't amuse myself, what's the point, right? It's not like anyone was paying me."

Josh scrolled with his thumb, then made a low rumble of surprise. "When was the last time you checked this?"

"Hours ago," she said, then winced. "There aren't a bunch of Brent's friends commenting, are there? Or maybe comments from him? I mean, I blocked all new accounts by him, but he could've found a way around it . . ."

"No," Josh said. "It's just . . . you know Lily's got a pretty big Insta following, right?"

She frowned. That was a weird observation. "Yeah, but that's what she does for a living. She's an influencer. I just fool around and share memes, make cheese jokes, and talk about pop culture stuff. Silly things."

"Yeah, well, Lily shared your cheese posts. She thinks they're hysterical."

"She did?" Tam repeated, shocked. She was grateful that the kitchens weren't too far from his house. After she pulled into his driveway and shut off the van, she made grabby hands toward his phone. "Show me!"

He turned his screen, and she looked at the post he was holding up—the one with her, Josh, and goat cheese.

It had a hundred thousand views.

"What the *hell*?" she yelped. "I . . . this was just . . ."

"Lily thinks we're 'cute together,'" Josh said, smiling. "So do a lot of other people. And I think there may be a bunch of people with torches and pitchforks looking for Brent."

She swallowed hard. "Is it wrong that a tiny petty part of me thinks that's perfectly okay?"

"He started this," Josh said. "And you handled it perfectly—with grace and with humor. It's not like you put links to his profile or anything. You did fine."

She squirmed. "I still feel kind of guilty."

"How about we go inside," Josh said, stroking her cheek. "I'll fix you some dinner, and then we can just relax for a while. And I'll help you forget all this. Okay?"

She nodded, smiling at how he might "help" her. "I'm here for that," she said.

"Am I really the GOAT?" he asked, his voice filled with humor, as they walked toward the front door.

"Hmmm." She pretended to mull it over, then tugged him to her and kissed him. "Only one way to confirm."

True to his word—he helped her forget, for most of the night. By the time she was breathless and naked next to him in his bed, the fact that he was the GOAT was unquestionable.

CHAPTER 29

"Am I dressed too casually?" Tam said, tugging at the sundress she'd pulled on before they'd left the house. "I didn't know where we were going."

They pulled up into a public parking lot in San Diego's Gaslamp Quarter. Normally, he didn't like going downtown if he could avoid it, but Graham Catering had an event that was big enough that Freddie was helping set up, and then he and Asad were planning to go out to dinner themselves. Since Josh needed Freddie's signature on a bunch of paperwork showing that Graham Catering was committed to working with Ghost Kitchens Unlimited, it made sense to meet them down there, and having dinner with them and with Tam sounded like a good time.

"You look great," Josh reassured her, and he wasn't just saying that to make her feel better. She was wearing a pastel lavender dress that was simple but still seemed to make her glow. She had more of a tan than she'd had when she got back from New York, as well as a bright smile. She just looked healthier and happier. He knew he'd do whatever he could to help her stay that way. "Besides, you know how it is. Nobody's going to judge you. It's San Diego, not Manhattan."

"Good point," she agreed.

Fortunately, the parking gods had smiled on them, and the Brazilian steakhouse that Freddie had suggested wasn't too far a walk. The evening was nice, too, and the sidewalks weren't too crowded. Music poured out of a few of the bars and restaurants they walked past. Tam smiled, and Josh felt all the day's stresses just melt away.

When they got to the restaurant, he instinctively guided her with a hand on her lower back, opening the door for her with the other hand. It felt natural.

It felt nice.

"Hey, sweetie!" Asad came over, giving them each a big hug. "Freddie's got the table—I was just freshening up. C'mon."

They had a table with a view of the street. There was the usual clatter and thrum of people's conversations and food being cooked and served, but otherwise, it was a low enough noise that they could easily hear each other, which Josh appreciated. He took a seat by Tam, with Freddie to his left and Asad across from him.

"Josh," Freddie said, shaking his hand and sending him a friendly smile. "You brought the paperwork?"

"Sure did." He opened his messenger bag and pulled out the folder. He'd marked each of the signature lines with arrow-shaped Post-its. Amber made fun of him, but his compulsion toward order made things easier in the long run. "You ready to do this?"

"More than ready," Freddie said confidently. "In fact, I'm still kicking myself for not thinking of it earlier. Asad, why didn't you think of this?"

He shrugged, laughing lightly. "Hey, I make things look good. I promise I can help brand the crap out of anything you guys do. I don't work on the inner business stuff."

"Well, Tam saved the day," Josh said, winking at her, and he was rewarded with a blush. He really wished he could kiss her. But despite their, *ahem*, nocturnal activities (and occasional afternoon or early morning activities), she hadn't said anything about them being a couple . . . and he got the strong feeling that she didn't want the rest of the Herd to know what they'd been up to. Not that he blamed her. If all they were was "friends with benefits," then he wasn't so sure he'd be thrilled hearing the townies weigh in on whether or not that was possible, or even advisable, especially for the two of them. As much as everyone had joked about Lily and Tobin getting together, people had honestly assumed that Josh would one day figure his shit out and get with Tam. They hadn't understood the dynamic. Tam and Vinh were good at hiding the shit their family was going through, so even though the Herd was aware that the twins' parents had had a tumultuous marriage, they hadn't known the full extent of the verbal barrage and sheer fury that the two could generate—or the emotional spillover that tended to damage their kids, in one way or another.

Vinh had been bonded to Emily—a relationship that was almost sickeningly sweet, until they'd imploded so spectacularly in college.

Tam, on the other hand, had Josh, and they hadn't messed with anything romantic.

Besides, Josh had been too busy getting caught up in whatever attention seeking and emotional manipulation the girls he dated could conjure up . . . a clear, embarrassing echo of his mother's relationships. He could argue that both he and Tam were following family programming, but by this point, he was self-aware enough to know what he'd been doing, and he'd course corrected by staying single for five years. Now, he'd done the dysfunctional thing, and he'd done the solitary thing. It was time to take a chance and actually have a healthy relationship.

With Tam.

If she'd let him.

Freddie signed the last page with a flourish before handing the stack back to Josh. "I am really excited about this," he said, his grin broad beneath his red beard. "Your kitchens are amazing, and I think that the delivery system is going to impress the hell out of Sherry. Not to mention the software, which I gotta be honest, I've never really thought about."

"And I made up some mock-ups of ideas for your bánh mì restaurant," Asad added, as he and Tam dug into the pão de quiejo appetizers, these cheesy, hot bread-ball things. *Because, of course, cheese.* Josh grinned at Tam as she let out a little happy hum of tummy-yumminess. "They run the gamut from high-end stylish to cartoony fun. You'll be able to pick what kind of vibe you're going for."

"Not too cartoony," Tam interjected. "I was thinking . . . something more traditional? A little. And good luck, of course. My mom might have some suggestions, actually."

"That'd be awesome," Josh said, smiling at her. She was a natural at this. Here he was, intent on helping her figure her life out, and instead, she'd just made his a million times better.

Was that what kept happening with the guys she was with? His smile fell. He didn't want to *use* her. He was trying to help her.

She must've noticed his change in demeanor. "You okay?"

"Huh? Oh. Sure." He cleared his throat. "How's the social media going? Still getting a lot of views?"

"I don't know if I should thank Lily or kill her," Tam said, her cheeks going pink. "Seriously, though. Lily was a sweetheart, but I wasn't trying to go viral."

"Although you seem to have pulled that off," Asad said with a sly grin. "And those cheese pairings? I was laughing my butt off."

She grinned back. "Thanks. I thought it was funny."

"I think it was brilliant," Asad said. "And if you play your cards right, I bet you get free cheese."

"Really?" Now Tam sounded excited. "Because I could really get behind that. I love cheese."

Josh snickered. "No. You?"

"Shut up," she said, nudging him.

They kept talking as their dinners were served. They all laughed over Tam's misadventures with the HandyJobs client, and then Asad assured them that he'd helped change the client's mind. "It actually looks quite professional now," Asad said with a grin. "I'd hire them."

"I don't know. If he'd stuck with 'HandyJobs,' he'd probably still get a lot of business," Tam said. "You know. Like Sofa King."

"Sofa King?" Josh asked, puzzled, before sipping his water.

She burst into laughter. "It's Sofa King good!"

He choked. "Ah. Gotcha," he said, when he could breathe again.

"All kidding aside, you're really good at this stuff, Tam," Freddie pointed out, in his quiet, serious way. "I hate talking about branding, and social media kind of gives me hives. You could do that."

"Hey, I do that, too," Asad protested.

"I know," Freddie said, rubbing the back of Asad's neck before leaning in and kissing his cheek. "But you are booked solid, remember?"

"True, but I always have time for you." He sent Freddie a smile of pure delight.

In that moment, Josh was purely, utterly jealous. He wanted what they had—the connection, the support. And he wanted it with Tam. It felt like a double date. He just wished he could *say* it was one.

But she just got out of a relationship. Is this really the best time for her?

He sighed. It wasn't ideal, he realized. He needed to give her space. Besides, he had his own full plate with the upcoming presentation to Darius's investment group.

"You two are too cute," Tam said, obviously on the same page as him. Somewhat.

Asad grinned. "So are you two. That picture, at the beach? Hot."

"Asad," Freddie warned, and Asad tried to look innocent.

"What? I'm just saying!"

"Well, I only posted the cheese pairings / ex-boyfriend stuff to feel better about Brent's crap, and I hope it came off as funny, rather than bitter. I can't say what's happening on Brent's pages—he blocked me, and from what Juanita told me, he's deleted or set to private all his social media," Tam said with a little sheepish smile. "But I know that a lot of people seem to have seen my side of the story and actually believe me. That wasn't the point, but it was kind of validating. And hopefully he won't be fooling some other woman anytime soon."

Josh nodded. "Good."

"Also, I've gotten a lot of volunteers to show me what I supposedly 'deserve.'" She rolled her eyes in disbelief. "I had to shut down my DMs. *Wayyyy* too many dick pics."

Freddie and Asad burst into laughter. Josh, on the other hand, felt his chest clench and his blood start to boil.

"You're getting *what*?"

"I had a few guys tell me that they could show me how a real man treats a woman," she said, not appearing to sense his growing unease. "One even said he'd keep me in all the cheese I wanted. Like a sugar daddy, but for cheese."

Asad hooted, and Freddie smiled, shaking his head. But Josh found himself growling before he could stop himself. He didn't have any right, per se. And he couldn't remember the last time he'd felt jealousy. Probably back in high school or college, when he was still dating drama queens. His last girlfriend, Callie, used to tease him by talking to her ex or flirting with guys when they were out. It was one of the final straws that showed him that the relationship was too toxic and he needed to get his shit together.

But Tam wasn't trying to make him jealous, and even if she was—she *wasn't with him*. God, he needed to get a grip.

"You okay there, stud?" Asad poked. "Guys are coming for your woman."

"Asad!" Freddie sounded scandalized.

Josh took a deep breath, counting to ten before he said something stupid. Then he looked at Tam, who was gazing back at him curiously.

"I think you can do better than that," he said to her, then forced himself to grin, winking. "I'll be your cheese daddy."

She let out a peal of laughter. "Oh my God. Cheese daddy. I have to put that in a meme somewhere."

"Talk curdy to me," Asad joked.

"Doesn't get any feta than this," Freddie chimed in.

"Brie my valentine, I'm so fondue you," Tam added, her voice full of laughter. "They write themselves."

"Best friends for-chèvre." Josh stroked a hand down her back, smiling at how happy she looked. Then he leaned in. "Selfie?"

She smiled, then pulled her chair next to him, snuggling up to his side and taking a picture of the two of them, his cheek touching hers. "Dinner out with my bestie, the GOAT, the man who keeps me supplied with cheese. In short, Mr. Perfect," she spoke as she typed. "Hashtag-CheeseDaddy. Hashtag-GOAT. Hashtag-BFF."

He swallowed hard. Then he looked up to find Asad staring at him shrewdly.

"Get you a woman who looks at you like she looks at cheese," he said, and Josh got the feeling he wasn't just kidding around. He was pointedly saying: *She looks at you like that. What are you waiting for?*

Josh gritted his teeth. Asad wasn't wrong. And after he gave the presentation, he'd finally put himself out there.

CHAPTER 30

By Saturday, Tam had shifted focus from her own "life design" brainstorming to helping Josh with his upcoming presentation. She knew it was a huge opportunity for him, and she knew him well enough to know that he was nervous as hell. It hit all her superadmin buttons. She'd helped him with his presentation design, something he'd considered begging Asad's help for, and proofed his slides. She'd watched him as he practiced his pitch, marveling at how smooth and competent he sounded as he quoted sales figures and market data and even food-waste numbers.

It was weirdly hot.

Then again, she found everything about him hot these days. He'd eaten a strawberry the other day, and she'd tackled him onto the couch and ravished him. Not that he'd complained, but she'd never responded like this to anyone in the past. Maybe it was the freedom that she actually *could* kiss him or touch him—or ravish him—whenever she wanted, that made the whole thing incendiary.

"I'm going in to the Tombs," Josh said.

"Do you need my help?"

He smiled, his eyes hooded. "Right now, you're too distracting," he said, leaning down and pressing a hot, sweet kiss on her lips. "Besides, I'm supposed to be helping *you*, not the other way around."

"I really don't mind," she assured him, and he stroked her face.

"I know. I don't deserve it," he said, his voice hoarse. "But I promise, I'll make it up to you as soon as the presentation's done, and then we'll talk."

She frowned.

Then we'll talk.

That sounded . . . ominous?

Before she could think too much about it, there was a knock on the door. She glanced over at Josh. "You expecting somebody? One of the Herd?"

He shook his head, walking over to the door and looking out the peephole. Then he opened the door. *"Vinh?"*

Tam felt her stomach drop. Shit. She was not expecting her brother.

She got up, rushing to the door. Considering they'd lived in the same city for years, she rarely saw him. They had dinner a couple of times a year, including some holidays. He looked like he always did: hair immaculately cut and razor sharp, gaze almost predatory as it swept over the details of Josh's house, and then Josh, and then Tam herself. He was wearing what he probably thought of as casual, a button-down shirt that was probably ironed and starched within an inch of its life, and a pair of gray slacks that probably cost as much as one of her boxes of clothes. His only nod to the Southern Cal atmosphere was a pair of black DC suede skate shoes, which made her smile. He'd loved those in high school.

"Hey there," he said. "Sorry I'm showing up unannounced—although I did tell you I'd swing by Ponto a few weeks ago, when we talked. I'm going to handle some business in LA this week, and I thought I'd surprise you," he said, his low voice sounding completely neutral. Which, unfortunately, was one of his most notorious tricks. If he was pissed, generally speaking, you wouldn't know it until you were bleeding out and he was smiling.

That was probably uncharitable, but she knew her brother. In response to her family's clamorous nature, she'd become a people-pleaser. He, on the other hand, had become a cold, ruthless sonofabitch.

"I was just headed to the Tombs—my business—anyway," Josh said with a sheepish smile. "You should check it out sometime."

"I was thinking I'd take Tam out, maybe grab something to eat," Vinh said in a tone casual for him. "But I don't have to be in LA till Monday, so maybe we can all grab dinner later and catch up."

Read: *we can have dinner so I can interrogate you about what, exactly, is going on.* She forced herself not to grimace.

"Sounds good." Josh turned to her and, apparently without thinking, kissed her. She tensed, and he stiffened, shooting a look at Vinh, whose eyes had narrowed. "Um . . . see you tonight. You've got your key, right?"

She nodded, unable to form words. Then Josh turned and walked out.

Vinh stared at her for a long moment, then let out a sigh. "So. You two finally together?"

"No!" she protested, then winced. That didn't feel right either. "I mean . . . yes? Sort of."

"That would explain the photos on your Instagram," he said, shaking his head.

"You have a problem with Josh and me being together?" she challenged.

"When you just dumped your most recent boyfriend a month ago?" Vinh said coolly. "A little bit."

She bristled. It wasn't his business, and she hated it when he got high and mighty on her. Still, she also felt a tiny, piercing sting of guilt as she thought that he probably had a point.

"C'mon. Let's go for a drive," he said. "We can catch up."

She nodded, locking the door behind her. In the driveway was a sleek silver Jaguar. She shot him a look, and he shrugged.

"Must be nice," she murmured, clambering into the passenger seat. "Where are we going?"

"Unless you're starving, I thought we'd drive around a little."

She nodded. For the first time, she realized that Vinh seemed . . . off. He was concerned (no surprise there), and sort of scowly (again, not a shock), and a bit judgy (completely expected). But there was some underlying melancholy. "You okay?"

He shrugged, pulling out and heading out of the cul-de-sac. "Tired," he finally admitted. "Long hours, corporate bullshit. You know the drill."

"I know those feels, bro," she said quietly. "Or at least, I did."

"What are you even doing now?" He probably didn't mean for it to come out as judgmental, but she still felt shades of it. "Just sitting around? Getting a tan? You definitely look like you've gotten some sun."

She sighed. "I know that Mẹ and Ba would probably scream if they knew what I was doing—or rather, what I'm *not* doing, I guess—but I was really going off the rails at my old job," she said.

"I know. I told you it was toxic and they were taking advantage—"

"I *know* you told me," she cut him off. "But the thing is, I keep getting the same kinds of jobs. Or at least, I kept getting the same kinds of jobs. The ones that had hellish hours for too little pay and no room for growth."

"Exactly," Vinh said, an edge to his voice. "So why don't you get a job with a chance for advancement? You're smart enough, you've got the degree. Granted, the job history's not great, but you could be a hell of a lot more than you've been, and we both know it."

She didn't quite know what to do with that mix of support and derision, so she scowled back at him. "I haven't even known what will make me happy! And I just . . . I keep getting these jobs because they're fallbacks. I know I can make people happy. *I know I won't fail!*"

She stopped immediately, stunned at that little truth bomb.

Shit.

Was *that* why she hadn't gone for any other jobs? Because she was afraid of failure? Because she didn't want to take a chance and risk being judged incompetent, or incapable? Or, worst of all, being fired?

Shit, shit, shit.

Vinh shot her a look, driving down El Camino Real before turning in to another neighborhood, navigating the maze of streets. "You know that you have to take a risk if you're going to get anywhere." Neutral voice, again.

"Don't start with me. I am having an existential crisis here," she muttered. "God. Please tell me I haven't spent the last however many years dating jackasses and taking low-end jobs because I've been a coward."

"I wouldn't call you a coward, per se," Vinh said, and at least now his voice was comforting. "But otherwise—yeah. Looks like it."

"Fuck."

He shook his head. "Well, now you know, and you can do something about it." He pulled over, parking the car in front of a house that had a bunch of preschool toys in the yard, a tricycle in the driveway. She frowned.

"What are we . . ." Then her eyes popped wide. "Holy crap. That's *our* house!"

"Used to be," he agreed. "Looks like they repainted. And obviously they've got young kids."

She took in the house that they'd grown up in, or at least since their parents moved them to Ponto Beach when they were eight. "It looks so much smaller than I remember," she murmured.

"Yeah." He leaned back, smirking. "Remember when we had the Herd over for a graduation party?"

She laughed, the memory rolling over her. "Yeah. Collin couldn't make it, and Keith walked into our screen door."

"And Mom made, like, a million appetizers," Vinh said, sounding both amused and somewhat sad. "And Dad sort of strutted around talking to everybody like he was cool."

She shook her head. "At least they weren't fighting that night."

They sat, silent, lost in memories. Then Vinh cleared his throat. "They offered me the vice prez job. At work."

She blinked. "That's great, Vinh," she said. "You worked really hard for that."

He shrugged.

"What, you're not happy?" Her heart ached for a second. Would her brother *ever* be happy?

"Maybe it just hasn't sunk in yet," he prevaricated. "It's like someone saying, 'Hey, it's Tuesday.' It's just something someone said, a series of words. Not any kind of . . . I don't know."

"You're taking it, right?"

He arched an eyebrow at her. "Of course I am. Don't be ridiculous."

"I don't know, you don't usually act this weird."

"C'mon. Let's go grab some brunch over at the Surfboard Café, before the new owners come out and find us creeping on their house," he said, sounding a little lighter. They drove off. "One other question."

"Hmm?"

"Brent." Vinh's voice sounded venomous. "He was cheating on you, then?"

She winced. "Why do you even follow my social media?"

"I know I don't call that often, and social media's easy to keep up with," Vinh said. "Besides, how else can I keep tabs on you?"

"You could text me."

He shrugged. "Maybe I'll do that next time," he agreed. "But why didn't you tell me what happened? And why you decided you needed to make those surprisingly amusing cheese comparisons detailing your breakup?"

"He decided to start shit on social media, and I didn't feel like letting him," she explained. She frowned, recognizing the ferocious gleam in his eye. "And it's *done*, so don't worry about it. Seriously. I don't need help on this one."

"Just because you don't need help doesn't mean I don't want to institute some payback," Vinh said in that deceptively mild voice of his. "I'm just saying: I could make him sorry for being born in about twenty-four hours flat, if you let the leash off."

She laughed, even as she knew, on some level, he was probably not kidding. Vengeance was his love language.

"I don't need you to terrorize my ex," she said, "but thanks for caring. And if it comes down to that, you're the first person I'll call."

"I just don't want anybody hurting my little sister."

"'Little' by only five minutes," she reminded him. Still, her chest felt warmed. They weren't close—not anymore, not since they'd both moved to New York. This reminded her, a little painfully, of how close they'd been growing up, when all they had in the face of their parents' unhappy marriage and subsequent emotional battles was each other. Then he started dating Emily, and she became friends with Josh, and the drift just happened.

Maybe they could fix that.

She glanced at her social media while he eased onto Highway 101, heading for the café. She saw a DM on Twitter and opened it. "Hey! It's Cloud City Creamery!"

"Those cheese guys you're obsessed with?" He smirked. "What do they want?"

"They say that the thread was amazing and want me to call them," she said. "I'll bet Asad's right. I'm gettin' free cheese!"

Vinh shook his head. "You going to call now?"

"Don't see why not. If you don't mind?"

He pulled into the parking lot. "I'll go get us a table." He headed off, into the sunshine-yellow building with a collection of longboards flanking the porch. She dialed the number from the message.

"Carl Brown," a voice said.

"Hi, this is Tam Doan," she said. "Um, I'm TamLovesCheese on Twitter?"

The man started chuckling. "I'm glad you called," he said. "Your thread, and the photos, were incredible. I've shared it with everyone in the office."

She grinned. "I'm glad you guys enjoyed it."

"More than that," he said. "By including us by name and tagging us in, we got a huge boost in followers. Especially since some news outlets picked it up. It's even on Buzzfeed."

She blinked. "I . . . was not aware of that."

"We've seen a bump in orders too," he said, sounding pleased. "It's early days, but we have a lot to thank you for."

She felt pride, that happy little boost of endorphins that came from a job well done. "You're very welcome," she said, then decided to shoot her shot. "Does that mean I can get some free cheese?"

Hey, it worked for that guy talking about Kerrygold on Twitter, she reasoned. And she was tired of playing small.

He laughed. "Well, if this works out, you'll be getting quite a bit of free cheese. On a regular basis."

"Really?" She knew she sounded overeager, but the hell with it. Maybe he was talking sponsorship? Not that she had a huge social media following or anything—her boost was purely due to Lily's intervention. She wasn't even sure she'd *want* to be a social media influencer, whether it was a viable career or not . . . "What did you have in mind?"

"Ever been to Seattle?"

She blinked. "Um . . . no?"

"Want to visit?"

"You mean like a factory tour?" That sounded so cool. Maybe Josh could go with her. She liked the idea of taking a vacation with him, especially after the stress of his presentation was over.

"No," Carl said, sounding amused. "I mean I'm offering you a job."

CHAPTER 31

It was the day of the big presentation, and Josh was nervous as hell. He'd been in the La Jolla headquarters of the Prometheus Venture Capital Group before, when he'd first gotten seed money from Darius. They'd signed papers in his office, and then Darius had taken him out to lunch, and they'd had a long talk about how to start pulling things together moving forward. Josh had been dazed then—the whole thing seeming surreal even in his memory.

Thanks to Tam, he'd relied more on Amber this time around, and realized that having two locations would be no big deal—he could easily turn the reins for Ponto Beach over to her and run the other one, or vice versa. Darius probably had his own ideas to tack on, and the man tended to think big . . . which was probably how he came up with his own millions to be a partner in the VC group and to have his pet projects, like angel funding Josh's ghost kitchen idea in the first place. Josh probably should've gone through Darius's portion of the pitch, just in case the guy wanted to propose opening twenty sites across the country or something, but Josh had been working with Darius long enough to trust him. Besides, Josh was the one with all the data, and if the investment group didn't want to go ahead with something so ambitious, it was fine. Josh wasn't going to count on it anyway.

His palms were sweating slightly. He stopped in the men's room, washing his hands thoroughly and giving his black suit a once-over.

Tam had given him a big thumbs-up, and helped him pick out the midnight-blue shirt and matching tie that he was wearing, but he hated dressing up to this extent. Professional, yes, but this bordered on pretentious.

He sighed, then stepped back out into the lobby. This was as presentable as he was gonna get.

"There you are." Darius looked dapper—did people still say dapper?—in a suit that was so deep plum it almost looked black, with a matching shirt and tie. Even though he was usually dressed casually when Josh met with him, the guy looked completely comfortable in his suit. Josh had to force himself not to tug at his tie. "You ready?"

"As I'm going to get," Josh said, trying not to sound grim. "I'll be okay," he added.

"I know. You get nervous before, but it's stage fright," Darius said easily. "Once you're up there, you'll be fine. And you'll knock 'em dead, just like you did with me."

"What're they like?"

"Well, there are four of us," Darius said, leading Josh down a hallway. The building wasn't too ostentatious, looking like a bank or maybe a somewhat fancy doctor's office. "Millie tends to invest in life sciences, Jen focuses on real estate, and Paul likes to throw the dice on tech startups."

"None of them have invested in restaurants before, then," Josh said.

"Nope." Darius smiled. "Good thing we're not pitching a restaurant, huh?"

"That reminds me," Josh said. "You said you were going to propose something a little more than I was pitching. Anything I should know about?"

"It's just a twist on what you're going to be presenting already," Darius said. "And it's nothing you're not capable of."

Josh frowned. "Why so secret?"

"Because I know you," Darius said. "If I run the idea by you, you're going to overthink it to death and try to work out all the kinks and control every possible variable and prevent any possible catastrophe. Sometimes, you just have to take the risk."

Josh quirked his lips. Seemed like the Universe was telling him that a lot lately.

"All right. Let's do this," Darius said and opened the door to a conference room. Again, nothing to write home about, other than the view out the floor-to-ceiling windows, which opened up to the ocean off in the distance. "Gang, this is Josh O'Malley, of Ghost Kitchens Unlimited."

The partners, who were sitting at the table and talking among themselves, stood. Josh shook hands with Millie Ono, who was wearing a pin-striped navy skirt suit, her hair cut in a blunt black bob; Jen Wojcik, a brunette woman who looked to be middle aged, wearing a pantsuit in a shocking shade of magenta; and Paul Fischer, a somewhat older man who was wearing an expensive-looking gray suit with a white shirt and bloodred tie.

"I'm still not sure why we're seeing a pitch about a restaurant," Paul complained to Darius.

Josh, who had been shaking everyone's hands, winced internally. He shot Darius a quick look.

Darius, on the other hand, looked unamused. "You didn't read the emails, did you," he said to Paul, his voice flat.

"Didn't think I needed to. Restaurants have a high failure rate . . . ," Paul pointed out, trailing off as if the sentence was self-evident.

Darius tilted his head, his eyebrow arching. "After the bad run of apps we invested in, I think that we're not necessarily in a position to throw stones," he said quietly but firmly. "And I wouldn't bring a proposal to the group if I didn't think it had a hell of a lot of promise. Which, if you'd read the proposal notes before the meeting, you'd know."

Paul grumbled under his breath but retook his seat. Josh was not encouraged.

I don't need this, he tried to reassure himself. *We're doing great. We don't need more funding. I have everything I need right now.*

But the lure of *more*, the possibility that he could make this work and succeed on a grander scale than he'd thought, was overwhelming.

Darius was right. He needed to take more risks.

He cleared his throat as Darius gestured to him to start. "Thank you for making the time to see me," he started. "I'm Josh O'Malley, and I own Ghost Kitchens Unlimited. For those of you who aren't familiar, ghost kitchens aren't restaurants, just like Darius said. They're a food delivery service that can incorporate . . ."

He kept going, forcing himself not to rush and to keep his voice even, just like he had when he practiced with Tam. He went through the details of the proposal: what the ghost kitchens were, why they were profitable, how easily they could expand. He handed out the copies he'd made of the company's financial history. It was probably too exhaustive, but he preferred to be overprepared. Darius wasn't wrong there. He also had a full marketing brief, with proposed next steps for the new restaurant and Freddie's plan for Graham Catering, along with proof of their partnership. Finally, he had data on price points, employee acquisition (especially hiring Phillip Nguyen), and his relationships with local suppliers. From there, he fielded questions from each of them.

"You're starting a new restaurant soon?" Jen said, pointing to the bánh mì concept.

"Yes. It's easier to pivot with a ghost kitchen, since there is no storefront or remodeling costs," he explained. "It's not much different than the software industry, actually, as far as ramping up."

At the term *software* Paul perked up, his eyes gleaming. He flipped through the sheets studiously.

Sorry you didn't read the notes now, huh? Josh hid the feeling of smug satisfaction.

"And you own the building?" Jen added. Now she looked intrigued.

"At this stage, we're just leasing," Josh said. "But because we didn't need to worry about things like parking or foot traffic or ambiance, we could get a great deal on commercial real estate and get it completely customized, and have it optimized for delivery. Later on, buying the building is definitely something we'd like to pursue."

Hey, if he was going to pitch this, he might as well swing for the fences.

"This is comprehensive," Millie said approvingly, flipping through the data. "And you have all this market data at your fingertips, rather than hiring a consultant? I'm impressed."

"Josh here has a beginning-to-end, integrated software system behind it as well," Darius said, standing up and walking to flank Josh. "May I?"

Josh nodded, grateful to sit down at the table and let Darius take over. He still wasn't sure what Darius's plan was, but Josh's throat felt sore, and he was more than ready to take a break. He poured himself a glass of water from the carafe on the small conference table, then took a long, refreshing drink.

Darius turned on a projector, something Josh should've probably thought of, but he liked giving hard copies.

"Now, if you'll see here," Darius said, and to Josh's surprise, he had slides of the various systems Josh had coded himself: the ordering screen, the inventory screen, the historical data of success. He'd sent them off to Darius at different stages in development, but he hadn't realized just how closely Darius had paid attention. "Josh built these himself."

"You're a coder?" Paul looked positively ecstatic, which was a far cry from how he'd been when Josh walked in.

Josh shrugged. "Self-taught," he said. "But I've always had an interest. Long time ago, I thought I'd be an electrical engineer or computer science major, and I like to build things when I can't find what I'm looking for."

"You did the graphics too?" Millie asked, surprised.

"No, that was my graphic designer, the one who does all the logos and branding for my restaurants," Josh said. "He does great work, by the way, and if you can get on his schedule, he's worth it." He always liked talking up a friend, and Asad was brilliant and easy to vouch for.

"The point is, we've got more than just a ghost kitchen here," Darius interrupted gently. "What Josh here doesn't necessarily see, but I think you will, is this: the business model isn't giving Josh another location to replicate. It's *selling the system*."

Josh jolted.

We're doing what *now?*

Darius just smiled. Josh snapped his mouth shut, staring at Darius in surprise.

This? This was what he was talking about?

"Think about it," Darius said. "We wouldn't be franchising a restaurant. We'd be franchising the ability to set up this *profitable* model, to any restauranteur, in any potentially marketable location. We could sell it as a turnkey system. Hell, we could also buy the property that they wind up using, giving them a launchpad. They'd have the market research component, the restaurant component, specialized accounting, and suggestions on packaging, delivery, and marketing. The software would be proprietary, naturally. And not every location would succeed . . . but we would be giving them tools and benchmarks to be as successful as possible, given those parameters."

"That's brilliant," Paul said, and Josh could all but see the dollar signs in his eyes.

"That kind of real estate investment could be golden," Jen added, with an excited gleam of her own. "You know, McDonald's made its money initially not on burgers, but on real estate. This could be just as lucrative."

"I am intrigued," Jen said, although she was more reserved. "This definitely merits more consideration, but my initial gut reaction is . . . this is a winner."

Josh looked over at Darius, who beamed back at him.

"I thought so too," Darius said. "Which is why I brought this up to you guys. I'm in, one way or another. I've already given him preseed and seed money, and there's a proven track record. He's ready for Series A for this system, I think."

Paul nodded, writing notes on the handouts. "This hits all my tech buttons," he muttered, nodding. "So, what are we thinking? Ten? Twelve?"

Josh frowned. What was he talking about?

"I think a standard fifteen for a Series A investment is more than allowable, if these numbers check out," Millie said, and Jen nodded, but paused.

"Actually, I think offering a bit over, to hit those real estate numbers, is probably wise," Jen added. "Maybe . . . twenty?"

Josh looked at Darius.

"We've invested more with less promise," Darius said with a wide grin. "Run the numbers—I am sure they'll satisfy you. And then we'll work on the timetable for how we want to roll this out and who to approach. I'll work with Josh on that as well."

They talked a little more, but Josh was in that same dazed, floaty state he'd been in when Darius had first invested in his ideas—and that was several hundred thousand dollars. He wasn't quite sure what they were talking about here. True, if he was marketing his "system" he might not need to do as much, other than packaging the software and making it more professional, as opposed to Asad's current fun design.

After a while, they all needed to go to their own meetings, and after another round of glad-handing and assurances that he'd hear back from them, Darius escorted him back out, all the way to his van. Then he shocked Josh by letting out a triumphant shout in the parking lot.

"What? What?" Josh stuttered.

"You are *in*, baby," Darius said, punching him in the arm. "They're going to do their due diligence, sure, but we both know your numbers are rock solid. Hell, you're generally too conservative for my taste. And I did my homework too. They're going to see just what I saw: you are sitting on a fucking gold mine. And we are going to market the hell out of that."

Josh's mouth dropped open a little.

"You're okay with this, right?" Darius said, reining himself in a bit. "I know . . . I should've prepped you. But you need to jump in on this, if you're going to do it at all. This isn't going to be a fresh concept forever, and while I see the market edge in your software and your system, it'll be easier if we strike now, while the iron's hot."

Josh's head felt like it was swimming.

"Whoa. You need to sit down or something?"

"They said twenty," Josh said. "What does that mean?"

"Million, Josh," Darius said with audible patience. "Twenty million. That's slightly above average, and I think we can manage with that."

Josh stared at him. "Twenty . . . *million*?" he finally gasped.

Darius smiled.

"Dollars?"

"Welcome to the big leagues, kid," Darius replied, clapping him on the shoulder. "You're on your way."

CHAPTER 32

Tam paced the hardwood floors of Josh's living room as she waited for him to return from the presentation to the investment group. He'd been so on edge about the thing she was feeling sympathy anxiety on his behalf. That was why she hadn't told him about the job interview tomorrow. She didn't want to distract him, and in the scheme of things, it seemed so much smaller. He was gambling on expanding his whole business. She just might or might not have a new job.

A perfect job.

The guy from Cloud City Creamery, Carl, had wanted to know if she'd be interested in their new social media manager position. She would be working closely with their marketing manager, but she'd be responsible for basically doing what she'd been doing for free. Talking up their cheese, making funny posts and memes. She would also need to keep an eye on making sure they didn't completely show their asses by posting stuff that was inappropriate or insensitive to whatever was going on in the world. It would have to fit in with their overall marketing and branding strategy, and unlike her usual just-for-fun social media exercises, they'd need to set performance goals and monitor insights. She couldn't help but feel a little excited. Okay, a *lot* excited. She liked the idea of having a job where she had measurable goals rather than just an interminable moving target, where she was praised in general when coaxed to do something (or, say, when she was asked to accept the fact that she was barely getting a pay increase during her yearly performance review). This would be tangible. And they sounded like they would provide her with her own body weight in cheese on a regular basis—which, admittedly, would increase as she indulged in her body weight in cheese. She grinned.

The grin fell as she thought about the biggest drawback to the job.

You'd have to move to Seattle.

She swallowed against the lump in her throat, deciding to walk out to Josh's backyard, hoping that his small and awkward view of the ocean would help calm her down. She could feel faint echoes of the sea breeze, despite the early autumn heat. She hadn't considered moving to the Pacific Northwest ever, but then, she'd never anticipated this curve ball of a job. It would mean leaving the Herd again.

It would mean leaving *Josh* again.

They were just friends with benefits, she reasoned, even if, for a brief moment, she'd considered what it'd be like if they were something more. And she knew she wouldn't lose him. If her bullshit in New York had proven anything, it was that Josh had her back, 100 percent. She could move to Timbuktu, and he'd still be there for her, in one way or another.

But they wouldn't have sex.

And she couldn't see him every morning, snuggling her, nuzzling her with his nose.

No more dinners on the patio after he got back from the Tombs.

No more pretending to watch movies on the ridiculously comfortable couch as they wound up making out.

Her heart kicked up a bit, and she pressed her fingertips into her chest, just under her collarbone, as the pain of that thought pierced her. She hadn't realized just how much she wanted to keep doing all that, until the thought of taking it off the table presented itself.

Maybe she should just tell them "no thanks" and walk? Take another admin job, one she knew she could do in her sleep. Maybe one with less monstrous bosses. And then . . . maybe she could suggest that she and Josh could take it to the next level, take a chance on being in a relationship.

But that felt wrong too. Too much like giving up what she had a chance at for a guy. And even though Josh was the ultimate cinnamon roll, a man almost too sweet to be real . . . it was too much pressure, on both of them. What if they didn't work? Then not only would their friendship be under strain, she might resent him after giving up what could've been a perfect opportunity. Just because she was in love with him.

And she was, she realized. She probably had been for over a decade. She just hadn't wanted to think about it because it was too frickin' scary.

She heard his van pull into the driveway, and she felt her stomach swoop like she was on a roller coaster. She clasped her hands together and fidgeted until she realized what she was doing and forced herself to tuck her arms awkwardly behind her back as she walked toward the front door to meet him. He opened it with a flourish.

"How did it—*mmmrph*!" she said, as he laid an enthusiastic kiss on her. It went on for a long time, or at least she thought it did. Her mind checked out, all sense of anxiety and confusion dissipating like mist in the wind as he tilted her head back and kissed her hard enough for her whole body to light up. Then he broke away, the two of them panting for air. "That good, huh?" she gasped, grinning.

"You would not believe," Josh said, stroking her face. "Hell, I don't believe how well it went, and I was there. The whole thing feels utterly surreal."

"Tell me everything," she said immediately, tugging him to the couch and sitting next to him. Sure, she was trying to avoid her news, but she had truly been waiting to hear about his pitch, and he looked incandescent with joy. She'd never seen him like this, and it warmed her heart. After all the shit that he'd been through, she couldn't think of a person who deserved it more.

"I pitched the idea of a second location . . . another set of ghost kitchens," he said. "I had all the numbers to show how easy it would be to set up, and how successful we are, and how replicable our system is." Josh's eyes shone. "As it turns out, my investor, Darius? Had an even better idea. He doesn't want us to set up another ghost kitchen. He wants us to basically patent and sell the whole system, to other ghost kitchen owners."

Her eyes widened. "That's brilliant!"

"It's a huge deal," Josh admitted. "It's way bigger and more complicated than anything I would've considered. It's going to mean doing a lot of stuff, like patenting the software and figuring out how we'd standardize things like workflow, but really, it's not as hard as I would've thought. Especially since they're probably going to give me around twenty million to get everything pinned down and rolled out."

Tam goggled. "Twenty million? *Dollars?*"

He laughed. "That's what I said! It sounds like Monopoly money, doesn't it? I almost passed out."

She couldn't help herself. She hugged him, hard. "This is fantastic," she said. "And it's perfect for you. You've made your ghost kitchen a success, and this is the next evolution. You are going to kick unholy ass."

He fidgeted. "Or fail miserably, I guess. That's a ton of money."

"None of that, or I will smack you," she warned, and he grinned again, hugging her hard and nuzzling her neck. She was going to forever think of the juncture of her neck and shoulder as Josh's spot. "You deserve this, and it's about time you just grabbed for it with both hands."

"It's going to mean a lot of work," he admitted. "But it'll be worth it."

She hugged tighter, kissing just behind his ear. "I believe in you."

"I know you do," he said, pulling away and looking into her eyes, his own blue eyes bright with emotion. "I could not have done this without you."

"I beg to differ, but it's adorable that you think so."

"No." He looked sterner, cupping her chin to ensure she didn't look away. "You are amazing. And I swear, we're going to find you something that helps you feel just as happy as I am with this."

She chuckled nervously. This was it. Her opening. "Funny you should mention . . ."

"Oh?" He immediately perked up. "You figured out something? Like what you'd like to do? Because I am all on board with that. If it takes you a while, or you need to . . . I don't know, take more classes, or apprentice, or whatever, you can stay here for as long as you want. And I'll help in whatever way I can."

There it was. He was so supportive. It was tempting for her to think about taking him up on his offer. Still, she cleared her throat. "I got a call Saturday, actually. When I was with Vinh."

He frowned. "Saturday? Why didn't you say something?"

"You were so focused on the presentation, I didn't want to distract you," she said. "And honestly, I needed to think about it."

"Who was the call from?"

She sighed. "Cloud City Creamery, if you can believe it."

He started laughing. "No shit."

"No shit. They saw the breakup cheese-pairing posts—God, it seems like *everybody* saw those things," she said with another sigh. "And they were impressed. They sort of dug through my older stuff too. Anyway, long story short . . . they want me to interview to work for them."

Josh smiled. "What job?"

"Social media manager." She swallowed. "I mean . . . it's a big leap. I've never done anything like that before . . ."

"Bullshit. You were doing social media for the ad agency and at least a few of their accounts, when they saw how good you were at it. All on top of your crazy admin stuff," Josh pointed out. "Just handling one account, for a product you love? Without having to balance budgets and order office supplies and deal with whiny account execs? You could probably do this job in your sleep and still knock it out of the park!"

She felt her chest warm. "There, um, is a tiny catch, though."

"You are going to kill it on this interview," Josh reassured her.

"That's not it," she said. "I mean, I'm a little nervous, but that's not the problem."

She took a deep breath, holding his shoulders as if for support. He studied her gently, that expression of unquestioning support clear.

"The job's in Seattle."

She saw the moment he froze. Those bright ice-blue eyes of his blinked twice, slowly. "Seattle?"

She nodded. "Their farm isn't in the city, obviously, but their corporate offices are. And a cheese shop."

It was like she could watch the gears in his mind moving as he processed the information. "Wow," he finally said. "That's . . . wow."

"I know," she said miserably. "I mean, it's the perfect job in so many ways. I couldn't come up with a better one if I brainstormed on a thousand Post-it Notes and doodled with a full rainbow of colored pens. But it's so far away. I feel like I just got home."

He sighed. Then he tugged her close. "Like you said—it sounds perfect," he said slowly. "Why don't you talk to them and see how you feel about them as a company? You don't have any pressure to take the job if you don't want it. But that said, I'd hate for you to cut something off, or miss out on an opportunity, just because you're scared."

"I'm not scared," she tried to scoff. Which made it sound like she was scared. "Nervous," she admitted. "Not scared."

He smirked at her, but there was some sadness around his eyes. "You're thinking small again," he said, and though his voice was gentle, it brooked no argument. "You could do this, I know you could, and what's more, you'd be awesome at it. It's scary to go to a new city, but it's not like you're going to lose us as friends. In fact, it's physically impossible for you to lose me, and I'd hate for you to stay just because of that."

She hid the wince those words provoked. Because a part of her really wanted to stay . . . because of him.

"Just see how the interview goes, okay?"

She swallowed. "All right, Mr. Millions," she said, as brightly as she could. "Enough about me. You've just had a huge day. How do you want to celebrate?"

His smile seemed a touch forced too. "Maybe we can hold off on celebrating until we find out if we need a joint party?" he said. "Want some dinner?"

She nodded, feeling awkward. And nervous.

And, considering how many good things had just occurred to both of them, a little sad.

CHAPTER 33

Josh knew that he shouldn't be eavesdropping . . . and yet here he was, in the hallway of his own house, listening to Tam knock it out of the park with her interviewer. He'd volunteered his home office for her Zoom call, and the interviewer seemed eager to bring her on board. To her credit, she didn't sound nervous at all.

"Why don't you tell me about your background in social media?" the man—his name was Carl?—asked. "What draws you to it? And what do you think is most important for a company to know about it?"

He knew she was nervous. She'd been nervous all morning, waiting for the call. He'd wound up kissing the hell out of her, and they'd had impromptu sex, which he had to admit had her a lot more relaxed. Now, she looked calm and confident, wearing makeup and smiling with a sort of assurance that he was proud of.

Josh had told Amber the good news about the big investment earlier and then told her he was planning on taking the day off, which she completely approved of. He'd be practically living in the office at the Tombs soon enough, more than likely . . . or maybe just putting Amber in charge of the Tombs and opening a new office somewhere to work out the details of the new business model. He'd never considered selling his system, and he didn't have the first clue of how, exactly, that would work.

But he couldn't focus on that today. He couldn't focus on much of anything.

Tam might move to Seattle.

He'd been riding such an unbelievable high after Darius had told him the good news, he was lucky he hadn't gotten a ticket when he'd raced back from La Jolla to his house. The one person he wanted to tell was Tam. It was more important than even telling Amber, or any of his other friends from the Herd. She was the closest thing he had to family, the closest person to him on earth. And her joy and support made him want to just wrap her up in his arms and never let go.

Then she'd told him about the job offer. It was like emotional whiplash. It had somehow literally never occurred to him that, in her quest to follow her bliss, her bliss might actually take her away from Ponto Beach.

Away from him.

Part of him clenched with the greasy vise grip of despair. He'd *just* gotten her back. They were finally together, in a way that he hadn't let himself think about. Even if they weren't living together, per se . . . they really were. They ate meals together, texted each other during the day. Made love at least once a day at this point, even if they identified it as "friends with benefits." She made him happier than he'd ever been, and he wanted to see her as happy as she made him.

He was planning on asking her to ditch the benefits facade. They were all but in a relationship. Why pretend otherwise?

Yeah, it was scary. Both of them had shitty track records in relationships, and even shittier role models for them from their own families. In their own ways, they'd been people-pleasers as a result of their histories—he'd chosen dramaholics and then fought to make them happy; she'd chosen self-centered jerks whom she'd contorted herself to please. As a result, their relationships tended to crash and burn—and then repeat. That more than anything had prevented them from getting together romantically.

So yeah, it would be a risk, and risk was something neither of them was historically fond of, as was probably evident by the fact that they kept doing the same thing, over and over, because it was *familiar*.

But for God's sake, he'd just gambled big on his business and had been rewarded in ways he hadn't even dreamed. Surely asking his best friend to become his girlfriend—maybe even asking her to move in with him, since they were already there—was a tiny risk, comparatively speaking?

But she wanted this job.

"I would say that social media isn't advertising," he heard Tam assert from behind the door, her tone clear and smooth. "It's easy for companies to make that mistake, but the best corporate accounts understand that it's a conversation. You have to know who you're talking to, know what they want, and then provide it to them . . . whether that's entertainment or information."

A new voice chimed in, a woman this time. "This is Theresa McCrae. I'm one of the founders of Cloud City Creamery. Just how familiar are you with our product line?" She sounded a little wary. "We're a small, family-owned company. I don't want someone to come in and make us out to be something we're not."

"I don't want that either," Tam assured her. "Trust me. I found you guys years ago, and I . . . well. I'm kind of obsessed with cheese."

Josh stifled a laugh. That was an understatement.

"You guys have an amazing product," Tam continued. "But you don't take yourselves too seriously either. Your brand is fun, not pretentious. And it's high quality. I miss that Basque cheese you did a few years ago, actually. I was so bummed when I finally ate the last of it, knowing it was limited edition."

"That was good," Theresa agreed, and Josh could hear the smile in her voice. "But we decided to focus on a different sheep's milk cheese. Not enough people understood what *Basque cheese* meant."

"I'd have done pairings, and some history. Kind of funny, keeping with the brand idea, nothing too long winded," Tam said. "Heck, if you decide to bring it out again, I could show you."

He heard Theresa chuckle. "Is this just so you can get more of it?"

"Guilty."

The trio laughed at this point. She was winning them over.

"The other trick is being consistent," Tam continued. "Slight variations between Twitter, Facebook, and Instagram, but a consistent posting schedule. Not blanket content. Interacting with other brands might be fun too. You guys have other brands in your gift boxes—which you could probably expand . . . I don't know, your marketing manager might have a strategy there—but maybe some cross-posting or special offers or whatever could work. Developing a social media calendar, with room for off-the-cuff stuff as things come up. Like how that movie *Army of the Dead* had Dave Bautista talking about how he wanted to open an artisan grilled-cheese food truck. You could springboard off that, talk about 'what's your favorite grilled cheese' or whatever. There are a lot of ways you can have a solid plan, plus room for improv and on-the-fly reaction."

Josh felt his chest expand, even as his heart sank. He was so proud of her. He was so thrilled that she was finally stepping into her own, not just taking what jobs she felt were safe.

He was going to miss her.

He retreated as silently as possible, feeling like a creep for listening in. He forced himself to settle down, deciding to make himself an iced coffee. Caffeine was probably the last thing he needed, given how nervous he was, but he couldn't eat and didn't want to pace.

The house was going to feel so empty without her. She'd only been here for a month, but already it felt like she'd been here forever. Or maybe it was just because the house had felt like a husk until she'd come in. He had been proud of it, sure—it was gorgeous, expensive, a shining example proving that he wasn't the worthless kid his mother had thought him to be. But at the same time, he was rarely *here*. He'd lived at the job. He'd just come back to sleep and shower. With Tam here, he'd had the Herd over, he'd cooked in his well-appointed kitchen, he'd spent time cuddled up on his couch relaxing.

He was going to miss her.

He gritted his teeth. The thing was, he wasn't going to be like her dickhead boyfriends. Collin had pushed her to move to New York so he wouldn't be alone, so he'd have a cheerleader and companionship, because he was socially awkward. Brent had apparently wanted someone to clean his apartment and fawn over his overinflated ego when his ex had gotten married. Tam had contorted herself to make other people happy, and convinced herself that it was what she wanted without checking to see if it really was.

He wanted her to stay. He wanted her to be with him.

But he wasn't going to ask her to give up what she was good at, what apparently would make her happy, just so he could be happy. That was a recipe for disaster. She might say she wouldn't resent him, but he wasn't going to be one of those guys.

He heard her gentle step down the hallway and schooled his expression to be impassive. "So how'd it go?" he asked.

She smiled, looking as dazed as he'd felt the previous day. "They offered me the job," she said, her voice shocked. "They want me to start as soon as possible."

He felt his throat clog and swallowed hard to clear it. "That's phenomenal," he said, walking to her and hugging her tight.

"Is it?" She looked at him. "Should . . . I mean, should I take it?"

"Are you kidding?" He put as much encouragement and enthusiasm in his voice as he could. "You were born to do this. And cheese. How can you say no to cheese?"

She smirked, but her eyes were still shadowed. "I think I could be really good at this," she said. "But I never thought about moving so far away."

"It's not as far as New York," he pointed out, even as his heart yelled, *It's still really far away!* "And Seattle's a cool city."

She shrugged.

"Besides, you're probably going to be busy doing . . . whatever it is social media managers do," he said. "And again: eating cheese. So that seems worth it."

"I just got back," she said, her voice small. "I'm going to miss . . . everybody."

He closed his eyes, then hugged her again.

"It's not like you're losing us," he said. "We're going to still be here, okay? And I promise, every time you want to come back, you can come here and stay with me. You can even keep my key, all right?"

She pulled back enough to stare at him, like she was trying to see inside him.

He couldn't take the scrutiny. "You'll kick yourself if you don't at least try this," he said. "You told me that. That I was meant for bigger things than just working the line or front of the house in restaurants I hated, because that's all I thought I was good for." He gave her another hug. "Your own words," he reminded her.

"Yeah well," she said, and she sounded sniffly. "Do as I say, not as I do."

He grinned. "Nice try."

She sighed. "It's scary," she said in a small voice.

"I know," he said.

"And I am going to miss you like whoa."

He swallowed hard. "Right back atcha," he said. He wanted to tell her she could spend every vacation, every holiday . . . hell, every weekend if she wanted. But he also knew that he would only be making it harder. She was ready to start a new life.

He had to let her do that, not keep her tied to him.

He chucked her chin. "You're going to be fine, sweetie," he said, kissing her softly. "You're going to flourish, I promise."

"I'm not going to ghost you all again," she said. "I want to stay connected."

"Okay," he said, even as his chest felt like someone had taken a sledgehammer to it. Surely she didn't just lump him in with the rest of the Herd? "Whatever you need."

"Like . . . could you text me? Like we do now?"

"Sure."

"And . . . maybe video call?"

The thought of staying that close to her, without *being* that close to her, had his heart breaking a little more. But he bucked up, nodding. "You got it."

"All . . . right," she finally said, drawing the words out slowly. "I guess . . . I'm moving . . . to Seattle?"

He hugged her tight. "Congratulations," he said. "Looks like we're both moving up in the world."

And he'd never realized just how much that was going to hurt.

CHAPTER 34

"Man, Josh, twice in one month?" Hayden said, clinking his beer bottle against Keith's glass. "I haven't seen your house this much since you moved in!"

"And both times parties," Keith agreed. "We need to start having game night over here."

"Yeah, but I've got a pool," Hayden quickly protested. "And Tobin's got the DnD set up."

"We can just add it to the rotation, is all I'm saying."

Tam listened, sipping at her own drink. And yes, she was actually drinking. Granted, it was a Kahlúa milkshake, hardly the type of thing that was going to get her hammered, but after contacting Carl and accepting the position, agreeing to start the following week, she felt a wave of panic and needed some kind of numbing agent.

It was really happening.

The job was going to be amazing. Probably. While she usually went into interviews with a sense of desperation and the need to prove herself, she'd felt looser when she talked to Carl and Theresa. Granted, the sex and shower she'd had prior to the Zoom call might've contributed to that. She looked over, seeing Josh joking with Tobin and Lily, who had just come in. He was smiling widely and looked happier than she'd seen him in a long time.

She was going to miss having sex with him, to say the least. No more stress relief on that front.

Oh, who are you kidding?

She was going to miss every single thing about him.

She tried to force herself to stay positive. The other good thing about working for Cloud City was she didn't get the same vibes that she had when she'd applied to the ad agency. The agency had emphasized things like "Do you work well under pressure?" and "We work long hours here—is that going to be a problem?" They'd essentially negged her—"Not everyone can handle what we do—we're not sure if you're cut out for this level of excellence." And Tam had bought into it hook, line, and sinker.

If anything, Theresa had emphasized that they saw the company as a family. "And not one of those horrible ones, like you see on reality shows," she'd added. They wanted work-life balance. It could be easy to get sucked into social media at all times, answering people's responses. Theresa wanted to institute some boundaries to protect her from burnout, and Carl had heartily backed her up.

Seeing that kind of support, especially after the bullshit of the agency, was kind of mind blowing.

She'd agreed to getting an already-furnished apartment in Seattle, after only seeing the online photos, close enough to the company's headquarters that she wouldn't need to buy a car right away. There were grocery stores and cafés and things within walking distance, and everything else she could Uber or Zipcar her way to or something. It wasn't New York, but that wasn't necessarily a bad thing.

She took a deep breath, then slugged back some more of her milkshake.

"You okay?" Emily asked, materializing by her side. "Congratulations, I mean, obviously. The job sounds amazing."

"It's all just happening so fast," Tam said, her voice shakier than she wanted. "It's a great opportunity, and I couldn't have come up with a more perfect job if I tried. But . . ."

"But you're thinking of Josh."

Tam hissed a "shush" at Emily, looking around to see if anybody else was looking. "No! Well, not exactly."

Emily quirked a skeptical eyebrow at her. "Tam, did you tell him you wanted to be in a romantic relationship with him?"

"Well . . . no." Tam grimaced.

"Do you think you *should* tell him?"

"No!" Tam felt every muscle in her body tense, and she crouched in on herself a little. "He's been so supportive. Hell, he's practically packed my luggage himself." And no, she wasn't feeling any particular way about that little fact. They'd stopped having sex, too, even though they were sleeping in the same bed. He'd work late, until after she was already asleep, and be out of bed in the mornings before she got up. He had to be exhausted.

She got the feeling it was for her benefit—or maybe it was just weaning off the "benefits" gradually so there wasn't a withdrawal when she moved. Whatever, it made her feel weird. Not like he didn't care. He obviously did. But she still felt odd about the whole thing.

"If he doesn't know how you feel, he's going to do what he thinks is best for you. You know how he is about you." Emily sighed. "I actually envy the hell out of that. He would jump in front of a speeding train that was on fire *and* had spikes all over it, if he thought it would protect you."

"I know," Tam groaned, tugging Emily into a corner. She lowered her voice so the rest of the Herd didn't clue in to what they were talking about. "Don't you think I feel the same way? I don't want him to feel like he needs to be in a relationship with me, just to make me happy. He's never felt this way about me, and trust me, we've had lots of chances. It's not just me being scared. If we were going to . . . be together, don't you think we would've done it by now?"

Emily stared at her. Then she slowly started shaking her head. "Wow. Just . . . wow."

"Don't judge me," Tam said. "We lost touch, and I'm not doing that again. If we can be friends, that's the most important thing."

"Well, I guess you're making baby steps, with the job thing," Emily said. "Honestly, it's probably better that you take the job. Much as I love Josh, it's a bad idea to give up everything for someone you love. You've got a chance at a life that makes you happy—not a life making someone *else* happy. If things with Josh went sideways, and that's always possible, then where would you be? You'd lose the friendship, and you'd blame him for not having what you want."

"I did think of that," Tam admitted.

"That's how I felt when I lost your brother."

Emily's statement brought her up short.

"I had to drop out of school," Emily said. "Not because of Vinh, obviously. When Dad died, and Greg started acting out, Mom needed help. She would've lost the house, and she just couldn't quite handle things. So I just left and did whatever I could to help her out."

"Vinh loved you," Tam said, but it felt weak. There were times when she wondered if Vinh *still* loved Emily, even though she rarely discussed it. Vinh was an emotional bunker at the best of times.

"Yeah, I know." Emily's smile was bitter. "But he had shit to do, and . . . well. It is what it is. The important thing is, if I could do what I loved instead of working the damned call center, I would be."

"It's been eight years, Em," Tam said. "How's your mom doing?"

"Some days better than others," she said. "But my brother's still a pain in the ass, and it seems like he comes up with new ways to just fuck up. I never thought I'd be twenty-eight and living with my family, but here we are." She looked at Tam seriously. "So what I'm saying is: take the chance. I don't blame your brother for leaving anymore. He's got a great life. You need to go out there and get your life too."

She knew that Emily was probably right. She loved Josh, might well be *in* love with Josh, but there were still too many variables. She at least had him as a closer friend now. She wasn't going to ghost him or lose him. And best of all, she didn't have a boyfriend in the picture anymore . . . no one to accommodate, no one to please. She needed to get her head on right before she could be in a relationship, anyway.

She hugged Emily. "Thanks for talking with me," she said. "I'm not going to let things fall apart again. I want to stay in touch."

Emily grinned. "That's what I like to hear."

Josh walked up. "How're you doing?"

"Congrats, big businessman," Emily said, hugging him. "I am so proud of you!"

"When you were in college, you were prelaw, right?"

Emily looked startled, then shrugged, her cheeks turning pink. "Sort of, I guess? I mean, obviously that's not really a major. But that was the aim."

"I'm going to be doing a lot of legal stuff, getting the business on track," he said. "I know you hate the job you've got. Maybe . . . I mean, if you wanted, you could look at paralegal, or even law school? I figure we could think of something, and trust me, I could use the help. Besides, you're really smart, and I know you work your ass off."

"That's sweet," Emily said. "Let me think about it. And no pity offers."

"I would never," Josh said, and Tam knew he meant it.

"Let me say hi to Lily—I hear she's back," Emily said, then walked away, leaving Josh and Tam alone in the corner.

"You okay?" he asked.

She nodded. "Just talking," she said quickly. "I'm going to miss everybody."

"Again: you can come back whenever you like." He squeezed her hand. "We're not going anywhere."

She sighed. No, she supposed he wasn't.

She just wished, for a moment, that she wasn't, either. But it was just too damned risky.

CHAPTER 35

Josh looked around the furnished studio apartment that Tam had rented, short-term lease, sight unseen. The people at Cloud City Creamery had recommended it, since a few of their company's officers had stayed there when they'd first relocated.

"This is . . . nice," he said.

"Well, it's not a total shithole, which I was kind of expecting," Tam said. "And it's bigger than I would've thought. In New York, you couldn't get a shoebox for the price they wanted. Especially not in the city itself."

He smiled at her, shaking his head. "The square footage was literally on the listing."

"Yes," she admitted, "but you know how I am with spatial relations. Everything's approximately ten-foot square, a mile away, or another twenty-minute drive."

He laughed weakly, even as he walked from one end of the studio to the other. The place was tiny. The door opened to the miniscule kitchen area, then there was a queen-size bed, a small round table with two folding chairs, a TV, and a bathroom. There was a little electric fireplace, and a postage-stamp-size balcony, which looked onto a building across the street. The skies were gray, full of angry-looking clouds. It was a portent of weather to come.

"It doesn't really matter anyway," she said with a shrug, steering her large new roller bag toward the plain gray dresser. "It's just going to be a place to sleep and maybe do some work now and then. Once I settle in and save up some money, I'll look at something more permanent."

His stomach roiled at the idea of her permanently up here. Still, he had to encourage her. She was his best friend, wasn't she? What kind of best friend would he be if he stood in the way of something that meant this much to her?

He helped her unpack her bags, which didn't take long. Then the two of them wandered through her neighborhood. He insisted on paying for her groceries, helping load up her fridge and cabinets so she had staples before she started work. That night, he took her out to dinner at a nearby gastropub. Ordinarily, he'd be much more analytical—studying the menu, wondering about their food costs and sourcing, what was popular, what wasn't.

Tonight, he only had eyes for Tam, who looked nervous but determined.

"You're going to be great," he told her. "Stop worrying."

She rolled her eyes. "I've never done anything like this," she said, her voice a little breathless. "What if I suck? As an admin, I did what people told me to do. I'm going to need to make some serious decisions and work quickly and prove myself. What if I screw up?"

"First: yes, you're going to screw up," he said, and she scowled at him. "But that's because you're human, and people do that. They're not going to fire you just because you make some mistakes. It's better that you actually make mistakes than freeze and do nothing."

She nibbled at the corner of her mouth, obviously processing this thought.

"As to the idea that you only did what people told you to—we both know that's not true. You are one of the best problem solvers I know, and when you see something needs to be done, you move mountains to do it. You don't wait around for someone to tell you how."

He was gratified to see the corner of her mouth—the one she'd been biting—kick up in a smile. Her eyes brightened. "You might have a point there."

"I know I do," he said. "I've heard your stories, and I know that as much as people drove you up a wall at your old jobs, you managed to get what was needed done. Regardless of their interference, not because of their instruction. You are more than ready for this."

He reached over the table, taking her hand in his, squeezing her fingers in a way that he hoped expressed comfort.

"And trust me, in a very short amount of time, they're going to know it too. You are amazing, and you're going to blow them away."

She smiled, so soft, so sweet, that his chest ached. "You always believe in me," she murmured.

That's because I love you.

He took a swallow of beer, pushing the rest of his gourmet burger away uneaten. "You've always believed in me," he said. "Even when I didn't think you should. Believing in you, when you've proven to be so amazing, is literally the least I can do."

She sighed. "What time is your flight?"

He glanced at his watch. He had considered taking an early flight the following morning, but Tam started her new job that day. He knew she was nervous, and he didn't want to distract her any more than he already had. Besides . . . if he stayed with her tonight, he wasn't sure how he'd be able to tear himself away. "My flight's at ten."

She frowned. "Thank you. For everything."

They walked back to her apartment, slowly, side by side. He bumped into her, and she smirked. Then she inadvertently bumped into *him*, and he laughed.

"People-magneting," she joked, something they'd done back in middle school when someone clumsily bumped into another while walking.

He shrugged, then indulged himself and put an arm around her shoulders, even though he knew he was ultimately making it worse on himself. The weather was misty, just short of rain. They stepped up their pace, heading into her apartment building just before the clouds opened. Still, their jackets and hair were damp by the time they made it back into her studio. She turned on the fireplace, its little propane flames dancing merrily.

"You sure you're going to be okay flying tonight?" she asked, looking out the window at the dark sky.

"It's just rain, not thunderstorms or anything," he reassured her.

"Because you could stay here," she said in a low voice. "If you wanted."

He looked at her. She looked so hopeful. And God, didn't his body scream at him. *Stay with her, you dipshit!*

But if he stayed . . . what would that do?

They'd missed their window. She had a whole exciting life ahead of her—one where she finally put herself first. And he was about to ride a rocket ship into the kind of success he'd never dared to dream of. They were going to be a thousand miles away from each other, and while long-distance relationships could work, they'd barely proven that they could manage a long-distance *friendship*. From now on, that was what mattered. If they tried a long-distance relationship, and it didn't work out . . .

He shook his head at himself. No. He wasn't brainstorming worst-case scenarios if it didn't work. If it didn't work out, then he'd lose his lover *and* his friend, and that was just too big a risk for him, even with his newfound tolerance for going for broke.

He sighed, stroking her cheek. "I gotta go," he said, and regret was rich in his voice.

She bit her lip, closing her eyes for a second. Then she took a deep breath. "Are you sorry?"

He dropped his hand, startled. "Sorry? For what?"

"For . . . you know. Us getting involved." Her cheeks turned pink. "Physically."

"No. God, no." He wrapped her in his arms, and immediately registered the mistake he'd made. The scent of her was intoxicating . . . the feel of her, warm and compact, and almost vibrating with desire, was overwhelming.

"Then maybe one for the road?" she asked, looking up at him from under her thick fringe of lashes.

He should have realized that there was no way he was going to avoid this. If he was honest with himself, it was exactly what he wanted.

They made love with slow deliberation. He'd been purposely tapering off—they hadn't had sex since her interview—but now, seeing her and knowing he wasn't going to be able to touch her or even say fucking good morning to her daily made him even more desperate to hold her close.

"Josh," she breathed, holding her arms up. He took off her sweater, then stripped her of her jeans and underwear and socks. She did the same to him, until they were both naked, both stretched out on the new sheets they'd purchased together, under the comforter he'd helped her choose and then packed with care.

He couldn't stop kissing her. She wrapped her arms around his neck, pulling him tightly against her as her legs wrapped around his waist. He groaned at the feel of her hot, damp channel brushing against his rock-hard flesh.

"Condom?" he asked between harsh, panting breaths.

"What, like I have some here?" she teased back, equally breathless.

The thought made him freeze.

"No, Josh," she said, obviously reading his body language. "I don't have any, and I don't plan on needing any."

He wanted to tell her of course she should have relationships. Or just sex. She could, and probably should, stock up on condoms and do whatever the hell she wanted.

I love her, but I'm not a fucking saint.

He growled. "Hold on a sec," he said, disentangling himself from her long enough to grab his wallet, where he had one last condom tucked away. After carefully checking the date, he rolled it on. They wouldn't have much time, not if he wanted to make his flight.

Fuck the flight. This was more important.

He found himself climbing beside her on the bed, his back against the wall. When she looked surprised, he patted his lap, where his cock jutted up like an obelisk.

She grinned and nodded, clambering to straddle him.

"Want to see you ride," he said, feeling a little foolish, but also way more turned on.

Her grin turned wicked, and she sheathed him in her wet heat in one long, smooth motion.

He threw his head back—and immediately regretted it, when his head hit the wall. "Fuck."

She let out a peal of laughter, then wound her fingers in his hair. "Feel better?" she said, simultaneously rubbing his scalp and rocking her hips.

He forgot the pain immediately, too fixated on the sensation of her enveloping him, moving slowly, tantalizing him. She shuddered, and he felt the muscles around him clench, then release.

"Oh my God," he rasped, his hips jutting up reflexively.

She had him scoot a bit farther out on the bed so she could wrap her legs around his waist. It was as if they were closer than any other position they'd been in. She tilted her face to kiss him, her tongue invading his mouth, her breasts and stomach pressed against his chest like she was trying to fuse to him, her hips moving like a dancer's. He gripped her hips, holding her tight, pounding up inside her as she gasped against his lips and rocked more violently, losing rhythm, losing control.

"Josh," she panted, and he could feel the rush of wetness as her pussy milked him like a fist. *"JOSH!"*

He let out an inarticulate yell and emptied himself into the condom, shuddering inside her, holding her like he never wanted to let her go.

They stayed like that, wrapped up in each other, their breathing slowly evening out. Then he kissed her forehead. She had tears dotting her eyelashes, he noticed, before she brushed them away with her fingertips.

He felt the same way, so he closed his eyes for a long moment.

When he felt back in control, they slowly disengaged, and he took care of the condom. He took the world's quickest shower and got changed. Then he went back out into her living space.

She was wearing a dark-emerald terry cloth robe—another new purchase, one he'd bought her. She looked warm and cozy and recently debauched, her lips puffy from his kisses and her hair tumbled from their exertions. Her sun-kissed skin was still flushed. He knew that he was going to picture her like this for the rest of his goddamned life.

"You know I love you, right?" he asked.

She nodded, staring at her feet in a pair of fleece-lined slippers. "You know I love you too."

"Best friends?" He held out his pinky.

She linked hers with his. "For-chèvre," she joked, but it sounded watery.

He kissed her, stroked her cheek. Said goodbye. Then went downstairs, where the car was waiting to take him to the airport.

He was going to miss her like oxygen. But this was the right thing to do.

CHAPTER 36

"All right! Bet you've never had a cheese tasting like this, amirite?"

Tam smiled faintly. "Well, no."

She was at a bar with her new "cheesemates," people she worked with at Cloud City's headquarters. She'd been there for a bit over a month at this point, but she was still getting her bearings. She'd spent time hashing out the new social media direction with the marketing manager, Carl, and taking in the company culture with Theresa (which, interestingly, had involved going to the farm over in Duvall and hand milking a cow that they had in the tourist section of the dairy). She'd been spending long hours in the office, but it wasn't like being at the ad agency. For one thing, nobody expected her to be there. If anything, Theresa and her partner, Agnes, kept telling her to go home.

But what did she have at home? Right now, not much. A fridge with some veggies that she was slowly letting go bad, some take-out containers. Some Jeni's ice cream in the freezer that the Herd had sent as a congratulations/housewarming gift. Some kind of plant that she'd bought on a whim and was struggling to keep alive. She liked the view from her tiny balcony, even if it wasn't of a particularly pretty building, and she didn't even mind the rain.

What she did mind was the loneliness.

Which was why she'd agreed to this outing, even though it was a cheese pairing with a tasting flight of hard ciders made by a local fruit orchard. She was looking forward to seeing what they came up with to pair with what kinds of cheeses, and she was taking photos like mad, despite the poor lighting conditions.

"You are an animal," Marcus, one of the cheesemongers, said with a grin. "A social media beast. Are these all going up on Instagram or something?"

"Some of them, staggered out, yeah," she said, feeling a little embarrassed.

"You don't have to," Theresa assured her. "We have stuff like this once a month to have fun and get to know each other. You don't have to keep working. You can just . . . relax."

That might be the first time—the only time—that a boss had ever said anything like that to her, and it took everything in Tam not to gawp or laugh nervously. "Don't worry. It is fun for me," she finally said with a sheepish shrug.

"Try some of the Blue Period with the Cider Master Reserve," Theresa encouraged. "Creamy blues love a champagne-style cider, I find."

"Loving your work is great," Agnes continued, "but you need to take a break from time to time. You know. Recharge."

"Tell that to my family," Tam said, then bit her tongue. What the heck was she saying? The cider couldn't possibly have caught up with her already. She'd barely had a few sips.

"Where is your family?" Marcus asked. "Any of them live up here? You're from California, right?"

"Um . . . my father lives in Saigon, and my mother lives in San Clemente—that's kind of between San Diego and LA—and my brother lives in New York."

If they thought her far-flung family was weird, they didn't say anything, just smiled benignly. "So you're from California. This must be quite a change . . . oh, wait, you gotta try this." Marcus pointed to a pink-tinged cider. "That's a rosé cider, from . . . I forget which orchard. But it's great. Got some quince in it, so it's got a pop of tart against the relative sweetness of the apple, you know? And it works perfectly with the young cheddar."

"Young cheddar?" she repeated, trying out the recommendations. They were really, really good, she noticed. "What goes with aged cheddar, then?"

Marcus took this in stride. "Hard farmhouse-style cheddar does better with the funkier stuff," he said. "I'd say that one." Now, he pointed to a darker cider. "It's got blackberries, too, but there's nothing too sweet or fruity about it. Barrel aged. It's got a punch."

She took a sip, then took a bite of the cheddar. "Wow."

"I know, right?" Marcus beamed. "Great job, isn't it?"

"Probably the best job I've ever had," she said truthfully, with a shy smile.

They smiled back. "Then let's hope we get to keep you for a good long time," Theresa said, and the rest of them cheered, raising various small glasses in toast.

"You enjoying Seattle?" Marcus then asked, as the various people around the table dissolved into their own conversations.

"I've been acclimating," Tam said. In fact, she'd forced herself to play tourist in her free time. She'd seen the Chihuly glass gardens, been to Pike Place Market, even checked out the Space Needle before remembering abruptly, at the base of it, just how much she hated heights. She still didn't have a car yet, something she meant to remedy soon, once she hit her temporary nest egg goal. In the meantime, though, she was enjoying what she could.

Or at least trying to.

"But I guess you miss the sun," Marcus joked.

That's not the only thing I miss. In fact, it wasn't even in the top five. Josh took up every one of those spaces.

"I'm not even from there, and I miss the sun," Agnes added with a laugh.

Carl gestured with his glass. "Thanksgiving's coming up," he pointed out. "Are you going down to see your family?"

She bit her lip. "My mother tends to spend the holiday with her husband's family," she said. "And my brother's going to be in the Virgin Islands or something, I think? Maybe Portugal?" She'd touched base with him after starting her job. "It's okay. I don't really celebrate the holidays as much anymore."

"Oh, I'm sorry," Carl said with evident embarrassment. "I didn't mean to make you feel uncomfortable."

"You didn't," Tam quickly reassured him. "Actually, I used to spend Thanksgiving with friends anyway." She smiled, remembering. "We used to do something called Leftover Hangover. We'd descend on one of our friends' houses at night, all of us armed with leftovers, and we'd have things like turkey and stuffing sandwiches with cranberry sauce, or mashed potato patties. And, of course, a ton of desserts. And we'd all wear the craziest pajamas we could find, and watch bad sci-fi movies or anime, and just gorge ourselves until we fell asleep."

"That sounds awesome," Marcus said. "Now I want to do that. What were your pajamas?"

"I have a rainbow unicorn onesie with a horn on the hood," Tam admitted, and they all burst out laughing.

"Okay, we're going to have to have Pajama Day at work," Theresa said. "We could even have a contest!"

"I see the accounting team being surprisingly strong contenders," Agnes added, and they laughed again.

Tam sighed. She did like these people. They were open, and amusing, and relaxed. They listened to her and acknowledged and respected her ideas. While so many other companies touted "we're a family," they usually meant one of those dysfunctional, inbred aristocratic families . . . where the workers were the serfs or something. Cloud City seemed to respect and support the people who worked there. Tam hated that a healthy dynamic was something she had to "get used to," but there it was.

And they all loved cheese—possibly even more than she did, which she didn't think was possible.

The thing was: they weren't *her* people. They weren't the Herd. And now that she'd had a taste of being back with her friends, feeling their love and support, she missed the hell out of them.

"You sound very close to your friends," Carl noted. He was like the "papa" of the group, seeing himself as an elder despite only being in his late forties. "How long have you known them? Since college?"

"Since grade school." Tam smiled. "I miss them."

"Well, their loss is our gain," Agnes said. "And you're more than welcome to share Thanksgiving with Theresa and me. We're going to have a bunch of friends over as well."

"Or my family," Marcus said with a warm, inviting smile . . . with possibly a hint of something else? "My mother cooks enough for an army, and she'd love to have one more, I promise."

Tam felt her cheeks heating, although she wasn't sure if it was from the camaraderie or, honestly, from the cider. "Thanks," she said quietly. "I appreciate it. And . . . I'll think about it."

She was forcing herself out of her comfort zone. Emily had been right about her making decisions based on the men in her life. And Josh had shown her she was used to living small, to dreaming small, and she needed to frankly knock that shit off. She couldn't have come up with a job more perfect for her if she'd designed it in a lab. Yes, she loved her friends, but . . .

You love Josh, too. Admit it.

She took a long swallow of cider. That wasn't the point. That had never been the point. She was making the smart choice for both of them. He had a successful business, she was on her way with a successful career, and the important part was: they were both still friends. She had to prove to herself that she could do this.

So she kept eating cheese, and sipping cider, and tried her damnedest to finally be fine with where she was, and who she was with . . . and not think about what could have been.

CHAPTER 37

It was New Year's Eve, and Josh was at Tobin and Lily's house—which still felt weird to him, that they were essentially living together. As always, it was a Nerd Herd party, which meant music, great food (provided by the ghost kitchens, which now included Freddie's catering company), and board games.

The problem was, Josh didn't feel up to *any* of it.

He glanced at his phone. It was barely after nine. At this rate, he was going to pretend to have stomach flu or something and bail. He could just as easily binge-watch *Sandman* at home or something, rather than act like he wasn't as miserable as he felt. Amber thought he was coming down with something, or that he was working too hard, which was probably true. Darius's investment group had approved the money, and now he was working with one of Paul's contacts to figure out the software trademarking, and figuring out how to package the workflow and delivery needs to "sell" to franchises. It was a lot.

It was not enough to keep him distracted from his real issue, however, and he knew it. No matter how hard he worked, or how far he ran in the morning, or how tired he made himself, he still thought about Tam, constantly. And he still hurt, constantly, missing her.

As promised, they'd stayed in close contact. He texted her funny GIFs and asked her how her day was. She sent him silly selfies that he couldn't stop staring at, her lips pursed in a kiss he could practically feel.

But at the same time, she told him about how well she was doing. She'd taken to the job like a duck to water, and he could see her blossoming in her new role. She also talked about the people she worked with. He'd seen a selfie of her with a few of her coworkers. There was a guy about their age who had an arm around her and a broad smile . . . Marcus, apparently. Some cheesemonger.

It would be hard to compete with a cheesemonger, he thought absently, then grimaced.

Before he could start to make his excuses, he was surprised when Darius walked up to him and shook his hand. "Hey," Josh said, surprised. "I didn't think you'd make it."

"Your group of friends sounded fun," Darius said with an easy smile, "and I didn't feel like dealing with some big fancy party. My family's out in Richmond, Virginia, and I went back for Christmas, but I wanted to hit the ground running with some of our projects when the new year rolled over. Anyway, I appreciate the invite."

Josh couldn't help but notice that Darius's gaze kept flitting over to Juanita. Maybe there were some other incentives to him attending. Of course, technically Josh was the only person Darius knew at the party, so Josh saw his avenue of escape get cut off. He'd just stick around till midnight, then. Maybe video call Tam, have the whole Herd say *Happy New Year*.

She'd probably get a kick out of that, he thought with a smile.

The smile quickly dropped off as he thought: *Unless she's not alone.* She might be celebrating New Year's a different way.

Say, with a cheesemonger.

His stomach knotted, and he almost crushed the cup in his hand.

"You okay?" Darius asked, but before he could respond, Tobin rapped on the table, and Lily turned the music down.

"First, thanks everybody for coming," Tobin said, his deep YouTuber voice resonating through the room and causing all other conversations to go quiet. "It's a while yet till the ball drops, but it's time that we address that other item on the agenda."

Josh frowned. Agenda? What agenda? What the hell was he talking about?

Juanita sneaked up behind him, giving him a gentle nudge toward the big table where they usually had DnD campaigns, gesturing to him to take a seat at the head of it. The rest of the Herd took up spots around him, with Darius looking curiously at the proceedings as Juanita sat him next to her at the opposite end.

"Am I DM-ing or something?" He hadn't been a dungeon master in a long time. Hell, he hadn't even been over for the usual DnD games for at least six months. "Because if I am, I missed the memo and don't have anything prepared," Josh added, feeling suddenly uneasy.

They looked at him with various expressions of frustration and pity.

After a long, uncomfortable silence, Josh cleared his throat. "Is this a New Year's party, or an intervention?" he finally said. "Because you're freaking me out."

"Bit of both," Tobin said with a shrug. "All right, just gonna lay it out there. You've been a miserable bastard since Tam left, and we all decided you needed to get some sense slapped into you."

Josh's mouth dropped open. He watched Darius's eyes pop wide as he surveyed the table. "Well. This just got interesting," he murmured with a small grin.

While promising himself he would kill them later, Josh gritted his teeth. "This doesn't feel appropriate," he said, but Lily put a hand on his arm, her eyes sympathetic.

"What the love of my life over there is trying to say," Lily teased, "is that we hate seeing you unhappy. Tam loves you, and you love her. Why is she up in Seattle?"

Josh sighed. "Because that's where she's supposed to be!" he said, the bleeding edge of his hurt making the words more cutting than he intended. "Listen, you guys don't get it. Every other boyfriend in her life made her believe that her dreams and her drive were second to what they wanted and what they were doing. I am *not* going to be that asshole. And I know you guys think it's ridiculous, but what we have? Our friendship? It was my fucking lifeline, and still is. And I'm hers. She's found something that makes her happy, and she's scared of losing what we've got. I am *never* going to be the unsupportive shit that doesn't respect that!"

They fell silent, looking at each other. Josh felt like he'd peeled off his skin and was standing there, raw and in pain.

Then, to his surprise, Darius spoke.

"This is your friend from New York, huh?" He looked thoughtful. "The one you were helping find a job, a few months ago."

Josh nodded.

"And you're in love with her?"

Josh grimaced . . . then nodded again.

"And . . . she doesn't know that?"

"Everybody knows that," Asad muttered, and Freddie shushed him. "What? We have all literally known. For years."

"Well, then." Darius opened his hands expansively. "I think you're being more than fair, but you're forgetting one thing. You need to give her a choice. She's a grown woman, from the sounds of it. If she's scared, if she's not interested, that's on her. But if she doesn't know all her options, then it's just . . . okay, not to be harsh, but it's just the two of you, being scared and miserable a thousand miles apart, isn't it?"

Josh gaped.

"Sorry not sorry," Darius added.

"Oh, I like you," Juanita said, her eyes positively beaming. Darius smiled and winked at her.

Josh crumpled back into his chair. "So what, I'm just supposed to say, 'Hey Tam, you've got this great job you love, and I don't want you to lose that, but could you move back to Ponto Beach to be with me?'" He shook his head. "Even if she does love me, that doesn't feel right."

"He's right," Emily said, her mouth in a tight line. "She shouldn't have to give up everything just because he's in love with her. No offense," she tacked on, sending an apologetic look to Josh.

"I call shenanigans," Hayden countered. "It's just a job. Tam can find one of those anywhere. Where's she gonna find another Josh?"

"Easy for a guy to say that," Emily shot back. "Don't even get me started on relationship expectations and roles across genders, pal."

Hayden frowned at her. "All right, point taken. But here's a thought. Let's turn it around. Why does Josh have to stay in Ponto Beach anyway?"

They turned to stare at him. Josh felt his eyes widen.

"I'm just saying," Hayden said. "Remote work is a thing, people. It's not like he's actually cooking the food over at his kitchens. Why does he need to be here?"

"Now we're on to something," Asad said, then got up and walked over to Tobin's whiteboard, which was conveniently empty. He picked up a dry-erase marker. "All right, we've done this a million times, since Josh has literally tried to Post-it and whiteboard all of our problems. Let's goooo!"

Then he wrote, in big letters:

HELP JOSH FIX HIS SHIT WITH TAM.

"First of all," Asad said thoughtfully, rubbing his chin, "it's got to include some sort of cheese."

Josh grinned as the rest of them started laughing. He felt foolish. But he also felt a bubble of hope in his chest.

He'd want everything to be perfect. Darius was right: he overthought things. And, like Amber said, he was a control freak.

But he could figure this out, if Tam was willing to give him any kind of a chance. He just had to take that risk—and make it count.

CHAPTER 38

Tam walked into Carl's office for a job evaluation. They'd discussed it when she got hired, and part of her couldn't believe the time had gone by so quickly. Another part of her felt like she'd been here forever. Not necessarily in the good way.

"Have a seat," Carl said. His office was clean but also scattered, with folders in haphazard piles and various cheese tchotchkes in the bookshelf and on the credenza. She took the seat across from him, and he sat at his desk. He looked at her, his hazel eyes kind. "How've you been?"

"Good," she said. "The cheesy lines campaign has been successful, even in all its iterations: cheesy season's greetings, cheesy celebration, and now cheesy love-you lines for Valentine's Day."

He nodded but looked at her with a half smile. "I know, I've been tracking the insights. Lot of engagement, and a lot of it is translating into more subscribers, more direct orders, and more sales," he said. "Which you knew. Even better, because we're getting more publicity and developing more national attention, we're getting interest from some larger supermarket chains." He looked excited.

She should feel proud. Well, she *did* feel proud. But at the same time, she felt . . . hollow. She tilted her chin up.

She knew that they were going to be discussing a pay raise today.

She had different plans.

"I wasn't actually asking about numbers or engagement, though," Carl continued. "You just seem under the weather."

"It is scheduled to pour tonight," she said with a half smile of her own. Yeah, it was a reach, and she knew Carl wasn't buying it.

"It's just . . . we love having you here," Carl said, his expression the textbook illustration of earnest dad. "And I was wondering: Is there something you feel is wrong here? Is there anything we could be doing to make working here more enjoyable?"

Her heart melted just a little. She really did love working with these people. They were unicorns: a company that really cared about their product and their people, to the point where they'd genuinely ask how they could make her happy. It continually astounded her and made her smile.

Unfortunately, it also made what she was about to do that much harder.

"There is something," she said slowly, "but . . . maybe it'd be better if we talked about my performance evaluation first."

"All right." Carl cleared his throat, then pulled out a folder with her name on it. "Exemplary across the board, really. Everyone you work with has great things to say about you, from the store staff to the cheesemongers, to upper management. You've helped boost our profile with imaginative campaigns, and you seem to be able to whip out answers or deal with simple questions easily. You've even made it clear that having an extra person simply to answer those repetitive questions, and make sure that people are being heard and responded to, is important and easy to train for. We're doing leaps and bounds better than I could have even dreamed." He smiled. "You should be proud of the work you've done. We would love to keep you on in the position of social media manager, and I'd like to give you a raise commensurate with that."

She nodded. "I really appreciate that, Carl."

He leaned back in his chair, studying her. "Please tell me you're not going to quit," he said.

"No. At least, that's not the plan," she said, aware that wasn't as promising as she could've made it sound. "Here's the thing. I love Cloud City Creamery. I love the cheese. I adore the people I work with. I like the challenge of the job, and I genuinely want you—us—to succeed as a company."

"But . . . ?"

"But . . ."

She closed her eyes for a second, gathering all her strength.

"But I want to work remote."

There. She'd said it. Over the past few months, the more she'd thought about it, the more she realized that there were different ways of thinking small. She'd encouraged Josh to pursue something bigger, and he'd done the same for her. The only problem was, she still wasn't used to asking for exactly what she wanted. And what she wanted, precisely, was having the Herd around her, enjoying Ponto Beach—and being in a relationship with Josh for real. All while holding the best job ever.

She didn't know if she could get it. But if she didn't try, she'd definitely never achieve it, and she was tired of settling. Tired of living in fear.

Carl's eyes widened, and he looked concerned. "It . . . we never thought about it being a remote position," he said. "Do you mean you want to work from home? Maybe just come in once a week or so?"

He sounded so hopeful she almost caved. The people-pleasing drive was strong, but her determination here was stronger. "No, I mean I'd like to move back to Southern Cal," she clarified, and his expression fell. "It's not that I don't love working with you guys here. I do. But it's not necessary. Social media doesn't need to be location dependent."

He frowned, obviously mulling it over. "I guess it never occurred to me," he admitted. "We tend to have people work in house. It helps with the team dynamic. And it allows for meetings, touching base. Social interaction, like the cheese tastings."

She nodded. "I admit, those can be important," she said with care. She'd given this a lot of thought. "The thing is, we don't work closely together. There's no reason we couldn't do meetings online." She grinned. "And, like the meme says, a lot of meetings could simply be emails."

He chuckled. She'd shown him that meme, along with a tweet that said, "This meeting could be an email, that email could be a fight in an alley," and he'd cracked up . . . then proceeded to tell her about how he used to work for a grocery store chain's upper management and how painfully true that was.

"For the sake of people with disabilities at the very least, remote work options should be more accessible," she continued, getting into a flow. "You've worked for toxic companies. You know a lot of them just want people on the grounds so they can micromanage and 'guarantee' that people are working. They assume that everyone is lazy, and they'd rather have the knowledge that you're working for however many hours of the day they assign versus simply achieving the goals that would be most effective."

"You know we're not like that, though," Carl protested.

"No, I know that," she reassured him. "That's why I thought you would be open to this work situation. I'd still hit our performance goals. I could come up and visit regularly, for company events or marketing meetings. But otherwise, I could just get the prototypes of the subscription boxes and set up my creative work there," she said.

His thick eyebrows pulled into a thoughtful expression. "Hmm. That's not bad," he said. "There really isn't any reason, I suppose, for you to physically be in Seattle."

She nodded, feeling relief start to course through her rapidly rushing bloodstream. "For me, it would combine feeling at home, surrounded by supportive people who love me—who are basically my family—and having that perfect job."

He smiled. "That's a strong argument," he said. "I think you're a good fit with our culture here, and I'm not going to say we're not going to miss having you around the office. That said, I'd rather have you happy and doing good work with us than completely gone. And maybe doing good work for, say, Creme de la Creamery."

"Those bastards," she joked with a wink. The "rivalry" between Cloud City and Crème de la Creamery was a running gag online, one that was boosting both their numbers.

He took some notes. "Let me run this by Theresa and Agnes," he said. "They might want to talk to you too. But I think we can make this work."

She felt almost boneless . . . as if adrenaline and anxiety had been the only things keeping her upright. "Thank you," she said.

He looked at his watch. "It's almost five," he said. "And the weather report's saying it's going to be a torrent. You have plans for tonight? It's Valentine's Day, after all."

She tried to smile, but it came out lopsided. She had not dated, not since she'd left Ponto Beach. Marcus had asked her out, but she'd gently and politely said no. She still texted Josh daily . . . no sexting, nothing romantic. Just because they missed each other.

It was making it impossible for her to move on, she realized.

She also realized she didn't care. She didn't want to move on from Josh. She wanted to move back—and for them to move forward. Together.

"No plans for Valentine's," she murmured. "Maybe I'll make a grilled cheese with some tomato soup, and watch a rom-com."

"The gruyère with the aged cheddar," Carl said immediately. "On maybe a sourdough?"

She grinned. These people. Cheese ran in their veins. "With the roasted red pepper tomato soup," she agreed.

"Sounds like a plan." He stood up, then shook her hand. "We'll talk soon, get this all sorted out. Enjoy the evening, okay?"

She nodded. She'd already scheduled the social media for the day—the "cheesy ways to say I love you" promotion she'd mentioned to Carl—and their new social media minion was diligently answering. (No kidding . . . the woman's name was Ursula, and she had *minion* written on her name tag.) With everything under control, Tam hurried through the pouring rain, back to her apartment.

The apartment still looked spartan. She hadn't gotten any artwork, although she'd put up some framed photos of herself and the Herd . . . and she'd printed and framed the Instagram picture of her with Josh, where he was kissing her neck. Because apparently she liked to torture herself. Otherwise, there was still only the rented furniture. She turned on the TV, looking for something mindless and fluffy to help her feel better. She eventually settled on *Love 020: The Movie*, because it was sweet and sort of silly, and it made her smile.

She was startled out of her little dream by a knock at her door. Her heart started pounding. She hadn't ordered any food for delivery, and nobody from work came to visit her. Maybe it was an irate neighbor? No, she tended to be quiet, and people kept to themselves . . .

She peeked through the peephole. Then, in a daze, she opened the door.

Josh was standing there, soaking wet, with a small duffel bag and a jacket that simply wasn't up to the task of keeping off the rain. His short hair was wet, and his long eyelashes were dotted with raindrops. He looked damp, and frazzled, and . . .

Wonderful.

"Josh?" she said, quietly. "What are you doing here?"

He smiled, so sweetly that it made her want to cry. Then he said the one word in the world she hadn't realized she'd wanted to hear.

"Goldfish."

CHAPTER 39

Josh was practically shivering with cold from the chilly rain that had managed to seep through his sweat jacket. At her gesture, he stepped into Tam's place, where she had her little fireplace going, the warmth of the room feeling like heaven after his sprint when the Uber driver dropped him off at the wrong door and then sped off. In his defense, the set of apartments did all look alike, and there was no parking—and the car behind them had been honking like a mad thing. Now, Josh no doubt looked like he felt: like a drowned rat.

Not the most auspicious way to tell a woman you loved her, especially on Valentine's Day. But there they were.

"Sit down," she said, before disappearing into her bathroom. She looked amazing, he noticed. Her hair was a little longer, falling past her shoulders, and she was wearing very comfy-looking flannel pajamas. She hadn't talked about having a boyfriend, or even dating . . . but then, she wouldn't, would she? Out of respect for his feelings? And he'd frankly been scared of her answer. He'd been working frantically since the Herd's brainstorming session on New Year's, and now, he was putting all his chips on the table.

She came back with a thick towel and tossed it to him. "You might want to get out of that jacket," she said with a note of concern. "You might catch a cold or something. It's not like Ponto up here . . . it gets brisk."

He nodded mutely, still trying to figure out how to get a grip on the situation. "Um . . ."

"So," she said with a soft, sweet smile that made him want to sweep her up in his arms. "Am I killing somebody, or do you need help hiding a body?"

It took him a second to realize she was parroting what he'd said to her, back when she'd left New York. He chuckled, shaking his head. "I need you to help me fix a mistake," he said.

"Oh?" Her voice was calm, but he could see her pulse beating hard and fast in the slim column of her throat.

"Yeah."

C'mon. Like you practiced.

He took a deep breath. It wasn't like it was his whole life's happiness on the line or anything. Like it wasn't the love of his life.

Stay focused.

"Here's the thing," he said slowly, toweling his hair dry. "I love you."

She smiled, but there was wariness there. "I know," she said, then, before he could call her out for a Star Wars reference, she added, "just like you know I love you."

"I do know that," he said. "But . . . I'm *in* love. With you. Obviously." He coughed. "And have been for a while."

She fell silent.

He felt panic grip him and plowed forward. "I should have said something. I just . . . we had so many good reasons, you know? And for so many years, you were my safe space. I don't even want to think about what my life would've been like if I hadn't had you in high school."

"Hard same," she admitted quietly, sitting next to him.

"You were just always my anchor," he continued. "And I kept telling myself that what we had was special. That no matter who you were dating, or even who I was dating . . . you had my back, and I had yours, and as long as we didn't mess with it, nothing would change that."

She nodded. "I felt the same way."

Felt. Past tense. Did that mean something had changed?

He shook his head. He needed to stay the course. "And I never, ever want you to feel like you can't pursue your passions, or achieve your dreams, because of what I want. I don't want you to feel like being a success in doing what you love, versus being with me, is some kind of . . . some kind of binary choice."

She stared at him wordlessly.

He was sweating, and it had nothing to do with the little fireplace or her heating system. "But I was also a chickenshit," he admitted.

She let out a little surprised laugh.

"I was so intent on making sure you were doing what you wanted that I didn't tell you that I . . . shit. I want to be with you," he said with all the passion and frustration and intensity that had been bottling up inside him for months. Hell, for years. "I want you to be happy. That's all I've ever wanted. But I have also been miserable without you."

Her expression softened. "Oh, Josh."

He swallowed against the grating harshness in his throat. "I want to be with you," he said. "I don't want to just FaceTime you, or visit on weekends. I want a relationship with you. I mean, if all I could get was a long-distance relationship, I'd accept it, because you're worth it. But I also know that I'm happiest when I'm around you every day. And I want to make you happy too."

She took a deep breath. She looked like she did just before a roller coaster did its initial dizzying plunge. And he knew from experience that she hated roller coasters.

Still, he knew exactly what she was feeling, because he felt the same way.

"I'm happiest when I see you every day too," she said.

He tugged at her, pulling her into his lap, and she looped her arms around his neck. "That's why I'm moving to Seattle."

"Wait, you're *what*?" she yelped.

"I mean, it's going to take a little while longer," he admitted, "but I've got the paperwork going. I'm going to put Amber in charge of GKU in Ponto Beach, and I'm going to set up a corporate office in Seattle—or maybe nearby. And we'll work everything else out from there."

"But . . . but your house . . ."

"It's just a house," he reassured her, stroking her hair.

"And the Herd!"

He felt a pang. "I will miss them," he said. "But it's not like I've been able to see them as much as I wanted to. And it's not like we can't visit either."

She stared at him. "You'd give that all up? For me?"

He sent her a lopsided smile. "I'd walk over glass and fire to get you a sandwich," he teased her, then added, "I'd give up everything I own to be with you. Because you deserve it. And I want to spend every day showing you just how much I mean that."

She looked teary. Then she leaned forward and kissed him soundly. The relief that flowed through him was immediate and overwhelming.

She pulled away for a second, cupping his face, looking deeply into his eyes. "I'm in love with you too," she said, her voice strong and steady and comforting, and he felt like butter in a sauté pan, just melting down to bubbles. "That's why I asked to work remote."

It took him a second to process what she'd just said. "Pardon?"

"I had a performance evaluation today," she said. "They asked how I could be happier in my job, and I told them I wanted to work from Ponto. I want to work from home—my real home."

Josh felt his chest heat. "You'd do that?"

"I want to be with you," she said. "And I want to be with my friends, who are basically our family. I want to be able to see the beach, and hang out with Emily and Lily and Juanita, and laugh at Hayden's jokes. I want to have double dates with Freddie and Asad. And I want to make out with you on the beach and have dinners on the patio . . . and fall asleep next to you every night."

He held her tight, almost crushingly so.

"We'll make it work," she reassured him. "One way or another. Because we've wasted enough time."

He kissed her again, because he simply couldn't help himself. Then he picked her up, which she responded to with a startled *eep!*

He put her on the bed, then grabbed a strip of condoms from his duffel bag, tossing them haphazardly onto her nightstand, which made her giggle. Then he started peeling off his clothes. "Don't want to catch a cold," he said cheekily, grinning at her.

She laughed. "Trust me," she said, wriggling to strip out of her cozy jammies, "get in bed with me and you may never feel cold again."

He shuddered at the thought. "God, did I miss you," he murmured, reaching for her as she dived under the covers and held them open for him.

The percale sheets were chilly for all of a second, making her silky skin feel all the hotter as a result. He wasn't even all the way in bed before they reached for each other, like they were dying for it. Like they'd been separated for a century and now were finally reunited.

"I missed you so . . . fucking . . . much." He pressed heated kisses on her breasts, her neck, all the special spots he'd mapped out in his all-too-limited experience with her. He was looking forward to finding even more places to make her gasp and writhe and moan.

"Oh! Oh, God," she breathed, pressing against him, hanging a leg over his hip. "Missed you too. I thought my heart was crushed. I was like a zombie. Total walking dead."

"I was an asshole," he admitted, kissing her. "Total mope fest. The Herd had to smack me back into shape."

"I can't believe we waited this long," she said, and her smile was like the sun.

He stroked a stray lock of hair away from her face, just staring at her for a moment. "I am so totally, utterly, completely in love with you," he whispered.

She smiled back. Then she kissed him hard, tangling her tongue with his, nipping at his lower lip to force him to open wider and give her more access.

They were side by side, and he twisted just enough to reach for a condom, opening it over his head and tossing the wrapper. Then he rolled it on, positioning himself.

"Gonna be fast," he warned her. "It's been a while for me."

"Same," she said. "I only wanted to be with you."

"So much same," he echoed. Then he pressed in.

She whimpered, wriggling, encouraging him to push deeper, her leg pulling his hips in tighter, until he was flush against her. She was panting like she'd run a race, and it was all he could do not to roll over and pound into her, the sensations ringing through him like a pinball machine.

They moved in perfect sync, meeting each thrust with increased pressure, until they were sweating—damp and sliding, grasping and nipping at each other, making little moans and cries of ecstasy. "Tam," he panted, "baby, I'm gonna . . ."

She nodded, then arched her back, her hips pistoning against his. He felt the ripple just as she let out a soft, high-pitched cry, her body clamping around him.

He lost it. He bucked against her, pulling her onto himself, thrusting until he felt his orgasm roar through him and he almost blacked out.

When they recovered, he took off the condom and threw it out, then stumbled back to her bed and gathered her up in his arms.

"From now on, no more pretending that we don't belong together, okay?"

She smiled—then held out her pinky.

He looped it with his own.

"So," she said. "Want a grilled-cheese sandwich?"

EPILOGUE

Six months later

Tam thanked the Uber driver as she got out of the car in Josh's driveway. Or rather, the driveway she shared with Josh. He'd put her name on the house's title and everything, which was both touching and terrifying. They'd been living together since Cloud City Creamery had given her the okay to move back to Ponto Beach and work remote. She'd still kept up her end of the bargain, meeting her performance goals and flying up for necessary meetings and special events. She'd actually just come back from the airport, after flying up for an overnight trip combining a fancy food-and-wine event with her second performance review.

"You've done wonders," Carl had said with his usual encouragement. "Our numbers look phenomenal, and we're getting more distributors. And we've been able to see how to work with more people who don't want to work in the office, or have mobility problems. It's been win-win-win, all over the place!"

That made Tam just as happy as her performance evaluation, actually. The raise that she received was just icing on the cake.

Other than her little day trips, though, she rarely was away from Josh, and she'd missed him. His new iteration of the ghost kitchens business was taking off and going gangbusters. He'd worked with someone at Darius's firm, a guy who specialized in tech, to get all the requirements for the software nailed down, and then they'd marketed the "system" of franchises—both the hardware he'd designed, like the conveyor-belt-driven delivery-sorting system, and the kitchen workflows, the front-of-house order and delivery elements, the marketing-research search engine, and so on—to a number of restauranteurs. He was also acting as consultant. They'd sold three packages and were on track to sell a lot more across the country. Darius was already looking at a global rollout. His investment group was over the moon, to say the least, and Josh was very solidly in the black.

She was tired, but it was a good tired. She felt like she was finally going somewhere in life—with people she wanted to be with.

She stepped inside, noticing that the house was dark, too, other than the hood light in the kitchen. She thought she could see the glow of the outdoor solar lights in the backyard. "Hello?"

She frowned. There was . . . whispering? Some kind of noise?

"Anybody there?" She made her way to the patio and opened the door.

Suddenly, a flash of twinkle lights lit up. "Surprise!"

She gasped. All the Nerd Herd were there, from the looks of it. Asad and Freddie, Tobin and Lily. Even Josh's investor/friend Darius, who had his arm affectionately around Juanita.

Tam laughed, even though her heart was beating fast. "You all scared the hell out of me!"

"Congrats!" Hayden shouted, accompanied by the barking of his dog, Tuna, who was dancing around Hayden's ankles, obviously enthused but not knowing exactly what was going on.

Well, that makes two of us.

"This is kind of a lot for just a performance evaluation," she said, bewildered, looking at Josh. "But I'm always down for a Herd party. Thanks!"

She wasn't sure why Juanita then smacked Hayden on the back of the head. Although, given those two, she was pretty sure he'd earned it.

Josh walked up to her, pressing a hot, lingering kiss on her lips. "Missed you," he murmured, taking her bag and putting it off to one side.

"Missed you too," she said, then lowered her voice, whispering in his ear, "and if you play your cards right, I'll show you how much tonight."

He grinned back wickedly, then cleared his throat. "Fun as that sounds," he said, "are you hungry? Because I made you a charcuterie board."

"You'd think I'd get sick of cheese," she mused, giving him a hug. "You'd be wrong, of course. But it would be the logical assumption."

"I really think you'll like this one," he said, nudging her closer to the outdoor table, which was decorated like a dream. No doubt thanks to Freddie and Asad, who could make anything both delicious and a visual delight.

"Well, I could have a nibble . . . ," she started to say, then stopped abruptly.

The board was gorgeous, a perfect combination of everything she liked. But that wasn't what caught her attention.

There, surrounded by a heart-shaped selection of cheese, was a small velvet box—and the winking brilliance of a platinum-banded engagement ring.

She spun to stare at Josh, only to find him on one knee beside her.

"I know this might seem sudden . . ."

"Are you kidding me?" Asad muttered. "This has been decades in the making!"

"Hush," Freddie murmured to him, pulling him tight to his side.

Josh just smiled, that amused, happy smile that she loved, and disregarded the interruption. "But we've loved each other for years, and I don't want to wait another day to let you know: I want to be with you forever. Will you marry me?"

She felt emotion clog her throat, but she nodded wildly, tears starting to spill. "Yes," she rasped, then swallowed. "Yes!"

He got up, grabbed her tight, and began kissing the stuffing out of her. And the Herd cheered in response.

"I love you so much," she said. "To the moon and back. To the ends of the earth. More than . . ." She frowned, trying to put it in a way he'd understand. "I love you more than *cheese*."

He laughed.

"And I love you more than anything," he responded, and kept kissing her.

Acknowledgments

I want to thank the team at Montlake Romance, specifically and especially Alison Dasho for being incredibly supportive throughout all this; Krista Stroever, for being not only a kick-ass editor but a fellow cheese lover; and Jillian Cline for helping to get the word out on these books I love so much. Also, again, I could not do this without the help of my agent, Tricia Skinner, from Fuse Literary, who I am lucky and grateful to work with.

Thanks to my family, especially my husband and son, who do whatever they can to make sure I can put dreams to paper.

Finally, thank you to the readers who have supported me and my geeky, silly stories.

About the Author

Cathy Yardley is an award-winning author of romance, chick lit, and urban fantasy. She has sold over 1.2 million books with publishers like St. Martin's Press, Avon, and Harlequin Books. She writes fun, geeky, and diverse characters who believe that underdogs can make good and that sometimes being a little wrong is just right. She likes writing about quirky, crazy adventures because she's had plenty of her own: she had her own army in the Society for Creative Anachronism; she's spent New Year's on a three-day solitary vision quest in the Mojave Desert; and she had VIP access to the Viper Room in Los Angeles. Now, she spends her time writing in the wilds of East Seattle, trying to prevent her son from learning the truth about any of said adventures and riding herd on her two dogs (and one husband).